The Altered Moon

By James Alan McG

The Second Edition edited by
Edits by Angie Greth

Reach out to me:
jamesmcgettigan@earthlink.net

If you're a writer in need of an editor, Angie Greth is a great resource: editsbyangie@yahoo.com

Interested in the rest of my series? Check out my website:

Contents

I
Final Assessment

The YTX-Krogen fighter jet engine roared just outside my cockpit as I approached a stable thirty-five hundred miles per hour. I flew at a low altitude and delightfully observed, as the hot orange desert that was Calinheim, a southwest sector in my home country of Utopian, swept beneath me.

"Criptous, your altitude is at sub one thousand feet. How about we pull back on the joystick and raise altitude by about four thousand, please?" a woman's voice from ground control told me over comms.

I shook my head. "Nah, you know me, ground control, I always like to live life on the edge; I think I'm good where I'm at," I replied.

"The YTX-Krogen may be agile, Alpha Criptous, but there's only so much she'll handle when we send the drones out. I'm not gonna tell you again. Pull up."

I chuckled at that. "Ground control, you speak as if this were my first time inside a Krogen's cockpit. Let me be the judge of what she can take. I didn't earn my way up to the rank of alpha by playing it safe. Go ahead and send out the drones. I'm ready." With that, I pushed forward on the throttle, accelerating the jet in a short burst, doing a spiral maneuver through a sizeable hole in the cliffside.

In the time that was spent twirling and jolting around the lower atmosphere, I spotted the first drone. A bright glint in the sky, about forty miles out. *Either you're early or the others are late,* I thought. A sudden burst of rays passed below my jet and hit the cliff beside me, rocking the Krogen just slightly.

A snarling curse slipped my lips as I stabilized the Krogen. *Movement, five o'clock!* I told myself as I came about. Whipping my head toward the second drone sweeping in fast on my position. The sensors picked up a third hot on my tail; dead ahead was a fourth. I spun sideways to avoid a collision. The enclosing drones evaded one another just as swiftly.

"I guess everyone's on time after all. Ground control, I have received contact. Engaging now," I said.

"Roger that, alpha. Good luck up there," ground control replied.

I raced through a maze of tall rocky pillars, twirling left and right while dodging a series of purple rays from a pursuing drone. Up ahead was a line of arching pillars, each one smaller than the last. Powering past the desert floor, I headed straight for them. A lone drone followed, keeping well behind me as I passed under the pillars. After the second passed over me, I jerked the joystick back, and slammed the throttle, propeling the Krogen over the third pillar. The rumble from the drone, as it crashed into the arch, shook the cockpit.

Climbing back into the atmosphere, with my heart thumping out of my chest, my was skin coated in goosebumps from the thrill of the fight. As I steadied my breath, fire trailed ahead of me as a second drone aligned itself behind me. I twirled my craft. Its triangular shape cut between every one of the drone's plasma rays, and descended back down. The drone followed, bearing down on me. I kept at my maneuver as we propelled to the ground. At the last possible second, I pulled back on the throttle and up on the joystick. The Krogen's nose flipped back toward the drone like lightning. I pushed the throttle forward, once again, and blasted the drone out of the sky. I pierced through the explosion, momentarily blinded from the burst.

The smoke cleared, revealing a third drone. I diverted back down towards the surface. This one patterned my every maneuver. Coming to this realization, a brief weight of dread befell my mind at the impossibility of evading this new challenger. However, my ego wouldn't allow my volition to be dampened in this moment. I applied every maneuver I knew to the chase; the drone was still able to land two strikes.

Baring my fangs, and a snapping bark at the drone, a daring tactic crossed my mind. Outrageously risky, but if executed properly, my victory would be secured. With a brisk tug on the joystick, the craft *thrusted* back into a flip. My chest pressed tightly against my straps and my breath deepened, as I found myself upside down over the drone. A swift action to an observer's eyes, but to me, it felt like I had all the time in the world. I never took my eyes off the drone as the nose of my craft came around. The drone propelled ahead. It was barely within range, once I aligned the shot. I took one final, deep breath as my sensors got a lock and fired! The shot landed and the drone split apart. I pushed forward on the throttle and boosted forward. My head whipped back as my peripheral view broadened.

I cleared my throat and shifted in my seat situated within G.M.E shielding that composed the cockpit. *One more*, I thought to myself. My eyes shifted back to the sky and saw the same glint of light flying high above me. *Come on now, let's get this over with.* The drone dove toward me, pulsing a sonic wave behind it. I pushed on my throttle and sped forward, maneuvering close to the cliffside as I waited for the drone to fall in behind me. *I pray Anua grants me sight to see a strategy to beat this final test.*

I soon learned, like the one before it, this drone was hard pressed on me, imitating my every maneuver, and staying one step perfectly behind me. I climbed just slightly in the atmosphere and leveled my trajectory. My sensors warned me that the drone was locking onto me. I braked my propulsion and looped underneath the drone. In just a few brief seconds, I had a shot locked, but the drone veered off before I could fire. I followed the drone, keeping it in my sight. Chasing it through the tall pillars, the drone fired upon one of them and sped past the debris. The rubble cast a shadow over my craft, swiftly spewing out across my path. My eyes went agape at the tumbling obstacles as I quickly veered away before it could hit me. Another curse escaped my breath as I recovered. *The drone must have Neural software. That would explain why it remained overhead from the others. It was studying me. Two can play at that!* I pushed on the throttle and sped forward. I knew exactly where to lure it.

Staying close to the cliffside, I slowed for the drone to catch up. My ears perked-up at the sound of sensors beaming, warning of the drone's closing pursuit. It was not at six, but twelve o'clock precisely. My eyes darted up. Just moments away from impact, I twirled the Krogen below the drone. The bellies of the two crafts were inches away from scraping against each other. The drone quickly shifted its course and came up behind me. I increased my speed and gazed along the cliffside ahead. There, I saw it: a tunnel near the top. I passed through it before, while waiting for the drones to arrive. It was a wide pass, big enough to make tight maneuvers, if needed. That's where I would take care of this drone. I pulled back on my joystick and flew into the tunnel with the drone close behind.

Now, I needed it to shoot at me, and fast. We didn't need to travel very far before we reached the opening at the other end. I eased my speed, so the drone would have an easy shot. My sensors warned me of the lock on. *That's it.* The shot was taken. I dodged the rays, which hit the cave ceiling overhead, and debris rained over us. My grasp on the joystick felt queasy; I loosened my grip as the Krogen rocked from the shockwave of the drone's fire.

My breath caught. Time slowed once again. Only this instance was different. It wasn't as if my focus narrowed. If anything, my focus broadened. I felt as if I was moving faster than everything else, including the Krogen. My awareness of it wasn't immediate, not until after I cleared the debris. Watching as the chunks of rock slowly spun passed me, I knew the drone didn't have a chance of evading it. With a bright, orange illumination of the cave, the final drone was defeated. I dashed out of the cave to an uproar of applause over the comms.

"That was some damn good flying, Amat. You earned your tour in Zeta. We'll have you shipped out next week," my commanding officer, Pac Yondugŭl, told me. "Come on back to base, alpha, and we'll celebrate!"

II
Restless Graduation

That night, Pac Yondugŭl poured everyone in the squadron a round of drinks—even the ones that didn't pass their final assessment that day. There were only a handful of us who had. Very few pass it their first time around. I counted myself lucky to be among them. My enlistment with the alphas started from the ripe age of ten; the training process, to attain the rank, takes five years. I would have signed on when I was five, but my parents wouldn't allow me. Laws of the Utopion Autocracy stated one could not enlist as an independent under the age of ten years.

Then again, maybe it was best I waited. If I signed on with the alphas at five, I would have received all the same training, but in more supervised environments and certain operations would have been restricted to me. Younger alphas were limited to less combative missions. Commanding gromrolls from afar. In rare circumstances, they operate as spies in neutral territories.

There were three of us who passed that day: Mae Kalbrook, Xeke Likenor, and myself. I wasn't particularly close to either of them, but Mae was a worthy competitor. She never failed to keep up with me in just about every training we were put through as a unit. Sometimes she even surpassed me. She arrived a few months prior to me and had also passed her first attempt at the program.

As we got older, I had the sense she developed personal feelings for me, judging by her tendency to frequently tease me. Whether it was a close run at first place, during a circuit drill, or even just bettering my tactics in simulated team-combat, she satirized me. Sometimes it was a simple look or lack of words between us. The space was so deaf that only the soft wind of the desert filled our awkward company. However, I always held back from any personal attachments that could've developed. I was there to become a soldier and to serve my country. That was my greatest desire, and it came before all else.

I stood idle, staring down into my rock glass, swirling the green liquor inside of it 'round and 'round. I didn't really like drinking, but I thought I'd humor my commanding officer by sharing a drink with him. Otherwise, I liked to keep a clear head; even when there seemed no reason to. Several members of my alpha unit congregated at my feet, idolizing me. They asked questions they wouldn't have been so curious to know the answers to a few hours prior. They practically worshipped me, and I hated every second of it. I didn't want to be adored. I didn't even necessarily want to be treated as an officer. I wanted to fight. Every moment I remained at Gallethol was time that could be spent taking out a xůté base or operative. Nevertheless, if the xůté's persistence kept as it had over the course of that year, within the next week, there'd be enough missions and targets to go around.

"This really has been a long time coming for you . . . really, for all of us, in due time. Have you put much thought into where you'll serve in Zeta?" asked Yuvara, a member of my unit. "Recent intel on the xůté says the freedom fighter's revolt will wage on for the coming decades if their current efforts persist."

A new member casually joined the gathering; one who's company I seldom appreciated. He beckoned to the group before I could answer Yuvara.

"Ah, yes, this has been a long time coming for you, Amat," said Ghivari, a pestering rival, who belittled my every success in the program. "But, while this is a day of celebration, there are some of us who could speculate at the obvious favoritism granted to you by Pac Yondugůl, Criptous."

I held a silence as I stared deep into Ghivari's yellow eyes. He showed no ounce of intimidation, the lips of his snout curled into a subtle, devious smile, at the anticipation of my reply.

"What are you getting at, Ghivari?" I asked.

"Well, it's been no secret, from day one, you're the son of the jinn-hid. And in all the time we've been in this program, this is the lowest count of graduates we've seen," Ghivari replied.

My mind was polluted with a fury, that I barely managed to tone down, at Ghivari's mention of my father. My father, who couldn't have been more disappointed when he found out that I signed on with the alphas. Something about *I wasn't doing it for the right reasons.* That only left me with a sentiment of restraint.

"Mm, maybe the alphas are becoming a dying breed, and less of those who join are vigorous enough to make the cut. But hey, I don't have a problem with that. Makes those of us who earned the rank more admirable." Ghivari frowned at my remark and revealed his fangs in a grimace. In that moment, I spotted Mae's gaze from across the room. "To answer your question, Yuvara, I am considering Névumbar, deep in the eastern front. Excuse me, friends."

Mae was talking to Aidra Dormon, someone I saw her socialize with regularly over the course of our training. They both gave nervous smiles as they saw me wandering over. I smiled back.

"Aidra, Mae, how are you two enjoying the party?" I asked. Aidra seemed ready to say something in reply, but Mae beat her to it.

"Oh, it's great! So nice to finally have an evening like this after all these years of vigorous training. What about you?"

"Desperately trying to get away from the inadequates that were crowding me over there," I joked. "I figured here would be as good a place as any." Mae giggled at that.

"Hey, what are you trying to say, Amat?" Aidra demanded as she lightly punched my shoulder.

"Don't mind her, Amat. Aidra's another one of those *inadequates,*" Mae said, shooting me a grin.

Aidra rolled her eyes and sighed.

"Speaking of which, congratulations to you, to us on our assessments," Mae said.

"Of course, we owe this day to ourselves. Ever since day one, we pushed one another to do the best that we can in this program and . . . it's been an honor, Mae," I replied.

"Likewise." Mae gave me a peculiar smile, one that said more about what she was feeling.

Aidra took one glance at each of us and caught on to some impression. I caught her eye and the excitement in the subtle curvature of her lips as she stepped away.

"You know I'm gonna be sad to see us part. I'm sure we would make a great team out there in Zeta," Mae admitted.

"I'm confident we would too. But maybe that's for the best. If you rely too heavily on another person to watch your back, you forget how to guard your own."

Mae acknowledged, "I suppose that's true. But if you rely too much on yourself, you can lead yourself astray or put others at unnecessary risk."

I nodded in agreement. "That's fair, I'll give you that. But then, isn't that what our training preps us for? To be the most advanced asset on the field, to the point that we require the assistance of almost no other?"

"Almost no other, doesn't mean no other at all. As one alpha, neither of us could hope to take on the full xǔté force in Zeta and succeed. We still need the backbone of the Utopion army behind us to win." Mae's confident tone backed her opinion.

I chuckled. "All good points, Mae, as are mine. I have to insist in my argument: as alphas and as warriors who were trained in every avenue of warfare, we stand, individually, as our own army."

"Oh, have we been arguing?"

The notion threw me off guard, and I stumbled on my words for a moment, which had Mae giggling.

"I'm kidding with you, Amat. It's always fun seeing you stumble in your ramblings."

"Mm, not as much fun as seeing you come second in almost every drill we ran."

Mae's jaw dropped. "Again, 'almost' isn't every time that's ever been."

"Well, I suppose you have me there," I replied.

There was a moment of silence between us, and my mind drew a blank at the sudden shift in the atmosphere. I could smell Mae's passion before it reached her eyes.

"Amat," Mae finally spoke. "I . . . I know it's the last night we'll likely see each other for a while. With that said, there's something I'd like to share with you before we part ways. Because, as you said, we've been such an inspiration to one another and . . ." Mae seemed to struggle to piece together what she wanted to tell me.

I could hear the words she wanted to say, but couldn't bring herself to express. Part of me was uncomfortable, as I had repeatedly told myself I didn't feel the same way. But then, part of me was also relieved and saw this as an opportunity to set the record straight.

"It's alright, Mae, you can tell me whatever you'd like."

Mae's cheeks grew red as her lips curled up. "Well then, in that case, I—"

"Amat!" Pac Yondugǔl shouted drunkenly. "Amat, where are you?!"

Good fortune shines on me! I thought, as I swiftly made myself known to my superior officer.

"Here, sir," I called. Pac Yondugǔl looked in my direction and spotted me, standing no more than a few feet away.

"Amat! Come here, my boy. Come, I'd like to make a toast." I promptly went to the side of the drunken pac, who had a half-empty bottle of Vitzkin in his grasp. A licorice-tasting spirit, that made your nose run and your stomach churn if you had too much of it.

Once at his side, the pac topped off my mostly full glass of Gilwitz, a less potent spirit that Yondugŭl poured me earlier, with the Vitzkin.

"Ah, there we are!" Yondugŭl said as he spilled some of the liquid onto my pants and boots.

I wasn't troubled by it. Even if I was, what could I do? The pac was my superior.

"I'd like to say something about this young man here. As I gather my thoughts, at this moment, I think what is there not to say? Amat, when you first arrived here, to Gallethol Alpha base, it was clear to me that your discipline was not flawed. There are many that start in alpha training, who put on a fad; they soon realize the training is more than they anticipated. However, in all the five years I trained you, I never saw you second guess yourself, and you've always pushed yourself beyond your limits. Such traits are seldom found inherent in a soldier. I know you'll do great things for Utopion, and I'm honored to have been your commanding officer. May Anua bid you safe journey on your tour. To Amat!" Yondugŭl raised his glass and everyone else joined in.

"As much as I appreciate your praise, sir, I think you're forgetting to acknowledge Mae Kalbrook. She could arguably be an equally best member of our unit," I announced, peering over at Mae.

I caught a glimpse of Mae's disappointed expression, but not from my remark. I faintly noticed it was from the moment I carelessly discarded her as she was opening up.

Yondugŭl raised a finger. "Ah, yes!" Yondugŭl drunkenly spat, walking over in Mae's direction. Mae put on an awkward grin as the pac stumbled to her. "Of course, Miss Kalbrook. You were practically inseparable from Amat in the time you've gotten to know one another. If I recall correctly, why, there have even been times that you bested Amat himself . . ."

I figured that was as good a time as any to leave the party. I knew what Mae was leading up to before Yondugŭl interrupted her, and I was glad he did. It would have been a shame to explain to her that I didn't feel the same way. Had we met in any other context, however, I might have. I did care for her, just not in that light. *She'll surely try to bring it up again,* I told myself. *It'll be impossible to avoid her for a week before we're all sent off. It would take some kind of intervention to keep her from chasing me around the base to tell me how she feels.*

III
Stinging Executive Order

I awoke to the sound of the comms alerting me in my room. I quickly got out from between my sheets and answered the call.

"Ah, hello?" I answered.

"Alpha Criptous." It was my pac's voice on the other side.

"Pac Yondugǔl? Is everything alright?"

The pac sighed. "Oh yes, everything is just fine. I'm sorry to have disrupted your first day off in a while, but I need you to meet me in my office, as soon as possible."

"Of course, sir. I'll be right over."

"Good, I'll expect you in twenty minutes."

Yondugǔl hung up abruptly, and I promptly dressed in my uniform. I exited my quarters and paced down the halls to Yondugǔl's office.

Along the way, I ran into Mae. Her eyes broadened at the sight of me.

"Good morning, Amat," she said.

"Good morning, Mae. I can't talk right now. I have a meeting with Yondugǔl, but we'll catch up later," I spoke quickly, but kindly. I didn't want to disrespect her. I also didn't want to get tangled up in a conversation that we would both regret having.

"Oh, alright…" Mae said, as I turned away from her.

When I entered the room, the air was filled with the scent of weco coming from the tab in the pac's hand. Beside the ashtray was a glass of water, a substance I rarely saw the pac drink.

"Sir?" I asked, pushing the door open.

"Amat." Yondugŭl examined the time on his wrist. "You are early, as expected. Go ahead and take a seat." The pac gestured to the chair sitting across his table.

"Thank you, sir," I replied as I sat.

Yondugŭl put out the tab in his water and leaned back in his chair. After holding a brief hush, he tilted his head and shook his finger at me.

"You know how fortunate we are to have clean water like that? How ignorant it is for someone like me to soil water with a tab? There are people . . . lots of people out there, Amat, who would rip each other's throats out just for a week's worth of water. Maybe even for a day's worth of water, for themselves and for their families. There are countless people who've never known the touch of a soft mattress to lay their back on."

I listened closely to my commander's words. His tone set a discomforting start to the conversation.

"What luxuries we are blessed with," I spoke nervously.

The pac leaned in close. "I trust you understand at this point that I'm about to reveal to you some unpleasant news."

I nodded my head. "I suspected as much, sir."

"Then, without further delay, I'll just come out and say it. Last night, I received orders for your reassignment, Amat." Yondugŭl turned his clear glass computer around and revealed the screen. A long message was displayed of the orders the pac had just mentioned. Before I could get down to what they were for, however, my superior spoke again.

"You won't be going to Zeta next week."

I bit back on my tongue as well as the instinct to retort the pac's statement.

"A flight was booked and you are to report to Jinn-hid Bod for further training at Base Lazithia, up north . . . to your father."

My expression furrowed into a scowl as my fists clenched around each other. My thoughts raced with disappointment and fury. Raging fury.

"I won't go. I've graduated from alpha training; I have responsibilities to my country. I'm wasted on further training at this point," I argued.

"This is not open for negotiation, Amat. I was given an order to relay unto you," Yondugŭl replied.

I snorted, planting my face in my palms. *All these years, this time and effort . . . just to have it stripped away by the old bastard?*

"Ah, it was him who gave out the order, wasn't it?"

"What?" Yondugŭl's expression went quizzical.

Unable to keep my temper dampened further, I sprang out of my chair, kicked it back, and slammed my fists on the desk. "My damned father was the one who stripped all I worked towards, for the passed—"

"Anua's Shadow blind you, Amat!" Yondugŭl stood up and met me at my level. "After all these years, have you forgotten how to properly address your superior officer? Especially while he recovers from a hangover?"

Pac Yondugŭl spoke sternly as we stared, grudgingly into each other's eyes. The pac bore his fangs after he saw I didn't back down. "Sit. Down. Alpha."

I tightened my jowls and growled as I took my seat, arms crossed. "Yes, sir."

Yondugŭl remained standing for a little while longer. "Now listen, this here" —he pointed at the message on his screen— "is an *executive* order from the second highest ranking official in the nation. Needless to say, his authority overrules my own. So, believe me when I say, under any other circumstance, I wouldn't wish this for you. I don't." Yondugŭl sat back down in his seat and stared at me in silence, with a kinder look in his eyes. "I can only imagine how great a disappointment this must be for you. Despite that, I want you to know and consider how fortunate you are to have clean water to drink, a soft bed to rest yourself on at the end of *each* day, and a father that loves you."

Springing my gaze back toward the pac, I squinted at him. Before I could retort, however, the pac continued swiftly, while maintaining his kind tone.

"You know, I signed on with the alphas at the same age you did. Only, it wasn't because I loved my country, or because I wanted to defend it. It was because, for the first ten years of my life, I had a father that would beat me within an inch of my life, at minimum once a week . . . just because he needed to let off some steam. Whether it was his work, his personal life, his childhood, me . . . I didn't know, I don't know, and at this point I don't care. What I did care about was feeling valued. Granted it was a little challenging to find that feeling at the start of my involvement in this program. But over time, I made friends, I earned the respect of my commanding officers, and I found myself the family I never had. I served with that family, and some died for me, for you, for us all. I don't claim to understand your relationship with your father, Amat, but with these orders here, came a personal letter explaining why. It seems he wants to resolve some tensions between the two of you before you go off and risk your life in the field. May the Goddess blind me in shadow if I'm incorrect in saying your father loves you, because my father never did me such a courtesy, *ever.*"

I wasn't moved by the pac's words. All I cared about was serving. Yondugǔl knew that and my father knew that. I wasn't sure if that motivation was pure or an idea planted and nurtured by the neuro-chip installed in my brain at birth. A device which routinely circulated Utopian propaganda into my thoughts. However, it was my greatest desire. My father was taking that away from me.

Although, I had to hand it to him, the infamous Bod Criptous had a reputation amongst many of my kin. He was a great man in his early days of service as a krollgrum. That was one of the early ranks that one can achieve in our regular army. He also operated as an assassin of sorts. He was contracted to take out some of the most dangerous people this world has ever known, without civilian collateral. My father didn't support the wars as such, but he did back himself on the services he performed. When he came home, he would often seek out opportunities to help people in need, whatever their circumstance, even if it meant putting himself at risk. I won't deny that I was proud of him for all of this. Although, the man couldn't seem to find it in him to be proud of me and of what I hoped to achieve. For that reason, I seldom sought an opportunity to boast about my connection to him.

I sniffed. "When do I leave?" I asked.

"Your flight leaves at two o'clock this afternoon," Yondugǔl replied.

I snorted in derision. "Will that be all?"

"Yes, that will be all."

Before I could exit, Yondugǔl spoke out. "There is just one more thing, Amat. If there is a final order I could give you, as your superior, it is this. Remember all those 'luxuries,' as you put it, that we've been talking about?"

"Yes, sir," I replied.

"I would encourage you to take advantage of each and every one you can find, especially the ones related to family. In this line of work, you never know just how much time or opportunities you have left with them . . . to show how much you care."

I nodded my head. "I'll be seeing you, Pac Yondugŭl." I swung the door behind me and got ready to head back home, to my father.

IV
Psyche Battle

"And where did you say you were going?" asked the kaw interrogating me.

It was standard procedure for militia to be inspected by Utopian law enforcement in airports, before travels. Especially, when one was armed.

"Lazithia, in Sanronmire, up-sector," I said, presenting the orders from my father.

The kaw scanned his eyes over the pages as he flipped through them.

"The son of the jinn-hid?" The kaw raised his eyes to me. "You're Amat Luciph Criptous?"

I slid my credentials to him next.

"That's my I.D. to prove it," I replied.

"And you just graduated from alpha training at Gallethol, under Pac Yondugŭl?" asked the kaw.

"Five years gone to waste," I replied. *This idiot couldn't tell by my coat?*

Before leaving Gallethol, Pac Yondugŭl presented me the alpha's decorated uniform with the insignia on the right shoulder. It was a broken triangle; the base did not connect with the other lines. Above the triangle's point was a crescent dome, and at either side of the point were two jagged lines. Each outline represented an alpha's mastery: the land was the bottom line, the point was the sea, the jagged lines were air, and the dome, space.

The kaw looked put off by the remark, but let it subside as he prioritized processing my documentation through an interface.

"Huh, well, everything appears to be in order." The kaw tidied up my documents and handed them back to me, along with my pistol. "Enjoy your flight back home, Alpha Criptous,"

Frowning, I plucked my belongings from the kaw and marched out of the interrogation room.

As I walked past the people in coach, I noticed many who saluted me on recognizing the insignia on the shoulder of my jacket. It didn't feel right, being saluted by the people on the flight. They probably imagined I served in Daikar, Donmar, Zeta, or in the restoration program. *I haven't done any of that; they pay tribute to a false idol.* A deep sense of shame overtook me.

On the screens of the plane, an ad was being broadcast for a new neuro-chip: code nine, they called it. It was an upgrade from the previous eight. At birth, everyone has a code one neuro-chip installed into their occipital lobe. Code one acted as a monitor of our vision, so to monitor our activity. It also broadcasted propaganda, through your thought process, about the Utopion autocracy, which one could choose to embrace or ignore. Any upgrade installment was done in the fashion of a punishment, as more control was induced into one's neural activity. This was to best ensure order, safety, and security among the Utopian people. Code two applies restrictions on your speech. Code three allows an operator to take control over your physical actions at any given moment. Code four manipulates your bowel movements. Code five shuts down your sex drive. Code six shuts down your sense of touch. Code seven shuts down your sense of taste. Code eight represses all memory of your life and installs new ones. However, it would seem code nine completely shuts down your sense of self. It makes you conform to an extreme. 'Embodying the perfect model citizen' was the slogan of the ad. 'if you know someone who may be a threat to Utopion security, please contact your nearest on-duty veteran…'

The message dissipated to my ears as I found my seat. I took off my coat and sat by the window. Moments later, a man walked up and took the seat next to me.

"Hey, how are ya?" the man asked as he loaded his luggage in the compartment above our seats.

"Not too great," I replied.

"Ah, sorry to hear that." The man took his seat, put his hand above his forehead, and flipped it over.

The action was not only a gesture of greeting someone, but also to pay respect and pass on the blessing of Anua.

"Zaith Dirkman," the man said.

I paid him the same respect with my own hand. "Amat Luciph Criptous," I replied.

"Well, Amat, whatever ails you, I wouldn't get too hung up on it. You're a very young man, by the look of you. Take my word for it, the problems you run into in your youth are minuscule to the ones you're confronted with when you get older."

"Even when your troubles concern your career?"

Zaith scoffed. "At your age, kid, you should be saying 'a' career. Like I said, you're young; there's a lot of opportunity in store for you. Life often surprises us, takes us places we least expect, when we're at one point of it versus another."

"That won't happen with me. I had only one pursuit, one desire my whole life, and I'm going to reach it one way or another."

"I'm sure if you had the power to recall the earliest memories of your life, you'd find that not to be true."

It's funny. When Zaith said that, I didn't quite recall what it was—the one desire I wanted to achieve when I was younger. It faintly surfaced to my conscience, along with the nostalgic ecstasy my young mind held about the ambition. Unfortunately, it swiftly faded. Something in my mind pushed it aside and forced me to draw a blank until I gave up altogether on my recollection. My attention returned to Zaith.

"I didn't know I was going to be a flicker writer until I found myself in my twenties. I was broke and determined to make it into reporting. Then, I met this guy on the levi-rail, and we got to talking about our views on the Utopion autocracy—about all the corruption, the demeaning force, and the spread of influence in this country."

My perception of Zaith had suddenly shifted. Receptors in my mind fired as my face darkened toward the man. I saw Zaith for who he truly was: a traitor.

"Zaith?" I was trying to get his attention, but he kept on talking.

"We discussed how we were gonna call it all out."

"Zaith?"

"And pretty soon we'll do just that."

I grabbed Zaith by the collar with one hand, and the other presented the alpha rank insignia on my jacket.

"Zaith!" I barked. "If I were you, I'd choose my next words about our great country wisely, while in my presence."

The look on Zaith's face was one of shock and awe. His jowls gaped as his eyes fixated on the insignia.

"Oh, sir, I had no idea you were *eh* . . . please don't turn me in. I was just trying to start a conversation; I'm not a fan of awkward silence—"

"You know, you talk too much," I said as I unholstered my pistol and held it beside my head, aiming it up as a warning. People across the way were looking at us and the plane went silent. No doubt, many passengers had become aware of the issue. "Now, as far as I'm concerned, I didn't hear the words that just came out of your jowls; I won't be hearing any more for the remainder of the flight. If I hear so much as a mumble escape your lips, I'll turn you over to the kaws. Nod if you understand."

Zaith nodded.

"Is there a problem here?" a female auxiliary on the craft asked.

By then I had put away my weapon and let go of Zaith's collar. "No. No, there isn't. Me and my friend here are just happy to see one another. Isn't that right?"

Zaith nodded his head nervously at both me and the auxiliary. "Yes, that's right," he said.

"We apologize for the disruption. I assure you it won't happen again." I smiled and the auxiliary's eyes passed over my jacket with the insignia. She smiled back.

"That's good to hear, alpha. Thank you for your service to us. May Anua bless you." The auxiliary presented the front and back of her hand beside her tall, pointed ears.

I returned the gesture. "And to you," I replied.

At some point in the flight, Zaith fell asleep and I caught sight of his wallet in his inner coat pocket. An unfathomable temptation to reach over, ever so subtly, and extract his I.D. to turn over to the authorities befell me. The neuro-chip in my head scrambled thoughts through my mind of how I had a duty to fulfill by turning this man in. He was obviously a threat to the Utopion autocracy.

Yet, a faint instinct spoke to me, some deeper empathy in my gut that argued the opposite. It urged me to let it be. It was something I sometimes felt when interacting with Mae. I wouldn't have called it love. It wasn't an emotion, but there was something about it that was soothing to my ego. The two urges created a strange hesitation within me as I raised my hand to reach for the wallet. My hand trembled as the messages from the neuro-chip intensified. I closed my eyes and sighed as I pulled back my arm, clenched my fist, and gave into that deeper empathy. After all, I promised if Zaith had remained silent to our arrival, I wouldn't turn him in, and he had . . . so far anyway.

For the remainder of the flight, I was tormented by the raging impulses of the neuro-chip within me. The neuro-chip flared signals from my thalamus and cortex, throughout my nervous system to induce varying levels of pain as a punishment. A punishment against my refusal to bring Zaith to justice, in the eyes of the Utopion autocracy. I can't put into words the psychological torment I endured until the plane landed and Zaith awoke. Zaith must have thought I looked dreadful. His expression was perplexed at the sight of me. However, before he could say anything, I grabbed him by the collar and spoke.

"*Finally!*" I growled. "You're awake. Listen to me very carefully, because I can hardly bear sitting next to you for much longer. I could have ruined your life today, but I restrained myself. Thus, I'm warning you to be careful of who you speak to about your profession in the future. Few militia in this world have the mental fortitude to withstand the commands of their neuro-chips. Especially for as long as I did during this flight. Do you understand what I'm saying?"

Zaith stuttered for words, but nodded his head.

"Good," I replied. "Now, kindly wait here as I get my things and exit the plane. The neuro-chip . . . it won't stop until I've either turned you over, or gotten as far away from you as possible."

I shoved Zaith back into his seat, grabbed my things, and marched off the plane, pushing aside everyone in my path. I had to get out of here. I had to, or I'd lose my mind before I even got to baggage claim.

V
Lazithia

By the time I got to the lobby, I started to settle down some. Along the way, I'd received several disturbed looks from the civilians walking by and even some from the kaws. In my march to the exit, one of the kaws bumped into me, grabbing my arm as he inspected my face.

After taking note of the insignia at my shoulder he returned his gaze to my eyes and asked, "Is everything alright, sir?"

"Quite," I replied, shrugging off the kaw's grasp.

"I hope you'll pardon my saying so, alpha, but you seem disturbed," the kaw replied.

I was silent as I held a squinting stare into the kaw's eyes before replying, "I'll admit I haven't been feeling my best of late."

"Any particular reason why, sir?" inquired the kaw.

"Truth be told, I'm a little home sick," I blurted the lie in hopes that it would swiftly conclude the conversation. "Although, I don't see how my health would be any concern of yours."

The kaw shifted as he narrowed his stare at me. "Do you have any documentation pertaining to your business in Sanronmire, sir?" interrogated the kaw. The subtle shift in his passive aggressive tone irked me.

A few moments after I started rummaging through my belongings, I heard a voice call out my name, "Eh, Alpha Criptous?"

I glanced over to the fully dressed duka, relived at the sight of her as she could corroborate my rank and purpose in Sanronmire. She would bring my nagging exchange with the kaw to a close.

"That's me," I said, finally locating my documentation. I pried it from my bag and handed it to the kaw. "And that's for you. Those and Duka . . . Ronkin here should put the question of my credibility here to rest. Keep up the good work, kaw." With a pat on his shoulder, I marched away as the kaw stumbled over his words. I assumed before he could protest further, he already saw that the documents were legitimate. Even if there was still the slightest suspicion that remained in his mind, I doubt a kaw would dare risk troubling a descendant of the jinn-hid.

***

All was much better once Duka Ronkin started driving me out to Lazithia. Duka is a rank just below my own, in the Utopion regular army—not quite at the level of an officer. However, it implied a certain level of experience.

The ride was mostly silent, aside from a brief, "It's an honor to meet the son of the jinn-hid," by the duka. In an effort to silence the torturous neural distortion flooding my mind, via the neuro-chip, I rested my head back and closed my eyes.

By the time we reached Lazithia, the day turned to evening. As we pulled up to one of the barracks, I couldn't help but notice a tall, motionless figure. If not for the light shining down on him, I would have thought he was a shadow in the dark. It had been so long that I almost forgot what my father looked like. Yet, there he was, waiting to welcome me. He certainly didn't have to, but the gesture didn't make me resent him any less for what he took from me that day. Once out of the vehicle, I averted my eyes from him. Even after I took out all my belongings, I couldn't bear to look my father in the eye.

"Amat," he said almost warmly, once I stood before him.

"Sir," I replied.

My father paused a moment and cleared his throat. "It's good to see you again, after so many years."

"Wish I could say the same," I replied.

My father sighed. "I'm sorry, my son. I know what I'm putting you through feels unfair. But if you could just try to understand the importance of—"

"Allow me to say, sir, I've had a rather long and exhausting day. I am tired and I'd like to rest. We can discuss whatever you have to say to me in the morning," I said, cutting him off.

I still wouldn't even glance at him, but I felt his gaze pressing on me. I could tell by the subtle sniff, before his reply, he started to well up.

"Very well," my father grumbled through his snout. "I imagine you had a rather unfortunate day. For that, I will show you to your bunk for the time being. But in the morning, we *will* talk about why you're here."

My father opened the door to the barracks and lead me past columns of snoring gromrolls to an empty bunk.

"This one here is yours," my father stated.

"What about my things?" I asked, my eyes finally managed a peer in his direction.

"I'll take care of them."

"When do we start training?"

"For you, not until the day after next. Don't you remember? Tomorrow's a holiday: Equal Night. Anua will be in her phase of rebirth."

"Right, I forgot about that."

"Such things are not wise to forget about, Amat. Anua took much from us, but she returned it in tenfold. She holds all in balance with one another. To disregard her days of tribute is to disrupt that balance."

My mind wandered intentionally and my ear twitched, giving me away.

"Amat, look at me."

I gave a huffing sigh through my snout as I looked up at my father and asked, "Can I rest now?" My father's eyes were sad; he shook his head. He seemed unable to recognize me.

"You may. Be in light," my father replied. He paused while he took up my things and looked back at me. "Remember, tomorrow, we talk."

"Looking forward to it," I said, with no hint of enthusiasm.

VI
Scars of Indoctrination

The next morning, I woke up just slightly later than I usually would. Sitting up from my bunk, I looked around the barracks; it wasn't very full. Though, there were a few who looked to be doing some small workouts, reading letters, or getting dressed. One of whom looked familiar. Despite the time that separated our last meeting, there was no mistaking him.

"Dilek?" I asked as I walked up to him. The young man quickly turned his head to me.

"Amat," his lips curled into a fang-revealing grin.

"By Anua's pale light, I didn't expect to see you here," I said as I embraced Dilek.

"Nor I you." My old friend and I shared warm looks. "I remember you telling me you'd gone on to alpha training. I would have thought you'd be on your way to serving by this time."

My smile dissipated. "Yes, well, considering recent events, fortune would not have it so."

"Ah, I'm sorry to hear that. But you are an alpha at this point, aren't you?"

"I am that much, yes."

"Well, congratulations then." Dilek gave me a brutish pat on the shoulder.

"Thank you. Are you and Lara still talking?" I queried, trying to change the subject.

"*Mm*, well, I don't know how you'd feel about this, but Lara and I got a little closer from the last time you saw us. As of a year ago, roughly." Dilek gave a smug smile.

I tilted my head as my face lit up with pride. I let out a brief howl of approval as I patted Dilek on the shoulder. "Why wouldn't I want to hear that, Dilek, that's great news! Although, I'm not incredibly surprised.

You and my sister were always close, in almost all the time we've been friends. Soon enough, I may call you brother."

"Yeah, we were all really close all those years ago. I have you to thank for where it's gone with Lara," Dilek replied.

My old friend and I laughed as we wrapped our arms over our shoulders and walked with one another out of the barracks.

Dilek and I spent the next couple of hours catching up on all we'd been up to over the previous five years. Much of what I shared related to training, since it was really all I did during that time. Dilek started his training as a gromroll two years after my enlistment, and he relayed how he achieved the rank of a krollgrum. He told me about a handful of missions he carried out over the previous nine months in Zeta. In fact, he was currently getting ready to fly out once again for another mission there. That stung a bit, knowing that Dilek received less training, spent less time in the army, and yet had more experience in the field than me.

At first, Dilek was hesitant to talk about any of his missions. His prolonged rumination seemed rooted in an awkward disturbance by the mission details and perhaps solemn oaths of secrecy. Indecision persisting ever more in Dilek's openness, I jocularly pointed out our differences in rank and demanded Dilek share the thoughts that occupied him. Though, in a joking manner, my curiosity had been suddenly kindled to hear of a true war story from someone I knew so closely and my tone may have come off more *naggingly* than jestingly. Dilek narrowed his eyes at me after my insistent request but in the blink of an eye, his offended stare subsided. My old friend blinked nervously. Still hesitant, Dilek opened with this:

"Eh, uh, well . . . there was this one time. It's always so vivid whenever I recall it. I was in Deki'Vaia, Zeta," spoke Dilek. His body language shrunk as he put his hands in his pockets and kept his arms tight by his sides. "Me and three other krollgrums were assigned to take out Muan'nei."

"The propogandist for the xůté?"

Dilek nodded. "A very pivotal and influential asset to the rebel force over there. Whom we underestimated the importance of . . ."

(Dilek)

There were four of us krollgrums; our drop point was located roughly forty miles out from our target area. The desert sands of Zeta were different from that of Utopion, in that they were a deep, velvet-red, compared to the rich, orange sands of my country.

The sands of Zeta were said to be rich with the blood of long since passed generations of ancient leaders and their armies. Anhìr Ŭmin, the Shrai'hen, was greatest among them. He ruled with a blood lust over the land, in the early dawn of man's coming into the world. Imposing his rule through war, the scorched lands of Zeta swelled the running rivers of their blood.

In that era, many things were scarce: shelter from the beating sun, food, and water in the dry land. However, many a ruined monument of ancient technologies still remained. The most common of those being the Latrodect monuments that resembled arachnids. In the heart of the country was a temple, built in the architecture of the lost Latrodect culture. There, an army of starving scavengers and humble folk tried to build a community.

The locals said these people managed to restore some of the technology within the temple, presumably through esoteric means. Much of which helped them to restore some of the land's natural biome, so as to farm and collect clean water. Try as they did, however, to keep this resurgence of natural growth hidden, the Shrai'hen and his pillaging army found the temple before long.

Without hesitation, the tyrant charged his army through the temple, slaughtering all who resided there. Armed with only delicate and or blunt weapons, in the good folk's arsenal, they were no match for Anhìr nor any man who followed in his wake.

When all had settled and Shrai'hen inspected the contents of the temple, walking over the bloodied corpses, something in the temple had been disturbed. Some said it was another rival god or goddess to Anua. Whatever it was had been greatly offended by the Shrai'hen's display of carnage. A violent wind picked up within the temple. A wind that tore at the shattered metals of the broken weapons, embusing them with the blood-stained sand. Caught in the whirlwind, Anhìr Ŭmin and his army cried out in terror as the sands tore through their skin and impaired their eyes. They were left to walk their final days out into the desert, cold, blind and bloody.

Thus why the desert of Zeta is called Pa'Zihnra, "Piercing fire." While no temple of the Latrodect design was ever found; no one has ever dared enter a Zetian sandstorm. For those caught in its wake, were met with the agonizing death of the sharp sands seeping into their eyes and under their skin.

We were driven into town by a hired, local operative. All the while my men and I remained incognito, with our fade-suits active.

Our man drove us five blocks into the city, until the civilian populous proved too dense an obstacle for his vehicle. I signaled him to pull off into an alley, where we continued our operation on foot.

We found our way to the roof tops, hopping gaps between buildings to bypass the crowds. We were a long way off from Muan'nei's position, near the heart of the town. Having a tight window to reach him, we moved. . . impetuously.

Within a kilometer of the target, we confronted a huge gap with a chipped wall for us to leap from. Guy at the back of the lineup didn't see the unstable step up and damn near fell to his death, barely making it to the other side. Crumbles of debris tumbled off the walls and *clicked* to the ground. The clash of his suit against the neighboring wall caught the attention of a few isolated civilians in the alley. One of them stared blankly at us. Of course she couldn't see us, physically, from the camo of our fade suits. All the same, she knew we were there, and what we would do next.

With the target finally in sight, we kept to the buildings and used our scopes to pinpoint Muan'nei's defenses. Before we could sound off the tenth hostile, we were under fire. One clear view and fifteen inches of being-at-the-right-place-at-the-right-time was all it took for Singens to take a bullet for me. The shot went through his eye; his body was launched back. With barely enough time to duck down, they already primed their heavy artillery and blew the roof from under our feet. We fell four stories, me and Kanham. We were lucky to have landed on some furniture, but Wetvern landed upright and broke his knees. We saw the bones protruding through his skin after the dust cleared.

A residing family of civilians cried and screamed at the intrusion into their home. A man, woman and child, presumably a family. All speaking in their native tongue. Despite not being able to interpret much of what they said, due to a multitude of reasons present in that instance, it didn't take much to recognize the enraged nature of the man. The woman tugging her child close as she struggled to argue and hold the man in place. My heart quickly hastened with adrenaline, even if my speech and awareness wasn't entirely lucid, I'd raised my weapon to the man as he persisted in his hostile mood. This proved to aggravate him further, pulling himself free from the woman's reach, he reached for a knife, wielding it above his head.

"Put the weapon down! Calm down and return to your—"

The door to their home burst open the moment the man charged at me with the knife. The intruding xûté were promptly distracted by the howling, charging man and opened fire on both him and his family with Zin-wave rifles. The weapons propelled high intensity, ultrasonic waves which burned targets from the inside out. The screams of the civilian casualties intensified. My gut churned as I momentarily witnessed their pale skin heightened to a deep red-brown; smoke rose from their flesh, their drying eyes turned yellow as all the moisture drained profusely from their eyelids. A scream I could hardly suppress, escaped my throat. Subconscious muscle memory took over as my aim shifted to the xûté. My finger pulling hard on the trigger in a wavering spray of ammunition. The xûté were mortally wounded. Blood-gurgling moans still reached my ear as they cradled their wounds on the ground.

Wetvern hardly noticed the xûté or the screaming family. Too shocked by the sight of his legs, hyperventilating, and crying for Anua, his hand trembled and hovered over his wounds. Finally, Kanham grabbed me by the shoulder and propelled me to my feet as we came to Wetvern's side, glancing over his bloody legs. Outside the door, sounded the voices of additional xûté in their native language. Kanham and I motioned to drag and move Wetvern to a more secure location. The moment we inched his body across the floor, his right leg snapped and was now completely severed. Next, another loud *boom* once again ruptured the floor from under our feet. After falling all the way down to the bottom floor, I came to; I was shell shocked, with Wetvern at my side. The side of his scalp was palpitating with blood, his lifeless eyes transfixed on me.

It wasn't the first time I was met with such a stare or seen a man in such a state. However, it was the first time I felt so close to death and had it stare right back at me, accompanied by the deafening ring of a shell shock. The shock of this scene permeated superstitious cowardice within my mind. I dared not move, lest the unseen spirits of the battlefield threatened to arrest and defile my soul, but no such assault occurred. Only the ominous presence of death itself, staring back at me.

Once again, Kanham came to my side to pick me up, his muffled screams barely managed to recenter my focus. Kanham limped us to the back of the building with the rumbling of the Xŭté Ankavi at our backs. We couldn't move fast enough to escape the sight of the turret gunner, but we made it out of there alive.

Kanham took a series of shots to the back, as we barged through a window. He fought through the pain to pulled us into the streets. With our fade suits as cover, we escaped the xŭté, for a time. Kanham was leaving behind a trail of blood. We only marched a few blocks, with the xŭté not too far behind, before Kanham told me to go on without him. With my thoughts starting to become more lucid, as it once was, I protested and tried to lift Kanham back to his feet. He shoved me off and growled his assertion for me to go on without him. I did not leave right away, and though I didn't see it, I heard Kanham pull back the hammer on his pistol. I knew it was aimed at me.

"Go!" he yelled.

He didn't want to shoot me, but I knew he would have. Only to make the point that I was a dead man if he remained at my side. With that, I finally withdrew. Half a block later, I heard the final cursing barks that echoed across the air, promptly followed by the sound of rapid gunfire.

(Amat)

"I haven't felt the same since. I've always carried this . . . sense of guilt, for making it out when no one else did," said Dilek.

I could see every detail my old friend had described. Though I listened in awe of his recount, the neuro-chip in my mind brought up feelings of attenuated my perception of Dilek, at his mention of cowardice and retreat of the battlefield. But I swiftly suppressed those emotions and cast them aside, as I did not wish to demean him at this moment of vulnerability. The opposition I'd posed to my neuro-chip a day prior had built up some resiliency against the immediate obligations contrived by the device.

Dilek moved on to other topics, things that occurred before his time in the Utopion army. A little about him and my sister, about which, I wasn't all that interested, but happy to hear how well they seemed to be getting along.

In our stroll, Dilek and I wandered past a gathering of the base's lower ranks, with a young man at their center. His face looked slightly more mature than myself, his features were more refined, with a bigger build than my own.

Upon the sight of him, something snapped in my mind. The way he grinned smugly, his eyelids just wide enough to give away his unease, and his barking speech . . . all his mannerisms reflected something in me. Something I promptly repressed at the moment of its resurgence.

"Who are they all sucking up to?" I asked. Dilek stretched his neck to see passed me.

"Ah, that would be Blick Vykin. He's something of an enigma. Nobody knows his rank, or where he came from. He's new to the base; he shares the same squadron as us. In the time he's been here, he's displayed the makings of a highly experienced soldier. I wouldn't be surprised if he's the most experienced trooper on the base, aside from the jinn-hid and the other training officers," Dilek said.

"I doubt he's better than a fully trained alpha."

Dilek smiled. "Ha! Well, only you put that to the test. You should pair yourself with him next time we have sparring training."

Dilek's unwavering smirk gave away his doubt in me.

"You don't think I could take him."

"He's three times your size, Amat," Dilek replied.

"I trained to fight bigger," I replied.

"Words only go so far, Amat."

"A leader is defined both by his words and deeds. As an alpha, I'm bread to be a natural leader on the field, and in life. I stand within thirty feet of a man who holds too much pride in his eyes, and a false sense of confidence in his grin. He's no leader, I can tell by the way the others congregate at his feet. He merely knows how to gloat so well as to hold their intrigue," I growled.

Dilek remained silent as I pressed my scowling stare at this . . . Blick. His instincts lured his gaze to me and his smile faded fast, as my eyes pierced through him. He quickly hid his discomfort with a subtle squint, his eyes staring back at me. We were both likely convincing ourselves that we were communicating the same thing: dominance. Although, what we truly felt, and what we truly displayed, was mere insecurity.

Shortly after that, Dilek and I went our separate ways. I proceeded to wander around the base, aimlessly trying to find some comfort about my new home. A part of myself filled with resent at the idea that I was starting to embrace my new circumstance. *This isn't where I should be. By wasting away in a program, I can gain nothing from, I am dishonoring my country and my vow to defend it.* To the west, there were several complex obstacle courses. At the south region of the base, rested a wide field of drat, a plant identical to that of grass, only purple in color. Given the rich orange desert beyond the field, it was obvious that the drat were artificially grown. To the west end of the base was a large, reflective dome, a matrix platform. It was used for training soldiers in augmented reality that could expand well beyond the dimensions of the dome itself.

"Ever trained in one of these at Gallethol?" a familiar voice beside me enquired.

I glanced over to discover my father standing at my side. I delayed my reply, contemplating whether to say anything at all.

"Many a time," I replied. "How long have you been filtering me?" I ground my teeth at the idea of my father using my own eyes to keep tabs on me.

"Just off and on throughout the day. I was going to approach you when I saw you awaken through your feed. But then, I saw you catching up with Dilek and I didn't want to intrude."

"How kind of you," I mocked. "Hack into my feed much while I was away?"

"I have always respected your privacy, Amat, and your decisions," my father said sternly.

"If you respected my decisions, you would have let me go on to fight in Zeta."

"In that regard, I respect your decision to serve. I do not, however, support your blood lust for war. That decision was made up for you by the code one neuro-chip festering in your mind."

I gave my father an intense stare. "And yet you have a neuro-chip of your own."

. "Be that as it may, I shield my thoughts from the propaganda that passes through them by the chip."

I chuckled and shook my head. "There's always an explanation," I scoffed.

My father and I stood in silence for a moment. He took a deep breath.

"I know you think you're here as a punishment. I know you think I'm holding you back—"

"Oh, there's no question you are. I have mastered the arts of land, sea, sky, and space warfare. What more do I have to learn as a soldier? What more could you teach me?"

"A lot more than you would lead yourself to believe!" my father barked, lifting his lips to bare his fangs in frustration. "There is always more to learn, even as a soldier of your rank. What I can and will teach you, Amat, is humility. You will not be discharged from my command until you learn and implement that trait."

I scowled at my father. I was so furious my head felt hot, and my face surely turned red. My father only gave me a stern look in reply, with his arms at his side. Neither one of us intended to back down.

"Be prepared . . ." my father finally said. "Your training will start tomorrow." He then turned his back on me, walked away, and no matter how hard I glared at him, he never looked back.

VII
Equal Night

I kept myself isolated from other members of the base as I continued wallowing in my own distress, my head hanging low. On occasion I butted shoulders with a random passerby, but I paid them no mind, even the ones who displayed a temper. The only thing that did manage to pull me out of my daze was a distant call of my name. Twice it came before I finally turned my head to the beckoner. Actually, two people. Their faces, as they came into focus, seemed faintly familiar. However, I couldn't quite pin who they were. What was obvious was one was their variance in age, by about three years or so.

"Amat? Do you remember us?" the younger one asked. My ears twitched in my moment's reflection before shaking my head.

"Well, it has been a while. I'll admit, I hardly recognized you myself, seeing as how you've grown so much. We're your cousins. I'm Olson, this is Log, my younger brother," he stated.

My thoughts were still tempered; I had to force a smile, not wanting to seem rude. "Of course, I think I remember you both, though I'll admit, not very well." It must have been the way I said it, because that caused the smiles to fade from their faces. I didn't consider it at the time, but I could tell I disappointed them.

"Well, perhaps we've caught you at a bad time. You do seem preoccupied, but maybe we could catch up later?" Olson asked as he put his hand on Log's shoulder and led them both away from me.

As they moved further from me, I reflected on my actions. *I need a distraction. If I keep walking around like this, I'll just sulk in woe all day.* "Hold on," I called out to them.

My cousins stopped and looked back at me.

"I could use the company, if you want to catch up."

Olson nodded his head and gave a reassuring smile. "I'm up for it. Log, what do you say?"

"Sure," Log replied.

The conversation started awkwardly at first, as I gradually doused the fire in my head. The more we got to know each other, the easier talking became. Olson was very patient with me and when things got quiet between the three of us, he'd always find a way to reinvigorate the conversation. Log came off very reserved and hesitated to speak to me directly. He had a lot of questions for me, my younger cousin. Like what I'd done, where I'd been, things of that nature, which only led so far. It was clear to me, however, that Log was curious about me, so I asked him some questions in return to make him feel included.

By the evening, we were all relatively well acquainted. I learned that my cousins weren't part of my father's squadron, but rather another officer, a pac: Rike Dolson. They told me how their two squadrons frequently competed against one another. From what I heard, my father's squadron often won thanks to the leadership of Blick Vykin. There was that name again. It threw me off, just for a moment, hearing how crucial he was to the squadron and his role in it. *Experienced soldier or not, I won't be kissing up to Vykin.*

As Anua reached her highest point in the sky that night, everyone gathered in union outside the buildings of the base to gaze upon Anua in all her pale beauty. Wandering around were several monds, priests of Anua's faith, who visited the base. They walked up to each soldier with a basket in one arm, filled with powder. The powder was to be thrown upon the faces of each soldier and officer in fistfuls, chanting blessings of protection and strength. Later the monds lit small torches of white flames and gave them out to everyone. It was a long time since I was a part of a ceremony like that. Such occasions were not celebrated at Gallethol.

Apart from the first day, every day I spent there was much like the one before. All I ever did was train, and all I was trained to do was to fight. Within just a few months of my training, the only thing I understood was war. Not the act of war itself, of course, but what I would have to become to survive it. From that, a war in and of itself was waged within me. To destroy any fragment of who I was or who I might have been before joining the alphas. *Who was it that I destroyed?* Suddenly my train of thought was interrupted and references to the war in Zeta, as well as remarks of Utopion's greatness, flooded through my mind. The reflection passed; I had forgotten all about it.

I stiffened my back and stood tall as I raised my white torch. The monds were vocalizing in deep chants, their heads tilted back, singing to Anua herself. All occupants of the base stood in a formation. Log, Olson, and I stood at the center of the front line. Before us, with his back to the formation, stood my father. He took a deep breath and let out a loud *howl*, crying out to the goddess. As the thoughts of who I was, before becoming an alpha, drifted from my mind completely, tears leaked from the cracks of my sealed eyelids, as I joined in the cry amongst my brothers and sisters. The monds continued their chant and one by one, all let out their own cry to Anua again and again and again . . .

VIII
Wolves at War

We continued to howl and howl to our fertile goddess until we witnessed her "descend" onto the planet surface, A reenactment of what many believed to be the true story of how life was catastrophically ended and abruptly renewed by Anua. Amid our rabid howls and barks, a sizeable, glowing drone, resembling the moon shot across the sky and landed somewhere out in the far distance, across the dry plane. That was everyone's cue to rush out and be the first to find it. Whoever did, had the honor of planting an ŭpa tree in its place. A type of scrub that, when its greenery plumed, it was so translucent it seemed to provide the plant with a chartreuse aura that would draw your eyes to its center like a kaleidoscope. I can't remember who won that honor, but I don't think it was me.

The remainder of that celebration was filled with gifts, and fortunes from the monds, as well as games and grog. One of the games being shadows and shards. A game that was held in the matrix platform. The environment was a deep, elaborate forest, where thirty glowing shards had been hidden. Ten masked individuals resembling "cursed spirits," aimlessly wander the forest, guarding the shards while four unmasked seekers maneuver through the dim forest to recover all the shards and present them to a mond, to liberate the cursed spirits. However, if a seeker is caught by a "cursed spirits" the seeker must offer some spectacle; a dance, jest or riddle to appease the "cursed spirit." If they cannot be appeased, the seeker is removed from the game, but if they can, they are released back into the forest, so long as they are not caught by the same cursed spirit twice.

Traditionally the celebration lasts the entire night and to rest early is an insult to the goddess. Though, I do recall my father cutting the celebration short before the night grew too old.

The next morning, dark and early, we were all awoken by a loud siren. My eyelids cracked open. I swiftly threw back the sheets of my bunk and got dressed. Everyone else in the barracks were doing much of the same, many of them sluggishly from the aftermath of too much grog. After a minute or two passed, I was in uniform, tying my shoelaces, when the doors slammed open. My father walked through, shouting and urging us to hasten our readiness and to fall in line outside.

Once I finished tying the second lace of my boots, I jogged quickly toward the door. It looked as though I would be the first one out with so many people still getting ready. I smirked at my father as I got within steps of the doorway, but just a moment later, a large figure raced through it and beat me outside. I almost stopped in my tracks, but as I slowed my pace my father shouted, "Move along, alpha, fall in line!"

I picked up my pace and was averse to stand beside the soldier who had beaten me. As I got closer, I recognized him from the day before—it was Blick. *Don't fuss over this, Amat,* I told myself. *It's only the start of the day, and by the end of it, Blick will know his place.*

The rest of the squadron fell in behind us, and my father stood before us all.

"At grace," my father commanded.

In unison, we all transitioned to less stiff stances.

"Listen up, gromrolls and krollgrums! Tomorrow, we have our next competition against Pac Dolson's squadron. I've observed each of your efforts on the matrix platform; you are all well-disciplined and dedicated. I'm proud of our victory streak in the last few weeks. There are some that I have even considered for officer training."

I didn't look back, but I could hear several of the men and women sharing whispers of caustic boasts and laughs.

"But!" my father's tone suddenly shifted and all fell silent, like a child would at the yell of an angry parent. "I heard that there was some rising tension between a select few of you and some members of Dolson's squadron. In that, I am *very* disappointed! Do not err in making enemies of your peers from another squadron. At the end of the day, we are all on the same side: fighting for Utopion. I should not have to reiterate this to any of you, at all! These individuals that I speak of, you know who you are. At the end of our training for the day, you'll face your consequences."

Where there were whispers of laughs and jokes, now there were sighs and moans.

"Your actions, as individuals, reflect on who you are as a squadron and who you are as a squadron reflects on me. In the past couple of weeks, some of you have made me look quite the fool, especially for my rank. As jinn-hid, I have many other duties that supersede you all. The superior training and battle strategy I bestow upon each of you is by *my* choice. Each of you were hand selected by me because your profiles showed promise for the makings of exceptional servants of war. Yet some of you have demonstrated that my standards for what makes an exceptional soldier of my training, is nothing short of dishonor and misconduct. For that, you'll all be putting in a little extra effort today. Fifteen laps around course C, I'll be filtering every one of you—your time, actions, progress, and failures. If any of you run a circuit over two minutes, you'll *all* start again. Is that understood?"

"Sir, yes, sir!" everyone replied.

"Good. Move out! Two laps around the drat field, twenty burpees, and then straight to the course! Move, move, move!"

We all raced our laps around the drat field, sprinting. Before long, Blick and I adopted a spot well ahead of the squadron. Neither one of us would let up; running so fast my legs felt numb, but my heartbeat steady, and my arms pumped with fluidity. Even when we turned corners, Blick and I seemed almost in sync. It took two laps two laps before I managed to surpass Blick. I wasn't sure how good of a lead I gained on him, all I knew was that I ran a faster circuit than he had.

My mind started to perceive things more slowly with each completed circuit, details in my vision seemed to stretch and became disproportional. Every breath echoed to my ears. My eyelids felt heavy, but not enough to close completely. Every impact of my foot touching and striding against the ground jolted my loose muscles and bones. Slowly, a large figure emerged at the corner of my eye. I didn't have to glance his way to know it was Blick, as he caught back up to me before I *kicked* into my stride and went even faster.

The first of our obstacles were that of bulbous, sanded tree trunks. We used the momentum from running to vault over one trunk after another.

Blick's heavier mass was the likely variable that propelled him further passed me, little by little. Being well behind, I raced Blick over to a patch of swampy mud where the hang-climbing obstacle was, leading to an array of dangling rings over muddied water. When close enough, I swung myself passed the final rings, to the ledge regaining my lead on Blick. Next was a series of long barbed tunnels we had to crawl through. Blick panted and growled as he struggled to nudge his way through. Clearing the tunnel with ease, I moved on to the flying bars obstacle. There were two columns, vertically inclined, side by side. One was for going up and the other for going down this obstacle, as well as a dozen, evenly spaced replicas of it. Once I reached the top of the left side, I flipped the bar and swung my body over to reach the right column. As I started on my way down, I saw Blick starting on his way up.

The sensation of calm breathing, and the perception of time slowing, occurred once again. An instant passed where Blick and I were at eye level and we shared a glance. The details that seized my attention seemed to stretch the time of the moment. An identical sensation to what I had experienced in the tunnel on the day of my final assessment with the alphas. I was caught off guard by the peculiar color of his eyes. The lower crescent of his irises were almost a glowing yellow, but on the upper crescent, they were a vibrant orange. Though they were not as rich as the red eyes of Anua's cho'zai. A select few of humanity were born with rich red eyes. In our culture, it was a sign that the individual was destined to be among our greatest warriors, and thus the course of their lives were decided for them. The most common colors were blue, yellow, and gray, but until that day I knew no man, nor woman, who bore orange eyes. *Ominous,* I thought to myself.

Continuing on my way down, my curiosity about the observation quickly faded. I ran downhill, to the final obstacle of a long rope I needed to climb and a bell at the top I had to ring. Cursing as I stumbled a few steps passed the rope after I took hold of it. Without another moment's hesitation, I started my climb, with Blick on the parallel rope. The bell was within reach as I eagerly stretched out my hand to flick it before Blick who also extended his own hand. At the time, I would have loathed admitting this, but I'm sure Blick struck it before me.

When we reached the bottom of the ropes, Blick rushed close beside me, nearly tripping me. Catching back up, I shoved him aside, snapped my muzzle at him, and growled. He looked over at me with a shift in his eyes as he bared his fangs and growled in reply.

After the seventh time around, someone did not beat two minutes. So, my father shouted aloud, for all to hear, that we were to start again from zero and it only started when we reached the beginning of the course. However, Blick and I remained neck and neck throughout it all. With every circuit we completed, the more competitive we became. My father caught us a few times while filtering, and warned us to knock it off, each time less and less leniently.

On our final circuit, Blick and I were drenched and dripping with sweat. We all were. But my competitive nature at this juncture did not falter. Up to this point, neither of us raised fists or kicked at one another. During this final lap, that would change. As we sprang over the trunks, closely beside one another, Blick managed to whip his legs around, mid-hurdle, and scrape the edges of his boots across my cheek. A likely accident, but I did not received it as such. Continuing up the course, I plotted how I would respond in kind. In the midst of working our way up the hang-climbing obstacle, I reeled my leg back and stomped my foot into his side without looking, so my father wouldn't see it on his neural feed. Blick immediately lost his grip and fell into the murky water below. To my father, it would look as though he merely slipped.

"Come on, Vykin, get up out of that water!" my father commanded sternly from afar.

Blick kept his eyes fixed on me, grinding his teeth as he made his way to the other side of the water and caught up to me. He skipped straight to the barbed wires and squirmed into the tunnel beside me, powering through the sharp metal. With his lead regained, he stopped, turned, and kicked down one of the pillars that held up the wire. The falling wire landed just ahead of my path and scraped across my scalp and ear. Unfortunately, I was looking down and not ahead, so my father wouldn't have seen that either. I growled as I pushed aside the wire with my arm. I crawled onward as blood trickled down the side of my head.

By the time I reached the flying bars obstacle, Blick was already on the second side and climbing down. I quickly took up a bar and climbed my way to the top. When at the top, the bell was within my sight, and my final strategy dawned on me. I swung my body forward and back, forward and back. In unison, I used my legs to waver myself until I was looping around and around and around. Finally, I launched myself forward towards the rope. I reached one hand high, ready to strike the bell as I stretched forward with the other to grab the rope. Blick was leaping up one of the ropes as he did previously. It almost seemed like he would beat me again, but I came in just before Blick. His hand slapped against the back of my own, as my palm sounded that sweet ring. I grabbed hold of the rope with both hands and slid down. He promptly made his way to me once he touched down, catching my attention with nothing but his stare. Despite our mutual distaste for one another, we could not will ourselves to speak until we caught our breaths.

"You don't say much, do you?" Blick asked.

"You know, I didn't hear that bell ring twice. It was my hand that rang it. You best climb back up that rope and do us all a favor, before we have to run another fifteen circuits." I slapped Blick on the shoulder and walked away, concluding our interaction for the day.

IX
Something More to Learn

The next morning, once again, the siren sounded before the sun came up. My father burst through the barracks, barking commands. My boots were strapped on by the time the doors slammed shut. With Blick trailing behind, I made sure I was the first one outside this time.

"Gromrolls, krollgrums, alpha, at grace," my father commanded once we were all in formation. "How is everyone? Tired? Sore? Good. So are the members of Pac Dolson's squadron. They too had their own vigorous drills set before them yesterday. As your commanding officers, we expect you all learned your lesson. Believe me when I say, consequences will be even more grueling should we hear any more news regarding unacceptable relations among the troops of this base." My father let that sit with us for a moment, then carried on.

"Today, you'll be in a doc-sim. Conditions will be harsh, it'll be dark. You'll be faced with Zetian programs, defending a sieged base, wired with an EMP. This exact situation occurred two weeks ago at the Quatel data center. The xûté infiltrated the facility, confiscating highly valuable data banks containing classified information. Any and all information that would serve them had been extracted and lost. The task force we sent in to neutralize their assault failed. Your mission will be to do what our own couldn't. Neutralize the targets and disarm the bomb before time runs out . . . alongside Pac Dolson's squadron."

Whispers suddenly picked up behind me. The response from members of my squadron suggested to me this wasn't a common occurrence—if at all.

"Now!" my father blurted, to silence the commotion. "We are going to be doing things differently today—for obvious reasons. Aside from forming a successful battle strategy, tactical coherence will be your *first* priority during this drill. Whether it's a friend you have trained with for years or a member of a competing squad, you need to learn to fight together and not against each other. We are all on the same side here and if you refuse to acknowledge another's value and or put aside your differences, you could get them or yourselves killed. Especially in Zeta, where the xŭté take no prisoners. A front, where I know many of you would like to be stationed."

My father passed his eyes over the formation, holding firm on me for an extended moment, then moving on. "But that will not happen if you are not the best you can be, in every way possible, which includes *teamwork*. Is that understood?"

"Sir, yes, sir!" everyone shouted.

"Good! Move out to the armory! Rendezvous with Pac Dolson's squadron at the matrix platform! Go, go, go, go!"

As we ran up to the armory, the last of Dolson's squadron was rushing out toward the matrix platform. I familiarized myself with the layout of the weapons; there was only one I desired. Gazing down, to the end of the racks, I found it: the electric shock-put 101. A weapon that fires small rounds of ball lighting that can be set to stun or tear chunks of an enemy's flesh to bits. The ammunition was in the form of crystal cubes holding surges of electricity, which, when loaded into a rectangular slot, it duplicated. When the cube reached the last of its voltage, it would spark and you could either fire the last of it, or take it out of the slot, throw it, and it would detonate a spastic shockwave on impact. I took up one of the shock-puts, as well as twenty cubes, that I stowed in a bag, strapped across my shoulder. I also armed myself with two knives, in case I ran out of ammunition. I picked up an earpiece for comms, a watch, infrared goggles for vision, and I dressed in a fade-suit. This was a form of armor that blends in clear as crystal with its surroundings.

I ran to the matrix platform where Pac Dolson, as well as his squadron and my father, awaited us. When they saw that everyone made it to the dome structure, my father spoke.

"Criptous, Vykin, front and center!" he commanded.

Initially, I was caught off guard by the abrupt callout, but I met Blick at the front.

"As I observed yesterday, you two seem to have some tensions between one another. Despite the promise you both show, I was not impressed with your childish quarrel," my father said. "However, I acknowledge that you pushed one another to do better than anyone else on the circuits. Which makes me curious as to what you could accomplish together. Thus, the both of you will share command over both squadrons during this sim."

My lips tightened into a frown and my claws dug into my palms.

"Hopefully, in having more at stake than just yourselves, you'll put aside your differences and work together to lead a successful mission. Can Pac Dolson and I count on you to do this?"

Blick and I, in unison, stood tall and raised the palms of our right hands to cover the right side of our faces.

"Sir, yes, sir!" Blick replied.

I, on the other hand, couldn't honestly make that guarantee. My father gave me a sidelong look; I didn't scowl or furrow my brows, but he sensed my distaste for the scenario all the same.

"Alpha?" my father growled.

My lips twitched in irritancy, revealing my fangs obscurely. Reluctantly, I replied, "Yes, sir, the team will be looked after under our leadership."

My father nodded. "Alright, move out then. All of you! Get in the dome! Go, go, go!" he barked.

The environment of the sim was not manifested yet, and the inside was dark. Although, along the walls and floor were teal numbers of ones and zeros, streaking down the dome's interior. The doors shut behind us, and my father's voice beckoned over the dome's speakers.

"The sim will commence on my mark. Three, two, one, mark."

The numbers expanded in size and depth as a life-like terrain was formulated. The sky was black, and burning vehicles sat idle, with clusters of fallen debris. A few buildings stood tall in the near distance. In the window frames, there were short bursts of flickers, followed by sounds of gunfire. Further beyond the buildings, thuds of explosions burst and lit up some of the darkness for the briefest of instances. A screech, getting louder and louder, came from overhead.

Blick cursed as he caught sight of the incoming ballistics.

"Scatter! Find cover!" I barked.

The team members moved, but not all of them fast enough to dodge the incoming fire. I took cover behind a crumbled wall and a few others slid beside me.

Once things seemed to settled, I glossed over how many we lost, and took note of the time. Six lay still on the ground not too far from where I initially stood. When you are fatally injured in a sim, you are not really physically harmed. The matrix tracks movement, presence, and impact of everything: from a single breath to how much damage a person could take from the simulated blasts. When it registers that someone was fatally wounded, it hits the individual with an energized frequency that knocks them out for the remainder of the sim. The downside was when you woke, it could leave you nauseous, depending on how long you were under.

"Amat," a voice over comms spoke. "This is Blick. We have six men down; the rest are scattered. Our targets are mostly positioned in the higher levels of the buildings, just due south of us. The Quatel facility sits two miles passed them, but the xûté have them fortified."

"Then, let's not waste any more time. Tell the troops to move up, take cover where they can. Don't fire till we're in a better position," I replied.

"Roger that." Blick opened a channel to all the members on our side and ordered them to move up.

I was ravished by the cool air blowing past my face and through my fur, the sweat dripping from my scalp, the adrenaline in my veins, and the projectiles that whizzed past.

Finally, when we were close enough to the buildings, I spoke on an open channel. "This is Alpha Criptous, those of you with pulse-cannons, get into position. Aim at the buildings off to the right of our position. It looks as if there may be more hostiles over there than on the left."

I ran and jumped into a wide pit, dropping onto my stomach, lying perfectly still. I was practically hiding in plain sight, positioned no more than a hundred meters from the nearest building the xûté took refuge in.

"Pulse-cannons, fire on my command. In three, two, one . . . Now!" Three deep pulses soared into the air, lightly kicking up the sand in their path. The waves blew past the buildings and, in the blink of an eye, pulled back with a great *thud*, tearing apart chunks of the structures.

The entire front of the buildings crumbled to the ground and there were none who fired from it any longer. I held my breath and shut my eyes as a thick, dust cloud swept over me.

"Move up! Use the dust as cover," Blick commanded on the open channel.

"No, wait!" I replied on the same channel. "Hold your positions till the dust clears. Pulse-cannons, aim your weapons at the buildings on the left to cover our flank! Wait till I'm clear."

Blick remained silent, as if he hesitated to respond as I stayed crouched and moved as swiftly as I could through the trench. Continuing up the way, the debris on either side of me became less and less bulbous, until I came to a clearing.

"Fire!" Blick's voice sounded over comms.

I whipped my head to the right, where I faintly saw Blick standing, and before I could protest in panic, the pulse-cannons sounded again. Without hesitation, I sprung flat on the ground, crunching my body and shielding my head. As the sound of the next few buildings came crashing down, I prayed to the goddess that no harm would come to me; none did.

I stood as the dust settled, glaring resentfully in Blick's direction.

"Glad to see you're alright, Alpha Criptous." I growled at the smugness in his voice.

"Move up! Take refuge in the ruins, and hold your fire while we scope out where to press our advance," I commanded.

I moved on my own, taking cover within one of the battered buildings and checked the time. Seven minutes had gone by. I quickly shifted in my stance and aimed my gun in the direction of whimpering sounds at my side. Registering the sight of a wounded civilian, an old man with a bundle in his arms, I lowered my guard. Coming to his side, I took in his features. The ash and soot coating his face made the sacks of his eyes glisten sadly, like the night sea. He had barely any fangs to count; those that remained were yellowed and chipped. I never saw someone so skinny before. His rib cage bulged and his skin almost looked molded to the ground. His fur was mangy and knotted, and his fingernails were disgustingly long. Despite the obvious sight of his strength fleeting him, his body relentlessly contorting, the old man's grasp on the bundle would not give. I didn't have to think twice about what might have been under those blankets. However, what did cross my mind was why this man and this toddler were here in the first place? Why weren't they expunged from the sim after the event was documented? There was no doubt in my mind that at one point this man and the child were here and were real. Although, I never witnessed such a scenario make it into a doc-sim.

"She doesn't cry no more," the old man said with a broken smile. "Before the building came down, she cry and cry. But now, she silent, peaceful. Anua take her." The old man laughed in a way that made him seem demented. The laughs quickly became wheezes and coughs. His breath quickened, until he gave out a final sigh and the life left his eyes.

I gently uncovered the bundle just slightly to find the child; its head bashed in from the falling debris. My heart sank and I couldn't help but fall back, jaw agape, eyes tearing. In spite of all I trained to do and to be prepared to witness, an encounter such as this was not one of them.

X
Last Man, Failed Man

As we waged forth, I dominated the command of both squadrons, treating co-commander's orders as mere suggestions, and acting on them when it suited me.

When the Quatel facility was finally in our sight, there were twenty minutes remaining on the clock before the EMP would go off and we were surrounded by heavy fire. We lost sixteen additional men and women in the skirmish, leaving us with a little over half of what we started with. Our options were limited; time was running out. Five minutes into the pin, Blick found me taking cover behind a smashed wall, returning fire when I felt it safe.

Blick grabbed me by the shoulder and yelled over the crossfire, "Amat, we are pinned down!"

I shoved his grip off of me. "I know!" I peeked out from my cover and fired some shots at the enemies hiding across the plaza. My sight returned to a very vexed Blick. "What? Did you expect praise for stating the obvious?"

"I've found an alternative route," he shouted. "It's not as direct, but if we travel east, there's a path that'll take us back around to the northwest, towards Quatel."

I was immediately unsure about this new course of action. "How much time would it add to our ETA, to the bomb?"

He tilted his head and shrugged. "We'd be cutting it close. I'm not sure we would even make it in time."

I shook my head. "I won't veer off from our path for a strategy based on hope. If we pull back now, our enemies here will surely move in on us and perhaps pin us down once again."

"At least we'd have a chance, which is more than you can say. If we push here, everyone will be mowed down."

"Is that a challenge?"

"Amat, this wouldn't be the time or place—"

"No, no, I've had plenty of say in our command over this mission. With our remaining . . ." I glanced down at my watch to check the time, "Thirteen minutes, you'll take the majority of our remaining troops. You will lead them down your alternative route, while I take two up the field and run straight for the base."

"Amat, don't—"

Before Blick could say any more, I opened a channel to all the remaining members of each squadron. "Attention all squad members, this is Commander Amat Criptous. You are to follow Commander Blick Vykin east and find an opening in the enemy's defenses. From there, push northwest, back toward the base. However, Olson, Log, and I will stay behind to sneak into the base and disarm the bomb. I am sending each of you lock-on locations of your designated commander. You have your orders. Criptous out." I closed the channel and walked past Blick. "Better step to. Time's running out," I reported to him.

I doubled back a little bit and waited in isolation for Olson and Log to come find me.

"Amat?" Log asked.

I said nothing in reply. I just sat there, perfectly still, on the hard, rocky ground.

"We're here, should we get a move on or . . .?"

"We're waiting, Log."

"For what?" Log replied.

I raised a finger. "Listen," I said.

I was referring to the sound of gunfire in the near distance. After a few seconds, it slowly started to die down and dissipate. "Ah, there it is: silence. Do you know what it means, Log?"

Log shook his head.

"It means the xŭté forces are moving out from their positions. Chasing after Blick and those under his command."

Olson had a puzzled look on his face; he knew there must have been more to what I was doing. "Amat, did you—"

"No time for further questions. We only got nine minutes left to disarm that EMP," I declared, interrupting Olson.

Together, Log, Olson, and I crept through the ruins of the battlefield and found our way back to the point where we were pinned down. We hid behind a large pile of pulverized debris and surveyed the area.

"There doesn't seem to be a xǔté in sight. Should be safe to cross the plaza here," I said.

Olson grabbed my arm before I could rush across the plaza. "Amat!" he shouted. "How can you be so sure . . . with such a limited view of the area?"

The way Olson asked the question indicated he already knew the answer.

I simply smiled at my cousin. "Trust me, Olson, and watch as I walk across this plaza without having to raise my aim in the slightest," I replied. Looking dead ahead, I stood and ran straight across the plaza with every confidence that I would reach the other side in complete safety. As I did. I turned around to look in the direction of my cousins and waved my hand. "All clear," I said over the comm system to them.

By the time we infiltrated the base, we had six minutes remaining until detonation. I didn't bother with updating Blick on our status. After all, he did say if he made it to the bomb, going his route, he would be cutting it close. My cousins and I raced through the interior of Quatel, down flights and flights of stairs. Blue lights flashed and spun, followed by a loud siren that echoed through the base. There were moments where my cousins and I were confronted by a xǔté or two. They would come out of nowhere and cut across our path. Where Olson and Log would pause to take cover, I refused to halt, moving steadily, and gunning down my enemies before they could even take aim.

"Amat, slow down," Olson called out to me after I'd resolved a handful of confrontations.

I had no intention of holding back; I wouldn't. My priority was the mission and the mission was to disarm the EMP before it went off.

Finally, I arrived at the level the bomb was located. Without a second thought, I barged through the door, breaking it open. Before me was a long hallway, with triangular pier screens at either side of it, and a large doorway at the end. It was guarded by a xǔté, armed with a wasper;

a long, narrow cannon, emitting a high-pitched ring before it unleashed its ten petawatt rounds. I looked back at my cousins, who were still coming down the stairs.

"Take cover!" I yelled as I hid behind a pier screen. Olson, who stood beside Log, pulled him to the side; however, Log was hit before Olson could clear him from the line of fire. I watched as a wave pulsed over Log and knocked him out. My focus remained unthwarted, despite Olson's distant cursing. The xǔté didn't let up in their suppressive fire. Heaving as I readied myself to go forth and move up the hall, I turned and stood upright. The gunman at the wasper vigorously thrust his aim and forced me back into cover.

The firing paused for moments at a time as the gunman shouted in his foreign language. Apposing shots were fired towards the wasper at Olson's arrival to the fight. As he took cover on the other side of the hall, I shot at the gunman to draw his fire to me and clear a path for Olson. Despite our aim, neither Olson nor I could land a shot on the gunman, for he was protected by a small, golden shield, which domed around him. I looked at my watch; we had just under three minutes left. In battle, that was a long time. The muffled sound of charging boots echoed from further up the hall, growing louder. Peeking past the pier screen, I saw more than a dozen xǔté taking positions at the opposite end of the hall.

"Olson!" I barked, taking out the ammo cube from my shock-put.

"Yeah?" he replied.

"If you have any sonic charges, let 'em rip, now!"

I threw the ammo cube down the hall, toward the xǔté forces. At almost the same instant, Olson pulled a pin and threw a sonic charge. The cube let out a great burst of electricity, stopping a chunk of the xǔté in their tracks. Some of the branching electric streaks grazed against the shield about the xǔté at the wasper, chipping away at its integrity. Olson's explosive filled the hall with a great whirling wind and a sonic *boom* that threw the xǔté so hard against the wall, their bones surely shattered. Now, all that remained was the xǔté on the cannon. With his shield still damaged he would have to take extra care in where he aimed his gun.

"Cover fire!" Olson yelled and I drew the cannon's fire as he moved up to another pier screen. "Go, go!" he urged.

I moved up to the next pier screen as Olson covered me. Unfortunately, the next time he tried moving up, the xǔté at the cannon didn't aim at me; he got some shots off at Olson. A wave fell over my cousin and he fell limply onto the ground.

As I observed Olson falling, he seemed to be moving so incredibly slow. I didn't pay it too much mind at that moment, being all too concentrated with the task at hand. All noise dimmed out, as the sound of my own breath filled my ears. Moving out from my cover, it was then I noticed the xǔté's movements were unnaturally slow as well. My focus narrowed on a gap in the shield, at the xǔté's right leg. Holding my breath as the xǔté and I took aim at one another, we both fired. Time sped up to its natural state. The xǔté's aim was thwarted upward and he fell back onto the ground as I finished him off with another burst of fire. Only then did it briefly dawn on me how peculiarly time shifted a few moments ago. *Perhaps it was a glitch?*

I kicked open the doors to the data chamber; at its center, was the bomb. Dashing and sliding across the floor to it, I quickly tore off its casing to find an assortment of colored wires. The timer on the bomb itself read fifteen seconds. By memory, I knew I had to find two black wires, parallel to each other, to disarm it. Sifting through wires of blue, purple, and green, until two seconds remained. Deep with the cluster, my eyes set upon them and in a desperate final effort, I extended my index finger around the cords and *yanked* them out of place.

My eyes sealed shut, and sweat trickled down my face as I waited to hear the sound of the sim ending. Like quicksand sinking into a pit, I could hear the grid of the matrix platform dematerializing. I opened my eyes to the sight as the ground seemed to condense and the world faded away while all the members of each squadron were dragged toward each other. They remained limp on the ground until all became still. Everyone besides me were taken down. Nevertheless, we won. Utopion won. The neuro-chip in my head filled me with such a tremendous patriotic pride, until that moment, I only dreamed of. It painted an image in my head of admirations and being honorably decorated, not in spite of the losses I'd suffered in the sim, but because of them. In the background of it all, I could feel signals from the chip firing to my broca, coming through as whispers. *You have done a great deed for the world, Amat, for Utopion . . .*

XI
Cold at Heart

When Blick awoke, he gave me a sour look. A lot of the men and women who followed him did as well. I cowered my sight from Olson and Log, as I exited the matrix platform. The doors shut to someone beckoning my name from behind.

"Amat."

I closed my eyes, sighed, and turned reluctantly to face my father. He walked up to me at a steady pace, which was neither flustered nor calm. "Let's take a walk," my father said, placing a hand on my back, guiding me forward.

The walk was quiet and seemed longer than it actually was. The longer my father held his silence, the greater a subtle sense of shame built within me. I tried so desperately to suppress the humiliation. My neuro-chip flooded thoughts through the greater part of my mind. Of praise and renown for the patriotic valor I demonstrated, but a faint conscience argued otherwise. However, my pride would not allow these conceptions to come to light before my father.

"Did they test you much in alpha training?"

I wasn't entirely sure what my father meant by the question. Of course, I tested in alpha training.

"Several times," I replied.

"In what ways?" The question was prompt and stern.

"I mean, I was tested in my skill of flight, survival—"

"That is not what I meant," my father's voice boomed and gradually settled. "Allow me to rephrase my question. Have you ever been put in a situation that seemed so simple, so straightforward, you wouldn't have perceived it as a test?"

I was still confused where he was going with this. My uncertainty and shame was starting to show as I strained to find my words.

"I . . . No. Not that I can recall."

My father stiffened his stature. "Then, I regret to inform you, you failed your first encounter with this sort of test."

"What do you mean I *failed*? I won the sim. I deactivated the EMP. I fulfilled the mission."

"The mission, Amat, was for *the squadron* to deactivate the bomb. As one of the commanders of the operation, it was *your* mission to see it done. Yet, you allowed more than half of those under you to go down a stray path, without your supervision."

"But they were under Blick's—"

"Blick lost his command long before you suggested he take the squad east. We both know why you didn't want to go that route. From what I observed, Olson suspected as much too. I'll admit, Amat, in your time away from home, I have filtered your feed. Enough to know that you stay up to date on the latest events covering the Zetian war. You read the report and viewed the footage of the assault on the Quatel facility. You knew that none of the troops made it back home because they were pinned down yards from the base itself. So, they took an alternative route. It was the very same Blick suggested. You used your troops as bait, Amat."

My father and I stood in silence for a moment. I parted my lips to speak, but before I could say anything my father reiterated, "You *used* your *troops . . . as bait.*"

I remained silent as my eyes trailed towards the floor, averting contact with my father's unwavering stare. He wanted me to feel the weight my indignity to the fullest.

"Do you . . ." I trailed off, making sure my father would allow me to speak, ". . . want me to say what I should have done?"

"What you should have done doesn't matter because you already did what you did; that will have consequences beyond the sim. You made enemies, Amat. I saw how the other soldiers looked at you when the sim ended. Worse than that, you proved something to me."

I exhaled forcibly. "Ain't that a shock."

"You are not worthy of your rank."

My eyes widened; my blood boiled at the thought of where this would lead the conversation. My heart skipped a beat and I glanced up at my father.

"Thus, I am stripping you of your alpha title. Since you were granted no ranks prior to alpha, you will be demoted to the rank of gromroll and be treated as such."

I took a few steps towards him until there was hardly any space dividing us. The shock of my sheer outrage, in that moment, was the only thing stopping me from exclaiming every cursed statement that came to mind.

"Words cannot describe the absolute dishonor you brought upon me . . ."

"You brought dishonor upon yourself—"

"As my father."

That caught my father off guard. I could see the weight of my words reflected in his expression. "I'm not sure where the man who raised me went. He must have died long ago, because I don't recognize the one standing before me." With that, I turned briskly and walked away. Before I could get far, my father spoke out, saying one final thing.

"I've often thought the same thing, as of late, regarding my *son*. I don't know what happened to the little boy who dreamed so fondly of traveling the stars and exploring the unknown, with an open heart."

That was it, my one other pursuit in life from a time long forgotten. In that moment, the significance of the recollection could not overpower my fury.

I clenched my fist and growled as I turned back toward my father. "He *grew up*," I snarled and continued walking, alone, without a care in the world, for my own was shattered.

XII
Humility

Wandering around the base aimlessly, I was drowned in the depths of my thoughts. Fussing over five years of training and effort . . . gone. There was no changing that. Regardless of whether my demotion was printed on paper at that very moment, it surely would be by the end of the day. My father was a jinn-hid, the second most powerful position in the country. His words may as well be printed as he spoke them.

To be demoted to a gromroll, of all ranks, was beyond outrageous. There was no telling how long I would have to wait before touring in Zeta now.

In my wandering, I stumbled upon my cousins, who were seeking me out. I ignored them initially, too enveloped with my own dilemma. Olson, who called out my name several times before catching up to me, firmly grabbed onto my shoulder and turned me toward them. The furrow in his brows laxed when he observed my woe-smothered face. Though, Log's scowl did not fade in the slightest.

"Amat, is everything alright?" Olson's tone shifted, as if feeling sorry for me.

"Nothing is anymore," I replied bluntly.

"Things aren't exactly sitting too well with me either, Amat," Log blurted.

I shifted my attention to Log and gave him a stern look.

"Log," Olson spoke calmly, trying to settle his brother.

"We know what you did, Amat. You sold out more than half your squadron under your command and although it was a sim, your heedless leadership took me out of the fight. Were the nature of that sim any more tangible, I'd be lying in a ditch right now," Log barked, snapping his jowls at me.

"You're not wrong, Log. But look at Amat's face, he knows the mortification of his actions. There's no sense in beating a man while he's down," Olson voiced.

I was almost further embarrassed at Olson's notion of referring to me as a man. Not that I thought of myself as one at the time, merely a soldier if nothing else. Without my rank of alpha, I felt I was nothing at all. *Perhaps that was all for the better. If I was nothing but a rank before, who am I now?*

Placing my hand on Olson's shoulder reassuringly, I spoke, "Log is right, Olson, don't douse his rage for not seeing through me. I knew exactly what would happen, and callously spent the lives of others to complete the mission objective. That was wrong of me and I have suffered *extreme* consequences, that fill me with an unfathomable regret, as a result. As for what happened to you, Log, I owe you an apology. I did not know what would happen in that hallway, but that does not excuse the lack of caution I exercised. A leader's mission is to the safety and prosperity of those under his command. I failed that directive."

Log seemed moved by my words; his expression suggested he found some sympathy for me.

"I'll understand if you don't want to talk to me anymore," I said to him.

Log peered up at me for a long moment and raised his hand, showing me its back and front. "I can't bring myself to forgive you at this immediate moment, Amat. But if your apology is true, I can bring myself to give you another chance at being my leader, my family."

I nodded my head. "I'll promise you, I'll look after you more closely in future sims; both of you." I placed a hand on each of their shoulders, as they did mine. "Unless, of course, we find ourselves on opposing sides during our training here," I joked, lightly. My cousins shared a gentle laugh.

Suddenly, my father's voice came through on the base intercom. "Will Jinn-hid Bod's and Pac Dolson's squadrons, please report to the gym. The squadrons of Jinn-hid Bod and Pac Dolson, report to the gym now."

Together, my cousins and I headed into the gym. There we changed into looser clothing and were armed with knives. I couldn't help but catch a few snarling glances from members on each squadron. They probably would have liked nothing more than to throw their blades past my head, or worse.

Everyone was split into pairs, each set to spar and hone their hand-to-hand combat with one another. My father likely paired me with Log deliberately. Assumably, he made the decision after having filtered my most recent engagement with my cousins. Each pair was designated wide, blue, square mats, with a large, gold circle on each. Everyone moved in synchronization at my father's commands. After a while, my father allowed us to train on our own, using whatever we wanted throughout the gym. Log and I decided to remain on our mats. I showed my cousin how to be fluid with a blade, tossing it from one hand to another between strikes.

It didn't take too long before Log and I started loosening up with one another and having fun. *Slit!* A flitting knife darted between myself and Log, just before we were about to engage each other again.

"Hey!" I barked, turning my head in the direction of the thrower and found Blick, with a few of the squadron members at his side, who were snarling at me earlier. I took a few steps in front of my cousin as the young men at Blick's side laughed and exchanged antagonizing jokes. "I won't play dumb and ask what that was about. But messing up in a sim is one thing; however, threatening my life with a blade is something else entirely."

I imposed a cold gaze at each of the soldiers which couldn't seem to unnerve any of them in the slightest.

"Oh, we're not threatening anyone here, alpha," said one of the men at Blick's side.

Surely they did not know yet, but being regarded as an alpha was a form of mockery in and of itself.

"We're just having a little target practice," the young man continued, repeatedly tossing and catching another blade in hand.

"Then, allow me to inform you that your aim is terrible; before you start something you'll regret, you should find an easier target."

All the men at Blick's side *oohed* and laughed at me while he and I shared menacing glares. After some time, I noticed he wasn't armed. He didn't say or do anything provocative, so I turned my back on him. Although, as soon as I turned, a second knife was thrown. The blade passed over Log's head, leaving a non-fatal cut along his scalp and trimming some of his fur. Log clasped his wound and fell to the ground crying.

"Log!" I shouted as I tended to him.

The young men at Blick's side burst in an uproar of approval, as Log cried for his mother. "Oh, come on, kid, it's just a scratch. Your mother probably received worse from cooking."

I clenched my fist as I examined Log's wound with my other hand. It definitely wasn't life threatening, but it was a large cut and blood was already coating half of his face. What little patience and humility I found, evaporated inside me.

I heard a voice yell out, "What's going on here?" I was almost certain it was my father's, but I didn't care, it was too late for intervention.

I picked up my blade, stood to face Blick and his companions, who looked away, and threw my knife. In a split second, a sound of fabric tearing echoed through the gym and he whipped his head toward me. His face grew red and his eyes went wide as he reached down towards his crotch. The knife tore through the cloth just below, but no blood dripped. Everyone went silent. After a moment, that seemed to last forever, my father howled a command, "Amat! Front and center, right now!"

"With all due respect, sir," I answered, walking towards my father. "I did not start nor encourage this. Blick threw a knife at Log, cutting his scalp, and he's wounded." I stopped just before my father, standing tall, ready for whatever came next.

My father growled. "*Vykin*, you too. Come here!" Blick stood beside me and cleared his throat. "The rest of you, leave the room! Pac Dolson, see to it that my nephew is taken to the infirmary and receives care for his wound."

"Yes, sir," Dolson said, as everyone else exited the room.

We all stood in silence until we found ourselves alone. My father shook his head and sighed. "I don't understand why you two have shown so much resentment for one another. You hardly know each other. Are you both that arrogant; that quick to judge? Blick, you've shown so much promise since you arrived here a couple months ago. But now you're acting like an rabid child!" My father turned his attention to me. "Amat, I filtered your interactions with Olson and Log before this training and from that, I trust you did not start this quarrel. Though you didn't start it or encourage it, you did engage in it. Which demonstrates to me that even after whatever humility you gained in the past hour, after losing your rank, you still have a temper that needs taming."

Blick looked over at me when my father mentioned that I lost my rank as alpha.

"Since both of you need disciplining, over the course of the next two days, you'll share in the chore of cleaning the bathrooms. Which I'm sure the custodian will be happy to hear. You'll still have training at the start of tomorrow. However, by the end of the day, I expect each bathroom to have sparkling fixtures and floors that squeak under my every step. Is that understood?"

"Yes, sir," I said. I saluted my father immediately, and Blick did too, only after he saw me do so.

***

In the days that passed, Blick and I continued to have our conflicts here and there. In fact, after the first day of us scrubbing toilets, he caught me off guard and beat me up. He assaulted me badly enough that I needed time to recuperate after he decided to leave me alone. Days turned into weeks, weeks turned into months; Blick and I were still at it. As time went on, I listened more and more to my father's advice and commands. I grew less resentful toward him and less arrogant within myself. Conflicts with Blick didn't seem as worthwhile to me anymore. Being a gromroll, I had less to prove.

Blick never let up. He seized every opportunity he could to rough me up. Early on, he had others at his side to help pin me down and to join in. Although, as time passed, I learned to get along with many of the soldiers. With the help of Log and Olson, they smoothed the tension between our squadrons.

I also learned a few things in the months that passed. I learned that it's natural for people to change for better or worse; that is necessary for growth. I learned how to have an appreciation for those in the lower ranks. In some ways, they experienced worse than what I endured through alpha training. I learned how to be more of a role model for others. Most importantly, I learned that some things aren't how you remember them, especially after they were lost for a time.

XIII
New Beginning

Two months went by. Even though I still held my country in high respect and resented those who spat on the might of Utopion, I humbly lowered bits of my self-esteem. I stopped feeling as entitled and better than those around me. In some ways, I even accepted the fact that there were those in my squadron who, at heart, were better than me. Young men and women, who were fighting to send every penny they earned back to their families in poverty. There were some who served to defend and participate in the reconstruction program across Galiza, helping those who were affected by Utopion's conflicts to rebuild. There were others who were serving to get their loved ones, who were falsely accused of treason, out of prison. I wasn't sure their loved ones were blameless in their crimes. Yet I couldn't deny how noble the cause of these men and women were. The more I learned about my squadron members, the more respect they earned from me.

She didn't occupy my mind too much since leaving Gallethol, but after hearing the stories of my squadron members, it made me wonder about Mae's reasons for serving. We were never close friends, at least I never considered her to be that, but we did know each other. As I reflected on our connection, I felt Mae deserved more cherishment than I showed her. There was no regret in acknowledging our relationship didn't become something more, but time from her made me wish I'd known her better. She obviously wanted to get to know me.

What hadn't changed, was my desire to serve in Zeta. Although, that was not out of bloodlust. It was simply a matter of how much time and energy I already invested toward it. I didn't want all the training I endured as an alpha going to waste. That also was something that continued to sour my heart: being stripped of my rank. Wanting my rank reinstated was not a matter of privilege, but honor. Ever since day one, I carried a great shame; I paid a price for my actions in the matrix platform. Except, my father didn't seem to think I learned my lesson, in spite of the progress in my character.

***

One morning, as per usual, I awoke to the sound of the siren echoing across the base before the sun's rays stretched over the horizon. I dressed myself promptly, but with no urgency of being the first to step out the door.

When we were all in line, my father gave his speech as he normally did. That day, he acknowledged certain improvements he observed about each of us and our relationship to Pac Dolson's squadron.

After my father came to a close, as the others ran to do some drills and laps, he called my name and pulled me aside. I wasn't quite sure what he wanted to talk about, though I was confident it wasn't in regard to anything bad. I'd be surprised if it was. Aside from a few quarrels with Blick in weeks past, I didn't do anything improper.

I walked beside my father as he led me towards the matrix platform. For a long moment, we walked in silence. I would have started the conversation myself, but it was obvious that my father wanted to talk about something in particular. When he was ready, he would speak.

"I am proud of the progress you made here, Amat. Truly, I am," he finally said.

I nodded my head in reply.

"You came a long way in the past two months. You bettered yourself as a young man . . . as a soldier. Though I didn't mention it in my speech this morning, I know you and your cousins are greatly responsible for the improvements between the squadrons. For that, I think you all deserve a reward."

I stopped and faced my father with intrigue.

"Today, after training, you'll go home to see your mother and sisters. Olson and Log will come over with Aunt Sally and Uncle Gordon. I've approved a week's relief from your training, for all of you."

I nodded my head and sighed. "A week?" I asked.

My father nodded his head.

63

"That sounds good, to see all of them again after so many years. Though this sounds more of a reward for them than for me." My father lowered his brows and parted his lips, but before he could speak, I clarified myself. "I'm not saying I don't want to go. But if I had a say in what I'd like in return is . . . my reinstatement, as alpha."

My father sighed, turned away, and kept walking forward, slowly.

I followed after him.

"Amat, I know you still want to serve in Zeta. As I said in the past, I don't condemn you for wanting to serve. But what I want you to realize is that war is a business, it's the root of how this country thrives. There are wars being waged simply for the sake of control and profit. These wars that I speak of, are the bloodiest and most . . . deceiving conflicts of the world. There is more to them than you are led to believe. Things that you would have a hard time embracing, knowing you as my son. Trust me as your father and as the jinn-hid, when I say that Zeta is one of these wars."

I raised an eyebrow. "You sound like an insurgent."

My father paused in his steps, turned to me, and spoke sternly. "Do you think I would be a jinn-hid if I was truly an insurgent?"

Caught off guard, I took a moment to answer. "No," I replied.

We continued walking. "I am not saying, Amat, that conflicts are carelessly waged by this country. There are plenty of wars being fought in countries like Rafik, Borthalon, and Druteika, where our forces are helping to defend our allies and rebuild their counties."

"So, you would have me go into the reconstruction program? As the countries you just listed are the most prominently associated with the program."

"I would have you stationed somewhere you'd be making a difference."

"Is there no way I can make a difference in Zeta?"

"You would accomplish *nothing* in Zeta!" my father barked, irritated by my incompliancy. My father took a moment to gather his next words. "Leave Zeta behind you. Choose to serve in the reconstruction program and I'll reinstate your rank as alpha. Make no mistake, you'd still get some action here and there in a place like Rafik. However, you wouldn't be taking back Zetian bases and annihilating xǔté forces, every day you're there. There would be threats for you to resolve. Those above you would seek out your various skills and training. Which would, no doubt, lead you to more opportunities. Consider what I have said, Amat, and give me your decision tomorrow morning."

I nodded. "Yes, sir," I replied.

I turned away to train with the rest of my squadron, but before I could get far, my father said, "If you agree to what I offered, I could have you stationed in any country of your choosing, as early as the day following your agreement. Apart from Zeta, Varkaten, and Tarconous."

Of course, I can't choose from any of the countries we're actually at war with, I thought to myself. "I will consider it, sir."

I ran to the drat field and fell in beside my squadron members who were running about the field, sprinting back and forth. When we reached the end of one side, we did ten push-ups; at the end of the other, we did twenty seconds of mountain climbers.

Eventually, Blick found his way beside me, and after doing a set of push-ups, he pressed his hand on my back and pushed off of me as he stood. The sheer weight of his mass, pressing through his palm, pinned me to the ground, deflating the air from my lungs. I grimaced at Blick as he ran off like nothing happened. *Leave it be,* I told myself, as I continued my routine.

Later, as we were sprinting across the field together, Blick stepped in front of my leg, slowing down just enough to trip me. I fell face first and slid across the drat. Growling and grinding my jagged teeth, I clenched my hand into a fist as I took a moment to recover. I thrust myself off the ground and spurred myself forth, faster than before. Exerting my frustration into my workout, the adrenaline in my system spurred my legs so swiftly, they felt numb. I kept an eye out for Blick to maintain my distance from him and avoid any further confrontation. But then, even while glancing all around me, somehow, I was punched in the gut. I caught a fading glimpse of who it was as he passed by me; sure enough, it was Blick. What was strange was how I didn't see him coming, and I barely saw his figure out of the corner of my eye. If not for that, I wouldn't have had the slightest clue about what, or who, hit me. The blow was so brutal, my core cramped and I stopped abruptly in my tracks.

Gasping for air, I felt a hand on my shoulder and a soft mocking voice in my ear. "Just stay down," Blick said. He shoved me forward and started to walk away.

Slowly, I stood up, groaning. "No. No!" I barked, gaining his attention. He stopped and we turned to face each other. I walked up to him, hugging my stomach with one arm. "I am tired of this . . . this competitive game between us, of who can get away with pummeling the other," I continued.

All the squadron members kept to their drills. Though, some that passed by did turn their heads our way.

"I tried to move past it by restraining my aggression, in the hopes that you would do the same. A task that seems impossible for you to perform, which is fine by me since I can't control your actions. However, by the grace of Anua, I will *not* stay down, no matter how many times you beat me. I'll die before I give you that satisfaction. Even then, I would still be the victor of this spiraling dispute between us. I'll fight to my last ounce of strength, and you'll end up before a court martial."

The nefarious expression on Blick's face faded. He shoved me back.

I sighed as I caught my balance, staring right back at him. "Do we have an understanding?" I asked.

"You could say that. For now," he replied and ran off, continuing his drills.

Shortly after that, my father and Pac Dolson called everyone in for target practice. Before I could enter the armory, however, my father called my name. He examined my dirtied uniform and bruises. "Have you and Blick been fighting again?" he inquired.

"If we did, Blick would look worse," I replied. My father gave me a pressing look. "There was some difficulty during the drills. But I did not encourage him. In fact, I swayed him, said some things that prevented the situation from escalating."

My father showed intrigue. "What exactly did you say to him?"

I took a moment to reflect on how I could summarize it. "I told him that our conflict was pointless. Somewhere down the line, one of us could end up doing something to the other which we would regret."

A smile grew on my father's face as he patted my shoulder. "I'm proud of you, Amat."

"For what?"

"You acknowledged a truth, saw beyond a challenge, and resolved an issue without raising your fists. That is something I was waiting to see in you since you arrived here. You should be proud too."

"Thank you, sir," I replied.

"Are you alright to carry on with target practice or should I send you to the infirmary?"

"I'll be alright."

"You're sure? Combat training will be right after."

I shook my head.

"Alright. Well, while you do that, I'll pull Vykin aside and talk to him about—"

"No," I said. "That won't be necessary." My father looked confused. "We have an understanding now; I think it would be better if we started out not pointing fingers at one another. I do not want to risk building another grudge, or creating more tension."

"You'd have Blick go without facing any consequences for this?"

"We both know he's done worse in the past. It's a few bruises. Turn a blind eye, just this once. I want to give him a chance at change as well."

"Very well. You've grown humble, Amat. But don't let the word of a former adversary cloud your judgment."

I nodded and my father let me walk into the barracks to grab a gun for practice.

"Amat," a voice called out.

"Hey, Dilek, how've you been?" I inquired.

"Better than you, by the looks of it."

"*Pff*, thanks for noticing," I said sarcastically.

"Yeah, sorry I couldn't be there for you this time," Dilek said.

"You say that as if I can't look out for myself."

"The bruises on your face prove it's a strain for you."

"Dilek, let's be honest. If I really wanted to, I could take Blick down with my bare hands. If it wasn't for my father stripping me of my rank and being so strict, things would have panned out differently on that field today." Dilek and I walked in silence for a moment, my tone getting heated.

"You're right, Amat. I'm sorry. I forget how much is at stake for you here."

"Ah, forget it," I said, patting Dilek on the shoulder. "On that subject, I had a talk with my father today about potentially being sent overseas."

"You don't sound too thrilled about it," Dilek replied.

"I'd be serving in the reconstruction program." I announced drearily.

"And this is a problem because . . .?"

"It's not Zeta,"

"It's a start," he replied.

"Are you seriously taking the jinn-hid's side in this?"

"No, I'm just saying it would finally get you out there. Although it wouldn't be your preferred front, you'd surely be transferred under a new chain of command with a new officer. Who knows, if you show your worth, get close with a pac-qua over there, they may grant you a way into Zeta."

"Yeah, because that went so well at Gallethol."

"We all have to start somewhere. I mean, if you look at it this way, at least you wouldn't be training anymore, you'd be serving. Isn't that why you signed on?"

I didn't answer Dilek's question right away. My mind drew a blank, with faint traces of propaganda filling in the silence from the neuro-chip. Although, those were empty justifications. Whatever the reason I joined the militia, it seemed pointless at that moment, as it could not be backed, for lack of recollection. "I don't know," I finally replied.

XIV
The Diramal

Dilek and I made our way to the range and took up positions beside my cousins. Log noticed us as we approached.

"You and Uncle Bod sure took your time talkin'. Everything ok?" he asked me.

"Yeah, it's just . . . the jinn-hid gave me a lot to think about," I retorted.

"All good news, I hope?" asked Olson.

I shrugged as I took a position beside Log. When the silence persisted for too long, Olson diverted his attention to Dilek.

"How've you been, Dilek? How was your last tour in Zeta?" Olson asked with a smile.

"Been good," he replied. "Did you hear about Lůkig Zůleba?"

"Yeah, I heard he was killed last week," I spoke, before Olson could.

Dilek's lips curled into a smug smile.

"That was you?" Log asked him.

"Sure was, and I was personally decorated by the jinn-hid himself, for my valor," he replied.

"Congratulations," Olson spoke warmly.

"Dilek, that's a big deal. That could be pivotal to the war now that Kiden Důmat lost his right-hand man," Log said.

"In war, right-hand men are easily replaced. It means nothing so long as they have Kiden still," I said. I turned my head toward Dilek. "Which isn't to say your efforts were for naught, Dilek." I turned to Log. "But it's likely they won't be as pivotal as you think, cousin." I continued shooting. "Still, you did the autocracy a great service."

Our attention narrowed onto our targets as we took aim, keening our every shot. "Now, that's something to think about," Log trailed off while I hit a target dummy dead in the chest.

"What?" Olson asked.

"Well, you guys were just talking about world leaders and it got me thinking. Have any of you noticed how little we know about our current Diramal?" Log inquired.

The Diramal, the icon of Utopion; her grand, all-mighty leader, I thought.

"Not really, but now that you mention it, it is very strange. Can't even remember the last time I heard his name," Olson said.

"While it is unusual that his character should be so illusive, such details are of little concern when you consider all he's done for this country. In the last decade alone, he has more than doubled our allies, rooted out insurgents across the land, and liberated eight countries. If a man can achieve so much, who are we to care about such trifling details?" I answered.

"I much admire the Diramal myself," Dilek said.

"Men don't keep to themselves for nothing. At the very least, the Diramal's likely got an ugly past or some ongoing conundrum that might ruin his image," Olson chimed in.

"It's impossible to know for sure exactly. Every time I asked the jinn-hid about the Diramal, he became agitated. He'd say I shouldn't be so curious about him. So, that's what I do," I said.

"Well, I heard from our dad that the Diramal and Uncle Bod worked together some years ago in SEF," Olson said.

I turned my head toward him. My mind burst with ecstasy as I came to find out that my dad worked for SEF. My childhood dream of becoming an astrometon was momentarily reinvigorated. However, I couldn't let anyone witness me in my awe. I quickly thought of something passive to reply with, "That might explain a lot."

"And if they have a history with the Diramal, and they resent him, it might be a cause to be weary," Olson said.

"Small world," Dilek added, to break the ominous tension.

"Alright, everybody, let's go! Head into the gym and change out for the sparring hall!" came my father's voice from across the range.

"Alright boys, let's move out!" Log said enthusiastically.

Log raced across the field, toward the gym, while the rest of us marched on. He was always eager to have a go at me, even though there wasn't any bad blood between us. He simply enjoyed the challenge and learning what he could from me, as I was the most skilled soldier at the base. Although my pride couldn't accept it wholly, there were times I speculated Blick might have been a more superior warrior. Each time we sparred, Log did demonstrate some amount of improvement. At least one new tactic would almost catch me off guard. Had he joined the alphas, he would have made a fine addition to their ranks, of that I had no doubt.

Log was so confident that day, he insisted on pairing with me for our first round. While he put up a good fight and lasted longer than expected, it didn't take much effort before I had him pinned and tapping out. Even as he recovered to his feet, my young cousin stood with a smile on his face, a rather daring one at that.

"You seemed like you enjoyed losing that round," I spoke sarcastically.

Log shook his head, still catching his breath.

"We both know, you barely kept up with me, that round," he replied.

We shared a laugh.

"I'll bet, you can't take on both the jinn-hid's and Pac Dolson's squadrons without losing at least one round."

I raised an eyebrow to the proposed challenge, even though I knew my father would likely never allow it.

"We'll never know that for sure, we've only got four more rotations before we move on to our sim training," I said.

"That's an easy answer for someone who's afraid to know the real outcome," he replied, walking toward his next partner.

While holding a conniving stare at my cousin, the corners of my lips turned up as my pride got the better of me

"I suppose we'll have to find out then, won't we?" I antagonized.

I pushed aside my next partner, who just got into his fighting stance, and approached my father.

"Amat, is there a problem?" my father questioned.

"I'd like to test myself," I replied with a nod. My father crossed his arms in reply as he indulged me. "I would like to take on the whole of the troops here."

"The whole of the troops?" My father's brows rose doubtfully.

"Think of it as a training exercise for them. Being the most skilled warrior here, each of the men and women might learn something from fighting me. The moment one knocks me down, we'll call it a day," I answered.

My father stiffened as he took a deep breath and considered my request.

"As much as I dislike admitting it," my father said, "hardly any of the troops here would have a chance at besting you. With the acceptation of one or two occasions, I almost never saw you fall to any of the troops here."

"Those few occasions were only lost to one individual in particular, and they were cheap fights."

"Be that as it may, there are some additional rules to which you'll have to agree. There are forty some odd members between both squadrons; we don't have all day for you to toy with each of them. You'll have three minutes to be pinned or knocked down. You go over the time limit with any one of them and this trial is over," said my father.

"Yes, sir."

"Another thing you need to do is keep your face clean. Going into hand-to-hand combat is likely to cause a concussion, or worse, if you don't protect your head. If you receive so much as a scratch that drenches half your face in blood, let alone take enough hits to puff your face and force your eyes shut, this trial is over," ordered my father.

"Understood," I replied.

With my body as bruised and battered as it was, I lost track of how many troops I beat. I was keeping to my father's agreement. I had each of the men and women down in under three minutes, though some were closer fights than others. I kept my face pretty, though some managed to land a hit or two across my jaw. Eventually, it came down to one final squadron member that I had yet to fight that day.

"Ha-ha-ha-ha, is there not one of you who can put up a half-decent fight?" I blurted as I helped a gromroll, by the name of Naků, up off the ground.

My father sighed notably and shook his head, unimpressed at the egotistical display.

"Actually," a voice deep in the crowd said, once it went silent, "in all the time we've known each other, Criptous, I don't think we ever had a clean brawl in the ring." Blick walked forward to reveal himself.

"If you're disappointed with the honor of our previous quarrels, I recommend you reassess your own fighting methods, Vykin," I replied.

The crowd "oohed," to my reply. All eyes were either on Blick and or me. He scoffed as he crossed his arms.

"Fair enough. You can rest assure, I'll fight fairly."

I looked over to my father and waited till he gave an approving nod. I gestured back and turned toward Blick. "If you don't, nor will I," I said, offering my hand to him. He looked down at it and back into my eyes.

"Understood," he replied as we shook on our agreement.

We took positions, opposite of each other; the other squadron watched in a solemn hush. Blick stood tall, stretching his limbs to get himself limber. Normally I would be doing the same. However, I felt something come over me. Suddenly, that strange feeling came back. It was the feeling I had in the cave, during my assessment, and during the last few seconds of the sim in the matrix platform. The expanding and deflating of my diaphragm seized my attention. A deafening silence filled my ears. A wave of my conscience seemed to pulse throughout the room. The fur about my arms and chest flexed while my temperature to rose. A dimmed shout called from afar. It started deep and slow, gradually picking up its pace until it echoed in a roar that carried across the room. Blick's first punch, which landed on my ribs, snapped me out of the abnormal sensation. Getting my bearings, he landed another across my chin as I stumbled back further.

As he reeled for another hit, I spun, grabbed his arm as it launched, and twisted it out to the side. Using my own momentum, I threw my elbow into his chest. The spectators let out shouts and cheers for the blows I landed. Those hits repelled him into a stumble across the mat. Then, we briefly stood idle as we caught our breaths.

Blick pounced off the mat, swinging his whole body around in midair and connected his foot against my head. Again, time slowed as I fell. The weightless shift in my legs was so graceful, as they were relieved of the weight from my body. My eyelids faintly blinked as I witnessed the ground rising out of the corner of my eye. *Not yet!* I stretched out my arm, barely catching my upper body from falling flat on the ground. Time sped up once again to its normal flow. I gazed up and over my shoulder to the bottom of Blick's boot hammering towards me. I rolled out of the way before it could hit me flat on my back; I recovered my stance. The crowds' spirits were raised once again.

It's quite peculiar how one can focus on something as small as a speck of dust, drifting in the faint wind right before them. The cheers were muffled again, but that was of little concern to me, as I was mesmerized by the tiny pieces of soot dancing before me. *What is happening to me?* I finally managed to ask myself. My lungs expanded as wide as they could from a deep inhale, my body laxed, and as I was breathing out, the . . . dust drifted beyond my sight. Something firm wrapped around my neck, from behind, lifting me off the ground. I couldn't breathe, gasping for breath and clutching at Blick's arms, with time *jolting* back to normal. When his grasp wouldn't budge, I shot my elbow into his side. He grunted and the lock around my neck loosened. No matter how many times I hit him, the lock remained intact. My vision started to dim. There were cheers all around me; I heard someone urgently shout my name. My eyes were squinting now, my fists clenched, and with a final lash of will, I *whipped* my head back into Blick's face. Blood spurted everywhere from his nose as he removed his arm and allowed me to stumble away. I coughed, catching my breath. I heard my name again and slowly turned my head toward my father, who had a concerned expression on his face. Blood seeped into my muzzle from my snout. I raised my hand to him and nodded to let my father know I was alright. My father sighed, crossed his arms, and nodded back.

I turned around to face Blick, who was bleeding worse than I was. Despite his injury, there was no more rage in his eyes than in mine. We were keeping to the rules. However, when he overstepped the boundary of choking me out, I broke his nose, which made us even. He and I circled around one another. Moments at a time, almost too brief to notice, he and everyone else seemed to be moving slower than they should have. Like watching a screen glitch and lag one moment and speed up or continue steadily the next. Standing my ground, ready for the next incursion, everything around Blick stretched out and vibrated. My eyelids grew heavy and my brow ached. He charged me, moving ever so slowly from my perception. The dizzy spell that came over me lowered my guard until he was finally just a step away from me, moving ever so gracefully.

I widened my stance and raised my hand to thwart him. The discrepancy in the relativity of our movements made it easier to push and redirect Blick's momentum. On contact, I snapped out of the strange time flow and Blick stumbled to the side, tumbling across the mat. The sound of the crowd cheering filled the room again. After having pulled myself together, I approached my opponent, offering a helping hand. Blick smacked it aside as he reached for my ankle. Anticipating this, my fist came crashing down onto his back. He snarled as he spun about the mat, kicking his foot into my legs and tripping me. Before he could do anything else, I rolled away, and recovered.

Blick threw one fist after another, landing two strikes on my face. I knew the second hit would leave a mark. Prior to landing a third, I caught his arm, but he promptly lifted his knee into my waist. I barked and snapped my jowls at his snout. That caught him off guard well enough to grant an opening for my nimble strike across his face, rocking his head. Wasting no time, I latched onto his arm, pulling him close, and shot my knee up, connecting with his gut. He stumbled back, slowly looking up at me: very slowly. A queasiness sent shakes down to my knees and filled my head with a pestering buzz, a ringing in my ears that dimmed all other sounds. Again, he rushed toward me; his movements were still slowed somehow. I began to consider the fact that I might have been the cause of this time fluctuation. How I was doing it, however, was still an enigma.

As my mind caught on to the surreal realization, my body and mind tensed. This seemed to hinder the strange ability, as my movements felt overbearingly heavier. In an attempt to dodge out of Blick's path, I found my knee weighed a *ton*. His charge momentarily quickened, as the pace of my heart jumped a beat. This constant change started to ache and weigh on me. A deep, pulsing, nasal wind seemed to *whoosh* around me. A warm vent of air left my nostrils for every rhythmic hurl that seemed to surround me; a tight pressure condensed my abdomen. It was then I noticed I was breathing too hard. *I have to calm myself.* The insight came instinctually.

Easing my breath until each inhale seemed to last minutes at a time, I was at last able to raise my knee. Extending it forth, the strike was so great Blick was shot back across the mat, where he remained still. The strike pulled me out of the time fluctuation, but left me in a daze. Fixated on Blick's body, I thought I killed him. The crowd let out its loudest uproar of barks and howls yet. Just before they congested me with their congratulations, I was relieved to see the faintest breath heave and raise Blick's back, then lax it back down. It was not before long I heard his coughs and saw him rise to his feet.

He gazed up at me, as the crowd hoisted me up. A knowing gaze boiled in his eyes as he stared at me. His lips sagged, and his jaw hung slightly in awe of me. It was not simply for the fact that I beat him, no. His eyes broke through me, seeing something I never knew about myself. I might have gone up to ask him why he looked at me so, if it weren't for— *clap . . . clap . . . clap . . . clap.*

We all turned toward the noise. There was an approaching figure in the shadows, tall and broad, his red eyes glowing in the dark as he came into the light. My father stiffened at the sight of the man and furrowed his brows.

The clapping figure laughed. "A most entertaining and satisfying display," the figure said.

"Attention!" my father shouted.

We all quickly got in formation and became dead silent.

"Diramal, we are honored by your presence," my father said, enthusiasm lacking in his tone.

"As am I honored by your son's performance, jinn-hid," the Diramal replied.

While the neuro-chip in my mind flared with gratitude and pride at the Diramal's praise of me, something in his tone felt discomforting. My father shifted his gaze from him to me. The Diramal towered above me as he inspected me with a strange, thrilled grin on his face.

"Meet my gaze, soldier," the pitch of his voice shifted in such a way that forced me to heed his command; however, I did it slowly.

I immediately took note of the Diramal's dark, blood-red eyes. *I almost forgot the Diramal was a cho'zai,* I thought. The eyes of the Diramal consumed my conscience, their stare tripped something in my neuro-chip. My regard for him was never higher than in that moment. The neuro-chip idolized the Diramal, compelling me to see him as a highly knowledgeable and stoic individual. From this, I felt I owed him my life, not out of debt, but for the glory of his tyranny.

"You're the strapping son of the jinn-hid, aren't you? Amat," the Diramal's stare was unwavering.

"Eh . . . That I am, sir," I answered.

"I read up on your profile from Gallethol; you were the best in your squadron. I must say, it made a massive impression upon me and the other high commanding officers, which would include your own father. Am I right about that, jinn-hid?"

The Diramal looked over to my father, the pitch of his voice shifting again, as he asked the question. "Yes, Diramal, you are. I am quite proud of my son's achievements and dedication to his training," my father's response was monotone. He quickly shook his head and collected himself as if something bewitched him. "However, he still has much to learn."

"Don't we all. But I should think his skills are better placed overseas. Perhaps, somewhere like Zeta. Surely, whatever might be left for him to learn could be discovered on the field? Wouldn't you agree?" the Diramal inquired, shifting his gaze as if he was asking me the question.

"I would not. Training is where a soldier learns best. There's no margin for error on the field of battle if he or she is underprepared in some capacity or other," my father stated sternly.

"Hmm, you may have a point, jinn-hid, even if I don't fully agree with it. You can rest assured, Amat, that the other officers and I won't take your militant ambitions lightly. We need you out there." The Diramal tapped my shoulder.

"My son's fate is his to forge and his *alone*," my father said.

The Diramal turned back to slowly face my father. "Of course it is. But there's nothing wrong in offering a little support; guiding the young man toward a career he already relishes with a passion."

My father grimaced. "All due respect, Diramal, but I don't think this is the type of encouragement *my son* needs to achieve his goals."

"We shall see. Like you said, it's the young man's choice. I'm willing to let Amat's cards fall as they may. Are you?"

The Diramal and my father stood locked in silence. A furious discourse seemed to be waging amidst their gazes, though not a single word was uttered.

"Well, the day is not over, and we still have much planned. So, if you would please leave me and Pac Dolson to finish our work with our squadrons, sir," my father said while lifting his left hand toward the exit.

"Of course," the Diramal said, smiling.

"It was an honor to have met you, Diramal," I said.

"Oh, no-no-no-no, son, the honor is mine." The Diramal gave me a gratifying smile as he turned and left the room.

XV
Green vs. Orange

"Alright, let's head to the matrix platform. Come on, move it!" the jinn-hid commanded as soon as the Diramal left the room. "Amat, let's get you to the infirmary. You look like crap."

I smirked. "Thanks, Dad." The jinn-hid encouraged Blick to accompany us to the infirmary as well.

He complied, but went at his own pace and kept his distance from us.

In the infirmary, the medics patched up some cuts and put ointments on our bruises. Within an hour, whatever sores that plagued me, dissipated.

I left the infirmary before Blick and headed to the armory. Olson and Log met with me shortly after I left, eager to share some pressing concerns I didn't put much thought into at the time.

"I thought you'd both be in the matrix platform by now," I said when my cousins caught my attention.

"We would, but we wanted to check in on you," Olson said.

Olson's unease almost amused me, as it felt so off the cuff.

"Regarding what exactly?" I asked, smiling.

"Well, don't tell us you didn't find it strange, the Diramal showing up unannounced and having a peculiar focus on you?"

I shrugged.

"Could have been a random inspection."

"By the Diramal? The man who practically *never* leaves the capital? Which, by the way, is nowhere near Calinheim," said log.

"Even for an inspection, that's an inconvenient errand to run for a man of his position," Olson added.

"He's probably just doing what he said—wondering why one of his best is being wasted on boot camp training among gromrolls and krollgrums," I returned.

Log shifted his neck and grimaced at the notion. Olson seemed partly taken aback as well, fighting the furrow at his brow and blinking repetitively.

"Then why wouldn't he send a cho'zai?" Olson finally asked. "The Diramal has a country to govern and dozens of fronts to lead. It just doesn't add up, him coming here for one man."

"Who can say?" I replied nonchalantly. "I'm not concerned about it, nor should *you* be either. If it gets me a spot in some *real* service, I'll gladly leap toward the opportunity and grab hold of it with both hands."

"Well, as much as I can understand your excitement, Amat, being so close to having something you always wanted, Olson still has a point. I have to say even I felt unnerved by the opposition between the Diramal and Uncle Bod," Log asked.

"While I can agree there was certainly some palpable tension between the two officers, your distrust in the matter sounds like mere superstition and conspiracy," I scoffed.

Olson let out a subtle sigh as his eyes analyzed the ground beneath him and contemplated a reasonable response.

"When closer one stands to a mural the less he sees of it," Olson finally said.

My eyes narrowed at Olson quizzically.

"Maybe this stems deeper than your circumstance, Amat." Olson continued.

"He simply extended me an offer and my father blew him off. That's all that happened."

"That 'offer' could have come in the form of a letter: orders straight from the Diramal himself, instructing your father to send you wherever our nation's leader saw fit. The fact that he came here, *personally,* to merely propose the idea and openly question your father, before you . . . It doesn't make any sense, Amat," said Olson with concern.

I stopped walking and both Olson and Log faced me. If Olson shared these thoughts with the old me, I would have counted them as sedition. The neuro-chip in my mind was slightly triggered all the same, but it did not thwart my natural response.

"Olson, as much as I appreciate your concern, I'm a highly valued, well trained weapon that's been placed on a rack for the past two months. So long as I sit in the barracks, my value deteriorates. If there's a chance someone will pick me off the rack, I'll gladly fire away," I said.

I walked into the barracks as Olson and Log followed in behind me. I picked up an electric shock-put 101. It was the only weapon anyone could use for this sim, for one reason: it was the only weapon that had a stun setting. I then dressed in a fade-suit.

"What about the way Uncle Bod spoke defensively of you," Olson said.

"What about it?" I asked, irritated.

"Amat, that's his senior officer. If he were to so boldly question and speak out against him – again, in your defense – I imagine there's a good reason for it. Your father cares for you sincerely. You're his son, for Anua's sake," Olson's tone had grown agitated.

I frowned and looked over at Olson. "Why should I be so weary of this opportunity, Olson? I barely know anything about their history. My father and the Diramal and the same could be said for you."

Olson held a silence as he looked into my eyes and placed a hand on my shoulder before answering.

"It is because you know so little of their quarrels, that you should be weary of them. A son often inherits the burdens of his father," Olson stated.

I scoffed, somewhat chilled by his words.

"How would you know? You still have your father," I replied.

"He need not be lost for me to know the weight of his misfortunes. The same goes for you, dear cousin."

I walked away from Log and Olson and entered the matrix platform. The environment was already set, but the match had yet to begin. The digital sun burned a radiant silver, the sky doused in rays of violet and blue amidst the tropical environment. Two beacons stretched high into the evening sky to the east and west of me. On the left wall, there was a panel with slots for placement on either team. I saw that there was only one open spot left for the green beacon. After our troublesome debate, I was uncertain of how the chemistry with my cousins would transpire. Without a second thought, I filled the last slot of the green team and headed toward the base.

To my surprise, when I arrived at the green base, I was greeted by Blick. Seeing as how I left the infirmary before him, I hardly expected to see him in the sim before me, let alone on the same team as me. "Ah . . . Blick, listen, I—"

"Nah!" Blick said, waving his hand to push me aside. "Don't worry about it. You put up a good fight. A little hesitant at times, it seemed," he chuckled. "But a good fight nonetheless."

Blick beheld me in a strange awe, his jaw hanging somewhat loosely, his eyes just wide enough to suggest some amount of perplexity. The cause for which, I couldn't begin to contemplate and left me discomforted.

"Thanks, I guess," I replied.

Blick finally adjusted his gaze and suppressed his unspoken impression upon me. *Were my abnormal movements so obvious to his eyes? If they were, how could no one else have noticed? Maybe it was apparent in—*

"I have to say," Blick disrupted the chain of my rational thought. "I noticed there were times where you were peculiarly fast in the fight." My skin trailed with goosebumps as he brought up the subject. "One might say you're . . . pretty light on your feet."

Blick seemed somewhat uncomfortable with the subject, as he shrugged and the look in his eyes shifted. The look seemed to suggest an unspoken question of whether we shared a corresponding knowledge, an inherent fact, about myself. I swallowed, looking to change the subject of the conversation.

"I could say the same about you. A few times when you landed a hit on me, I didn't even hear your footsteps."

Blick stiffened and his brows raised ever so subtly to know I made him nervous.

"I suppose we have that in common." There was a certain familiarity insinuated in his words. This sudden shift in his character was all too strange for me.

"It may be arrogant of me, but I should like to start anew with you, Amat."

"Start anew?" I asked.

He nodded.

"Not to overlook the rivalry we built up over the past couple months, but to see what we could accomplish together: as brothers in arms. The events of today made it apparent to me how childish we've behaved toward one another, and I merely seek to make amends," said Blick.

I stood with my arms crossed as I considered his proposal before extending my hand to him. He approached and joined his grasp with mine. "No hard feelings?" he inquired.

"No hard feelings," I replied.

"Attention all gromrolls and krollgrums!" my father said over the intercoms. "The selected leaders for this match are Olson Criptous as the prime officer, and Log Criptous will be second officer on team orange. On the green team, we have Amat Criptous as the prime officer and Blick Vykin as the second officer. The match will begin in ten seconds . . ."

Blick and I approached the cluster of troops standing closer to the base entrance.

"Alright, huddle up everyone," I said, as I grabbed a stick off the ground and drew a large circle. "Considering I studied both my cousins' stratagems closely in the past couple months, I have a pretty good idea of how they'll launch their assault. While Olson and Log are over here in orange base, in the west." I drew a second circle apart from the first. "Olson is most likely going to send Log up the middle to cut down our numbers." I drew an arrow pointing toward our base, symbolizing Log's movement. "While Olson and the other half of his troops hold a position closer to or within their base. I think we can all agree Olson likes to govern his troops in waves, but even then, that's a broad stratagem to consider, in its execution. My guess is that there could be anywhere between two to four fronts situated between us and their base."

"If you expect their forces will be so divided sir, why not hold here and wait them out? Cutting down each wave as it comes, gaining us the upper hand in our fortifications." Gromroll Klo-en questioned.

"Because there's the unaccounted variable of them gathering in full force before launching their assault, in that tactic," I replied. "If we solely utilized the base, it would completely block off our sight of the opposing team, giving rise to dozens of unforeseen infiltrations and attacks. Even with everyone having access to fade suits, we might as well be caged vermin dodging bullets. Which isn't to say that couldn't work, Klo-en, but we'd have a much better chance at winning if we meticulously pick apart each of our enemy fronts, one by one."

The camouflage suits we had access to completely blended with our surroundings—nearly making us invisible. To keep us from losing track of each other while our camouflage is active, the suits also have sensors on them to track body heat. The suits then send scrambled codes, interlinked to the visors attached to our helmets. The codes are specified to each team or unit, thus, keeping both sides cloaked from one another.

"Assuming your correct, what did you have in mind for a counterattack?" Blick interjected, a cogitative look on his face.

"I suggest we divide into pairs, pressing forward as a dispersed unit, covering a stretch of approximately a hundred-fifty meters. Keeping vigilant to the environment before us."

"Thus, minimizing our disturbances to the terrain that would otherwise give away our positions?" Blick posed the question for clarification.

I nodded.

"Odds are Log's already out choosing a position with any number of troops under him. If they're not still advancing, by the time we meet them, chances are they'll have taken stationary positions on the ground. There's a lot of brush in the environment of this sim, so if they are on the ground, watch for compressions and body-sized indents in the terrain. Keep in mind, lying prone makes the guised target more perceptible. If we take our charge slow and Log makes that simple mistake, the tide could be easily swayed to our favor."

"Though this wouldn't be the first time you've been on opposite sides of a training ground with your cousins, Amat, how can you be so sure of yourself?" Blick asked.

"I've made a calculated assessment, based on the favored stratagems Olson has adopted in the time I've trained with him. That doesn't make what I've said here, foolproof. But, to account for a margin of error, we'll designate two pairs, to either side of the formation two-hundred meters north and south of the larger force. That way, if we're overwhelmed or met with something unaccounted for, we'll fall back and regroup with these numbers."

I passed my eyes amidst the faces and characters I'd gotten to know in the last couple months.

"Krollgrum Reiser," her ears perked and her spine stiffened as I called out her name. "Should both Vykin and I get taken out of the game, you'll take over the command in our stead."

"Yes, sir," replied Reiser.

XVI
Stopping a Ball of Light

The transparency of the fade-suits, when activated, is so lucid that even the outline of one's body would barely show in a full sprint. That being said, the liquidating processors built into the suits were at their strongest, the more gracefully one moved. Thus, when on the lookout for armored enemies with the tech, one had to be mindful of the most subtle details: footprints in the dirt, divots, rustles in the brush. Through our neuro-chips, we accessed one of its many modified features, which are granted strictly to military and law enforcement personnel, a comm channel that facilitated a telepathic form of communication.

"Alright, can everyone hear me?" I asked. One by one they all complied. "From this point forward, keep all exchanges strictly through the neural comm link,"

"Yes, sir!" my teammates replied in unison.

Almost half an hour had gone by by, and we still didn't seen any sign of Log or Olson. We searched and searched, looking for any visible transparency, and found nothing.

"Halt! Everyone, whatever you're doing, hold your positions," I commanded.

"Is something wrong, sir?" Blick enquired.

"Yes, there is. We've reached the center of the grid, which means if we haven't seen the opposing forces by now, and we haven't, we will soon. Look there." I gestured with my finger. "That's the entrance to the matrix platform. It's possible that we might be right on top of them or we might have passed them."

"It's possible they could be further up the map, closer to their own base," Blick suggested.

"No, trust me. They're here. At least some of them are. In fact, I think I spotted them."

"How far?"

"Roughly fifty meters directly ahead of us, though I can't quite tell how far their positions span. We'll move in, then on my mark, the left and right wings of our line will create an encompassing formation seventy-five meters in diameter from my location. Krollgrum Reiser, cover our flank and hold positions an extra twenty meters outside our assault unit."

"Yes, sir!" my squad replied.

We closed the gap by about fifteen meters in a wending approach.

"Hold, *mark*," I announced.

Like embracing wings, my troops formed a circuit about the opposing team's position.

"The team is in position, Amat," Blick said.

"Good, now let's pick out our targets. Everyone take note of the indents and outlines in the brush and dirt. Anything that looks like it could be a body, lock your aim to it," I commanded.

"By my count, I'd estimate there's at least half a dozen sitting here."

"Only one way to know for sure."

I pulled out my gun and cocked it. "Everyone, be ready to fire on my command in three, two—"

Bang!

I was startled and my aim was thwarted as I winced. But the shot didn't hit anyone, at least not that I was aware of at that moment. Once again, my perception and movement within time somehow slowed; however, it was far more intense this time around.

Almost everything and everyone was frozen in place. My eyes widened at the surreal vision of a large ball of electricity frozen in its trajectory, just inches away from my chest. The subtle turn of my head to Blick dampened my vision briefly and made me woozy, as if I had a blood rush to the head. Collecting myself, I observed another ball of electricity was fired at Blick as well. It was frozen no more than a few feet away from him. *Should have been more gentle cocking my gun. I'm sure that's what gave us away.*

Though I seemed so sure of the location of an opposing team member, or two, just a few moments prior, bewilderment became me and I could not hone my attention on anything beyond the two static rounds. Still I estimated the direction from where the shots came. I took my aim and fired. Time started to speed up again, gradually. The ball of electricity coming toward me started picking up speed. Stumbling to get out of its way, I fell over Blick and managed to push us both out of harm's way. Impacting the ground *jolted* time back to its normal flow. We landed behind a hollow, where we took shelter. Blick let out a growl and shoved me off of him, coughing vigorously as he removed his helmet.

"Jeez, Amat, how much do you weigh?" he asked once he caught his breath. He gave me a queer look, as if he was curious to know the answer to something else.

"Everyone, return fire!" I ordered through the neural link, ignoring Blick. I barrel rolled into a line of sight where the shot came from and sprayed my fire throughout the brush. As we fired and hit members from the opposing team, their camouflage gave out and revealed their positions.

Once I noted the halt in opposing fire, I ordered my men to cease fire. "Investigate the area. Make sure everyone's down."

I took a moment to process everything that happened during this third altered time experience. Even though I still didn't quite understand how this phenomena was occurring, something occurred to me. *It seems to transpire in moments of distress . . . Like a defense mechanism.* Then I remembered Blick. I walked over to him. He was still lying behind the hollow, breathing heavily, hugging his side where I fell onto him. *At least I'm not going crazy.* If he was clutching where I hit him, it meant my velocity was fast enough to hurt several times worse than if time was flowing normally. Our impact was not so harsh, as I recalled.

I deactivated my fade-suit and offered him a hand. "Anything broken?" I asked.

"I don't think so," he said as he also deactivated his fade-suit. He took my hand and I pulled him up. Blick grunted loudly as he stood.

"You're sure?" I asked.

"I'll be fine, it's just . . ."

"What?"

"It's strange."

I was about to say something about what happened, but before I could speak, someone called, "Criptous!" I turned my head.

"We should check that," Blick said as he walked past me. I followed after him.

"Sir, not all the enemies are down. This is only half of the team. We've counted twenty bodies total here," said Reiser.

As expected, I thought, giving a nod. "Any casualties of our own?" I asked.

"Yes, sir. Fourteen of our members are down."

"At least we still outnumber Olson. Has anyone found Log? Is he here?"

"I just counted the losses, sir, I didn't take note of the faces," said Krollgrum Reiser.

"That's alright." I put my hand on her shoulder as I walked past. "Dismissed."

All the soldiers on the ground were grunting and moving very slowly from their rankle wounds. Even one grazed hit of a stun round to a limb would be enough to make the world spin. Usually, it's enough to knock the target out for about an hour before they wake up feeling nauseous. As I walked among the cradled members of the opposing team, I saw Dilek lying flat on the ground, breathing heavily, his eyes narrowed. I crouched down to him; he didn't seem to notice me at first. I patted him on the shoulder.

"I knew all too well . . . you'd discover our position," he said, grinding his teeth.

"You share that with either of my cousins?" I asked.

"Tried . . . Log convinced Olson it would work . . . covertly overwhelming you in . . . numbers."

I chuckled lightly. "You look like you've gotten used to being stunned. You're not clutching at yourself like the others."

"Just 'cause I can take it . . . d-doesn't mean it . . . s-sucks any less."

I smiled and Dilek tried to chuckle, which immediately became a cough. "Hang in there, Dilek. Remember, the shakes won't last long."

"A-p-p-preciate it," he said.

I stood and walked away from Dilek.

I continued my search for Log, to ensure he was down, while my teammates awaited further orders. Eventually, I found my younger cousin.

He tried to make it appear as though he was still knocked out, but I knew better. I knelt beside him and felt his pulse. When I felt it wasn't irregular, I jabbed at Log's torso, hoping it would tickle him.

"Huh, not so much as a twitch or a smirk? I'm impressed," I said. Certain members of my team shared estranged looks, but I paid them no mind. I whispered, "Log . . . I know you're faking. I see your lips curling. I must say, I can't wait to see where this little 'silent but deadly' act is about to take us. Do you remember the time you overslept on Red Eve and Olson and I—"

Suddenly Log lifted up his arms with his gun in hand and aimed it at me. I saw the movement coming and ripped the gun away from Log's grasp.

"Whoa, okay," I chuckled. "I thought that one would get you."

Log was chuckling along and I could see he was struggling not to. "Anua blind you, Amat, you said you'd never bring that morning up again," he said.

"See, but I didn't fully bring it up, did I? I only mentioned it because I knew you wouldn't let me share it for all to hear."

Log shook his head.

"A cheap blow to expose my cover."

I scoffed. "What cover? I already knew you weren't stunned. Your pulse was as steady as a tide."

My team members gathered around.

"I don't think you're giving me enough credit for holding a straight face for as long as I did," Log said.

"Oh, I trust you did your best and applaud your effort regardless. Yet I can't say I'd do the same for your battle strategy."

"It's worked almost every time we use it with the fade suits. Especially in a map like this. I'm surprised at how well of a jump you got on us."

"'Almost' isn't assured. Strategies are meant to be fluctuated to keep the enemy on edge. You should know this by now."

"I guess." Log sighed. "So, I assume you expect me to tell you where Olson is?"

"Actually, I already know where he is."

Log glanced around nervously at all the guns aimed at him, each of their safeties turned off one by one. I raised my hand to them.

"Ah-ah, unnecessary, stand down."

"Uh, no, it's alright. Suppose it's past time for that anyway," Log said.

I shook my head with a smile. "Oh, Log, sometimes you surprise me on the rare occasion you show your bravery. You build that and maybe Olson and I will stop making you the butt of our jokes all the time."

"If you know what's good for you, you'll both cut that crap out sooner rather than—"

I stunned Log. For a long moment, his body spasmed and his eyes rolled back as he growled, grinding his fangs. "Well, I think we had enough of that for the time being." I stood and sighed, glancing around; all eyes were on me.

"Alright, come on now, the show's over. Let's move!" I shouted. Everyone reactivated their fade-suits, and we all headed out to the orange base.

XVII
Lone Stealth

We held our position a few clicks from the entrance of the orange base. There was a rough, forty-foot diameter of open field surrounding the base with no cover. If we all crossed it and anyone was guarding the outside, they'd surely spot us. Blick and I snuck ahead in an attempt to infiltrate and scope out the perimeter. After all, up to half of the opposing team remained and there was a lot Olson could have done with twenty soldiers, even if he played out his typical strategy.

Granted, in sims like this, Olson would make subtle changes to his plan, but often it was the same layout. Send any given amount of troops out to fight on a front to mow down enemy numbers while the rest guard the base. As we moved around, being mindful of our surroundings, minimizing how much we shook the leaves and made noise, Blick and I found at least half a dozen soldiers guarded the perimeter of the base, judging by the number of man-sized divots in the drat.

"Six guards seem too few for what they have left. Why would Olson reserve most of his troops within the base?"

"Do you think it would be wiser to take them from the rear?" Blick asked.

"Regardless of how we take the guards out, we should be more concerned with the formation that'll await us within the—"

Suddenly, gunfire from several different positions was unleashed in the direction of my team. Six from the front of the base, eight at our flank I growled.

"Come on," I said to him, as more lines of fire were exchanged by members of my team.

I ran out into the open and dove onto the ground, on a small field of drat. Then, I took aim at two of the six guards, as they revealed themselves from their line of fire, and shot. Blick took down three, before the last one noticed our position and returned fire. Her shots passed over me and without hesitation, I fired back, stunning her. All fell silent and when I felt it was safe, I looked back. Blick's position was compromised; his fade-suit deactivated and he was out.

I carefully ran across the field and checked back in with my team, counting the numbers. They were all down, as were the eight soldiers that flanked my team. That meant two things: there were six enemies left—*inside the base, would be my guess*—and I was the only one who could take them down. *Well played, Olson.*

I went down into the base; my footsteps echoed in the dimly lit hall. The hall led to a tall room with three levels. Still, my footsteps echoed, and although I couldn't see them, I felt Olson and his teammates looking down at me. I stood motionless and silence filled the room.

Suddenly, shots were fired; my breath caught, I fell back, and I shut my eyes. However, when I realized nothing hit me, I cracked my eyes open and saw six frozen spheres of electricity. I shook my head and stood so abruptly that I felt light-headed when I found my feet. *I suppose I should have known this would happen. The question is, how do I control it?*

I maintained a steady breath, remembering how that impacted the fluidity of my movement in this altered flow of time. Taking deep breaths, the pulsating beat of my heart eased subtly.

I tried to formulate a strategy, but even my thoughts took longer than usual to gather. They all came flooding to me like overlapping whispers that steadily grew to shouts, repeating the same thing over and over again. But what were they repeating? What was I trying to think?

Then I heard it, clear as crystal. *Two are right in front of me.* I could tell based on the trajectory of the electric spheres. It was then that I noted the spheres started moving nearer—time was flowing again. I sprayed my aim, dead ahead of me. By the time I took cover, everything went back to normal and I saw two of the opposing team fall before me.

Treading lightly, I made my way up to the second level, as I was able to overhear what Olson and his troops were saying.

"Am I missing something, or did we seriously hit nothing just now?" one of Olson's men blurted.

"Maybe he got lucky and pulled back just in time to dodge our fire," another suggested.

"Doesn't matter, Kidra and Adrin are down, which means someone entered the base and is a live threat still. I don't know how he did it, but if anyone could slip out of an attack like that, it would be Amat," Olson said.

"What should we do then?"

Whatever Olson told them to do, he must have done it over a neural-channel because I couldn't hear what they discussed after that.

The sound of incoming boot-steps from further up the room was my que to move forward. I climbed over the ledge on the left side of the second floor and hung off it, facing outward. Once Olson's men walked past me unsuspectingly, I swung my body up until I managed to do a handstand on the ledge and gracefully set myself down on the floor. Their boots left stomp-prints on the dusty surface. I switched the fire rate on my gun from auto to rapid, took a deep breath as I raised my aim, and let loose, hitting and revealing all four of the soldiers there.

"What the—?" Olson shouted. He dropped down to the second level and investigated the scene.

Olson landed right in front of me—a few more inches and he would have crashed on top of me.

"Well, this is awkward," I said. Without another moment's hesitation, I fired before Olson could react. I stunned him.

The sim of the matrix platform started to dematerialize into code and everyone was pulled to the entrance of the platform.

My father came in to congratulate me. He didn't say anything, just a simple nod and salute. I returned the gesture.

Clusters of medics came into the dome and tended to everyone stunned, giving them injections that would help with the nausea.

"That should conclude everyone's training for the day. If you're ready, we can start heading home," my father said.

"What about Olson and Log?"

"Your Uncle Gordon and Aunt Sally are on their way to pick them up. Besides, it wouldn't be wise to take them on a ride so soon after they were stunned."

I nodded. "Lead the way then, sir."

95

XVIII
Two Orange Triangles

About halfway through the ride home, Dad finally ended his extensive conversation with my uncle over the phone. A comfortable silence fell over the car for a time.

"You excited to see your mother and sisters?"

I nodded my head. "I suppose so."

"They'll be excited to see you. Lara may seem a bit down though. She won't tell me or your mother why. We were hoping since you two were so close you might be able to get her to open up?"

"That was more than five years ago."

"Still, maybe she'll feel more comfortable around you, being her older brother. Your mother and I are concerned, but we can't help if we don't know what the problem is."

I nodded.

"I'll see what I can do."

"Thank you, son" my father said.

My ears perked and an invigorating chill ran up my spine. Though it wasn't the first time my father had been with me, since our reacquaintance, it *was* the first time he'd expressed a sense of gratitude toward me.

"I'm glad I made an impression upon you and the Diramal," I said. My father didn't answer immediately.

"Yes, about that. . ." my father sighed, a lethargic shift in his tone. "Amat, let me tell you something. This interest the Diramal has in you, it's not genuine. He only sees you as a body to support his own agenda."

My neuro-chip triggered me involuntarily. The vagueness of my father's words set off something in my psyche.

"As critical assets to the Utopian militia, should *our* agenda not be aligned with our Diramal's?" It was the first time in the while I'd been so outspoken toward my father. I wouldn't have phrased my response as such if my father's previous statement didn't sound so suggestive.

"That there is a prime example of what I'm talking about." My father whipped his index finger at me. "While I observed that it doesn't occur as often, that tone you take with me at times is *not* you, Amat. It's the neuro-chip, with preconceived praise and propaganda that keeps you from thinking for yourself and at times, for others."

Reflecting on my reaction, I reserved my train of thought in that moment.

"Now, I know you can't be entirely blamed for the way you think, in that respect. The more we adhere to and acknowledge the neuro-chip's programing, it represses our natural characters."

"I know; I've tried to be more aware of that," I replied.

"I know you have. I'm not saying your progress has gone unnoticed. But the fact that you still have deep-rooted desires to serve in Zeta, Amat, is concerning. It's the latest war Utopion has waged, it's the main conflict our government is urging every able-bodied man and woman to join. You have to ask yourself: is it truly your desire, your genuine *choice,* to go out and fight in it?"

My neuro-chip became agitated by father's speech, spewing raging thoughts of treason towards my father in that moment. However, I remained silent and did my best to reflect on all my father said.

I opened my jowls, took a breath to speak, but my words were momentarily caught as I uttered the word: "N-no."

"No what?" my father lightly persisted.

"It's not my choice, wanting to go to Zeta." My eyes started to well up, but I did not cry. It lacked all logic of my ideology, yet it felt so… true in a way I couldn't put into words. "I can't fully . . . accept that. But I know it's the truth, deep down, I know."

My father placed a comforting hand on my shoulder as I wiped away a falling tear.

"It's okay, Amat. That's a start and I'm *so* proud of you for it."

I flicked my head in the direction of my father, who wore a gentle smile on his face. An expression I seldom saw him wear. Something about it was enough to console me then and there, which subsided my discomfort.

"With that said, I want you to keep your distance from the Diramal. If he isolates or approaches you again, you tell me immediately. Understood?"

"Yes, sir," I replied.

The circumstance of the conversation abruptly brought to light a subject my father and I spoke of earlier.

"You know what, all this talk reminds me of what we discussed about the reconstruction program—"

"Hold that thought, Amat," my father interrupted. "Look there, up at Anua, do you see what sits upon her?"

I was speechless when I set my eyes upon it. My mind couldn't comprehend its authenticity; it was almost as if I was trying to convince myself it wasn't real. Yet there it was, a fraction of the moon's size, yet large enough to be seen from the surface of Galiza.

"By the Goddess! I haven't seen anything like that in—"

I whipped my head over to my father. "Wait, you mean . . . you've seen something like that before?"

"Never mind what I said. We have to get home, *now*."

"Well, what is it?"

"I don't know, Amat!"

My father drove faster and faster as I stared up, dazed by the two stacked, orange, triangular objects sitting atop Anua.

XIX
Family

We made it back home in a rush. Dad stormed in like a madman, yelling my sisters' names to see if they were alright. All while I still couldn't get enough of the strange ship on the surface of Anua. My father found Lia and Lara in their rooms, both unaware of the Goddess' unexpected visitors.

"Daddy!" Lia shouted in delight. My father turned to her and squatted down with his arms reaching out to her. My father stood as he took little Lia into his arms, squeezing just firmly enough to make his grasp inescapable but not crushing.

"Oh, thank Anua."

"Why were you so worried just now?" Lara asked.

My father gave Lara a strange look. "Has the news said nothing on it yet?"

"You think we watch the news?" Lara replied.

My father sighed. "Where is your mother?"

"She went out to get Amat his welcome home gift."

"And you haven't heard from her since?"

"No."

"Alright, well, I suppose if she hasn't figured it out by now, she will soon enough."

"Find out what?" Lara asked.

"Well," my father hesitated, glancing from Lara to Lia. "I don't see any point keeping either of you in the dark about it when it's plane for all to see. Follow me outside."

I watched as my father took the girls outside and showed them the grand, triangular, alien ship on the moon.

"Anua has a crown now!" was my little sister's response.

Lara, on the other hand, seemed completely unfazed by the situation. A unmoving, dejected expression lingered on her face. *I guess Dad wasn't kidding about Lara. I wonder what the matter could be.*

"Yes," my father replied awkwardly. "Anua has a crown." He put Lia on the ground and got down on her level. "But . . . we don't know how it got there. I think it would be best if we all stayed inside the house tonight, at least until we hear further news about it. Alright?"

Lia nodded her head. "Okay," she replied in a whisper, as if she'd just been told a secret.

He turned his head. "Lara?"

"Yeah, fine, whatever. It's not like I have anywhere to go anyway."

Though he claimed he was just as clueless as the rest of us, as to how or why the ship arrived, his attitude toward it suggested otherwise.

My father's phone started to ring. He pulled it out of his pocket and once he saw who it was, he asked me to take the girls back inside the house.

(Bod)

"Hello?" I answered.

"Bod! Are you and the children alright?!" Judi asked over the phone.

"Yes, Amat and I made it home safe. The girls are fine. We saw the . . . ship on our way home. I haven't noted any aggression from the craft, and we haven't heard much about it on the news as of yet."

"Oh, thank Anua. I haven't heard any bad news either, but I just wanted to be sure that you and the kids were alright."

"We are. Will you be home soon?"

"Yes, I'm just making my way back to the house with some gifts for Amat."

"Lara told me. Are you doing alright?"

"Well, I'm disturbed, to say the least, but so long as the world is still intact and you're all safe, I'll be alright. What about you?"

I held my silence, uncertain of how to answer.

"For now . . . I'm just happy that we're all okay, like you said."

Judi paused before replying.

"Bod, do you know what that ship is? What it means?"

My gaze trailed across the street to a silver car parked with two cho'zai within, staring intently at me from afar.

"Let me know when you get home, I'll help you haul things in," I said to Judi.

"Alright, I love you."

"I love you too."

I hung up and marched boldly to the cho'zai. Even as I stood just outside the driver's door, they only stared and kept their window up. I knocked twice on the glass barrier; it slowly dropped down to reveal the never blinking, red stares of the cho'zai.

"What does he want?" I asked.

The wide grin of Cho'zai Xaizar's face extended to his eyes in a twisted pleasure of intimidation.

"Why do you always hold such prejudice against us—"

"Save it, Cho'zai Xaizar," I interjected. "There's no clouding the purpose of your being here. You are among the Diramal's most esteemed cho'zai, and the most spineless at that."

Xaizar's grin faded.

"What does he want?" I repeated.

"You might have noticed there's a concerning presence seated atop our moon. The Diramal chose you to lead a squadron of troops to investigate the craft," Xaizar replied.

My eyes narrowed.

"A squadron?" I asked.

"Anything more and it would spread panic, the Diramal wants—"

"I could *not* care less what the Diramal wants, *cho'zai*. A mere squadron is a death sentence against the technology those beings possess. If he's so confident a single squad is adequate, tell him he can lead the mission himself."

The cho'zai and I held menacing stares. My eyes trailed down to Xaizar's side; his hand, placed on his sidearm, ready to unholster it at any moment.

"You might want to check yourself before proceeding with whatever's in your mind right now, Xaizar. A cho'zai assaulting the jinn-hid wouldn't reflect well in the public eye. How that would sit with the Diramal," I stated.

"Not if there's no witnesses," replied Xaizar.

"My wife is about to turn the corner. Down the street, a neighbor, Fjöra Gūndar. Two houses down is approximately forty-three paces away and closing from the east. Two strong witnesses to make a trustworthy story. If you don't believe me, filter their neuro-chips. You have about twenty-two seconds before your window closes and one of them gets a clear look at you."

Xaizar looked ahead anxiously to Judi, who was arriving in her car up the road.

Xaizar let on a smile of annoyance as he gazed back at me.

"And what is my alternative?" he asked.

"Leaving would be a wise choice," I replied.

He scoffed.

"You'll be hearing from your superior before the end of the day."

I stepped back, keeping my gaze locked on the cho'zai, as Xaizar scrambled to get the vehicle started and sped forth down the street.

"Bod?" Judi beckoned from behind.

I finally broke my stare from the car and acknowledged my wife.

"Who was that you were talking to?" she asked.

I sighed.

"Cho'zai, from the Diramal," I replied.

She turned her head slightly.

"What did they want?"

"Something they won't get in the manner which it was asked," I spoke reassuringly as I brushed my fingers past Judi's cheek. "It's good to see you again."

Judi gently took Bod's hand as she glanced down, a bit of gloom in her expression.

"And you," she continued. Her face lit up as she smiled softly at me.

"Come, see our son. He waits just inside."

(Amat)

"Welcome home, Amat!" Lia wrapped her arms around me as tight as she could.

Lara gave me a nod and half a smile.

"Hey, Lia, you remember me?" I asked.

"A little. Enough to miss my big brother!" she replied, gazing up at me. "I'm happy to see you again."

I kneeled down to her level as my little sister's ecstasy filled me with delight.

"And I, you," I replied, brushing at her snout with my finger.

Lia's shoulders tensed up and her arms squeezed together as she smiled wide, her tongue hanging out slightly. I stood to acknowledge Lara, easing my way into her space as I went to embrace her. Lara awkwardly put her hands around me in return.

"Are you feeling alright, Lara?" I questioned. With her dejected expression, she avoided my eyes as I looked upon her.

"Yeah, I just . . ."

I looked down at Lia and said, "Hey, Lia, uh, you're still the artsy sister, right?"

"Yeah!" she exclaimed.

"I bet you made me something for the occasion, didn't you?" I asked with a smile.

"I did!"

"I'd love to see it. Why don't you go get it for me?"

"Okay!" she said.

Once she was out of the room, I turned back to Lara and tried to see what was going on.

"Lara—"

"It's nothing," Lara said, cutting me off.

I sighed. "Mom and Dad don't seem to think so."

She scoffed. "Mom and Dad don't know the half of it."

"So I heard," I said, taking a seat beside her on the furniture. It was then I noticed, in the shadow of her sleeve, there was a fresh bruise. I reached out with my hand to reveal the wound, but she saw me and pulled the sleeve down.

"Lara?"

She shook her head.

"Who did that to you?" I asked. I didn't need to think too hard before finally piecing together a rational conclusion for the likely identity of the culprit.

"I heard a few months ago, from the man himself, that you've been going out with Dilek. Is that true?"

Lara's breaths got deeper at the mention of his name. My heart twisted as my lips lifted, momentarily revealing my fangs in a rictus of betrayal and ire.

I sighed and repositioned myself in my seat. "It's okay, you don't have to talk, just nod or shake your head, alright?" I asked as I took my sister's hand.

Lara stared off into the distance but nodded in reply.

"Have you and Dilek had problems?" I asked.

She nodded her head, and her eyes were starting to glisten.

"Have you been seeing someone else recently, other than Dilek?"

With a head *shake*, she frowned. That made me tilt my head.

"You've still been seeing Dilek?"

She nodded as a tear rolled down her cheek. I held my sister's hand tighter, swallowing as a deep sense of guilt and empathy filled me. I had to ask a question I already sensed the answer to, but couldn't believe it unless my sister confirmed it.

"Lara, I need you to be honest with me. Has Dilek hurt you?"

She gave a heavy sniff and started crying.

"*Shh, shh*, it's okay, I'm not going to tell anyone. But I need to know, Lara, where did the bruise come from?" I asked.

She finally turned her head toward me. "You said his name half a dozen times at this point."

My jaw dropped and my eyes widened. I swallowed.

"Please don't tell Mom and Dad. Please . . ." she said as she leaned into my shoulder and held my hand tight. I placed my other hand on her back in comfort.

It didn't even compute to me. Dilek didn't seem to change in the slightest since we reconnected. *I guess memories can be deceiving.* "It's okay, I won't," I finally said. "But hey, look at me. Are you still seeing him?"

Lara shook her head. "I . . . I was, even while this was going on. But after last night . . . it was too much. It was just too much."

I took a deep breath.

"How many times has he laid hands on you like that?" I asked.

"I don't know, I haven't kept track, but more than once," she replied.

I didn't think it wise to judge her, despite the criticism that flowed through my mind at that moment. I didn't know the first thing about how the relationship was decaying. So, I simply said, "You're never going to see him again. I don't care how often he comes by or how he may seem. You're never going anywhere or doing anything with him, *ever*."

She nodded her head.

I didn't say it, but I was prepared to take measures, as soon as an opportunity presented itself, to make sure Dilek got the same message: that Lara was off limits, now and forever.

"Alright, now pull yourself together," I said, brushing Lara's shoulders. "Or it'll raise questions from Dad." Lara nodded and sniffed as she wiped away her tears.

"There you go. I'm sorry. I'm so sorry I couldn't be here sooner for you. But it's going to get better, you deserve better. If you're going to give yourself to someone else, make sure they are going to be nothing but loyal, and above all, respectful to you. Remember that."

Lara nodded her head. It was then that I could hear the quick footsteps of my younger sister racing down the hall.

"Lia's coming," she said.

"I heard," I replied, looking in Lia's direction, then back at Lara. We shared a smile with one another.

"Amat, Amat! Here you go," Lia said as she handed me her gift.

"Oh wow, look at this. It's all nicely wrapped and everything," I said. I gave Lia a smile with a sidelong look. "Did you do this yourself?"

"Yeah!" she said with a big grin, bouncing in place and playing with her fingers.

"Marvelous job," I said, unwrapping her gift.

The wrapping revealed a small but fascinating . . . thing that she glued and attached all kinds of materials to, with two dots that resembled eyes, and a pink slab of paper that resembled a crooked smile.

"And who is this?" I asked.

"Her name is Shina." She always named the things she handcrafted.

"*Ooh*, hello, Shina. I'll treasure her," I said.

"And I also made you this!" Lia said, handing me a second gift. It caught me off guard by how much longer and heavier the second gift was.

"Oh, two presents!"

"Me and Mom helped her make this one for the most part," Lara said under her breath.

"Did not!" Lia blurted.

I unraveled it from the paper and found a wood carving of a ship, an explorer, like the one my father must have traveled in during his time in SEF. Then, for a brief moment, I was taken back to when I was a lot younger. When my dreams of exploring the stars were so strong, filled with passion.

"*Wow*, this is *very* nice, Lia. I am impressed, I'll take extra care of this one, thank you."

I glanced over at Lara while Lia wasn't looking. *Thank you*, I mouthed.

"When are Olson, Log, Aunt Sally, and Uncle Gordon going to be here?" Lia asked.

"They'll be here soon," I said.

Moments later, the front door to the house opened.

"That's probably Mom," I said.

"Oh, yay!" Lia shouted excitedly.

We all walked down the hall toward the family room.

"Amat!" Mom said as she embraced me with open arms. "*Ohh*, welcome home."

"Thanks, Mom," I replied.

"Hi, sweetie," Mom said as she crouched down and gave Lia a hug and a kiss.

"Hi, Mama!" she said.

Mom walked over to Lara and gave her a hug, wrapping her arm around Lara's wounded side. She winced. "Lara, how are you feeling?"

Lara looked over at me. "A little bit better, I think."

"I had a feeling," Mom said as she stroked Lara's cheek with her thumb. "You've been crying. Crying is good for the heart when it's sick."

Lara nodded her head and gave a nervous smile. "Are Gordon, Sally, and your cousins here?" Mom asked.

"Not yet, but they will be soon," Dad said as he approached.

"Well, I better get a jump start on dinner then!" she said. With Lia still in her arms, she went to grab one of the bags off the ground, but my father beat her to it.

"I'll help you," he said.

"Can you carry me too, daddy?!" asked Lia as my father picked up the bags.

"Oh, not right now, sweetheart, my hands are full."

"Aw! But Mr. Njöri could do it!" protested Lia.

My father tilted his head at the mention of my father's self-made nickname among his children. A njör was a great, woolly animal on Galiza, with eight legs, and a wide boney head. Ferocious mammals, commonly found in the colder parts of the world. Any time his children would get upset or frustrated, instead of escalating the situation, my father would turn himself into "Mr. Njöri." Proclaiming himself a great behemoth that would chase his children throughout the house tickling them till their frowns turned upside down.

"You're right, Mr. Njöri could do it," he spoke conspicuously and brought a smile to Lia's face. "You better run before he gets here."

She giggled and shook her head vehemently.

My father wiggled his torso and bent forward as he ran after my little sister, up chasing her through the kitchen, where he dropped the bags. Continuing their chase, he caught up to her as she squealed, picking her up and spinning her around.

"Oh, you have a belly full of giggles?" he deepened his voice playfully as he asked the question.

"No!" she laughed.

"You can't hide your laughs from Mr. Njöri, he can always sense the giggles in your belly!" my father continued.

He set Lia over his knee, pressed his lips to her belly, and exhaled loudly, causing her to erupt into laughter.

"Wah! Mr. Njöri always finds your giggles," he said, finally letting Lia go.

He rejoined my mother in the kitchen. Their voices dimmed and suddenly my mother burst into laughter. A nostalgia filled my heart that nearly brought tears to my eyes. I couldn't say I felt as delighted as my mother and youngest sister in that moment. But seeing this other side, this playful… fatherly side to my dad that I'd been so robbed of for years, it ignited something in the atmosphere. Some lost aspect of my character; youth.

***

"Amat!" my aunt and uncle exclaimed in pleasure.

"Hey, Uncle Gordon. Aunt Sally," I said, giving them a hug. "Come and make yourselves at home!"

"With pleasure," Log said, as I led him and Olson into the family room.

"Have you all seen Anua?" Sally asked, agape.

"We have . . ." My thoughts returned to the alien craft on Anua's body. "It's curious, to say the least. The ship I mean."

Gordon cleared his throat, interjecting himself in a quick effort to change the subject. His brows sagged and his eyes were unnerved at the mention of the craft.

"So, where are your parents and sisters, Amat?"

"In the kitchen, Uncle Gordon," I replied.

"Perfect." He nodded at me. "Let's go say 'hi' hon'."

"Oh, alright, you boys have fun."

Olson nudged me with a small smile as we made our way to the furniture.

"Hey, good job in the sim," said Olson.

"Thanks," I replied.

"How'd you get passed that barrage, by the way, when you first came into the base?" he asked.

Log looked quizzically at me, as his ears perked.

I took a deep breath as I quickly thought of something to say.

"Eh, I could hear your guns cock a mile away. I dove back from your barrage the moment you opened fire and sprayed in the direction of your two troops on the first level," I confidently replied.

"I wouldn't doubt it. If Amat's eyes were sharp enough to notice half a platoon of troops lying prone in a brush, his ears could probably hear the breath leaving your snoot, Olson," Log joked.

Olson scoffed; his expression suggested his mind still stirred with something.

My cousins and I sat down as my aunt and uncle found their way into the kitchen. I sensed we all had a mutual urge to discuss the alien craft on the moon.

"So, uh . . . Did you guys hear anything about the craft on the way over?" I inquired.

Log shifted uncomfortably in his seat as Olson glanced over at his younger brother.

"Not really. They . . . mentioned it, obviously, but in a very illusive way," Olson replied.

"Well . . . it's not like there can be much said about it," I laughed, awkwardly. "I mean, what all could be said about it? At least they acknowledged it."

"Maybe we could find an update, if we switch on the news," Log suggested.

"Well, let's test that theory," I returned, grabbing the remote and aiming it at the glass rectangle on the wall.

A news channel immediately appeared on the screen, with a reporter discussing the rebellion in Zeta.

"Not exactly what we were looking for, but I—"

"Wait, listen to what they're saying. They're talking about Zeta."

My neuro-chip fired with its propaganda programing, filtering my mind with thoughts of how glorious it must be to spread the Utopion autocracy.

"We just received a report," the reporter started. "That the xǔté killed their national leader, Ceodric Xanadarom, in response to the loss of their second-highest ranking officer, Lůkig Zǔleba. The Zetian and the Utopion militaries were pushed back very close to the western borders of Zeta." My thoughts deteriorated into outrage at this loss. "It would appear that the war there will wage on to maintain the peace and the righteous autocracy of the world. May the goddess favor our government's cause in uniting our world and peoples. Now, in other news—"

Out of frustration, I turned off the television and looked over at my cousins.

Damn terrorists, smiting our autocratic—

"Well, this doesn't seem to have lightened the mood," Log said sarcastically. His words broke my train of thought. I was momentarily frustrated, but then the lessons of my father that he'd been instilling into me came flooding back.

"Amat? You alright?" asked Olson.

I cleared my throat.

"Oh, yeah, I'm alright." The thought crossed my mind to bring up how I just had a minor episode with my neuro-chip, but I figured, *Why bother?*

Olson nodded. I took a deep breath.

"Should we try one more time to see if there's any coverage on the ship?" Log suggested, trying to shift the mood.

I sniffed; the scent of dinner was in the air.

"Yeah, sure, we could check real quick," I replied.

I switched on the screen and before long, we found some coverage on the subject.

"—still don't know much about this object or where it came from," said a reporter's voice, narrating over footage of the craft. "For reasons unknown, the Diramal has remained silent on the matter. However, we've received reports from Cho'zai Zothra, one of the Diramal's most esteemed soldiers, that the nation's leader intends to send a manned mission to Anua. He plans to accomplish this through the long-retired Space Exploration Frontier. The mission will be led by SEF's top technicians and biologists. The group will be escorted by a small squadron of Utopion's alphas and krollgrums, should things turn ugly in this historical encounter."

Alphas . . . if only I remained one, perhaps I could be among the few to escort the mission.

"—Zothra says that although SEF's exploration program has been inactive for over a decade, both the alphas and scientists received prior training in piloting the craft that will be used to visit the surface of our beloved mother. And that the public should expect to see this mission launch tomorrow morning, eight a.m. western time. We'll have more on this as the story develops."

I lowered the volume to hardly anything. "Well, at least I'll have something to watch over the next couple of days or so, depending on how long they investigate that ship," I said.

"You wish it was you that was going," Olson said.

I snorted in derision and turned toward my older cousin. "You catch onto a lot of things, Olson. Something I observed in my time back here. But be careful, catch onto the wrong thing and someone might give ya a dirty look."

I meant it as a joke, but at the same time, I didn't appreciate the intuitive notion. I loved Olson, but that part of me, the part that wanted to be an astrometon, was long suppressed. A young boy's dream that could easily be taken for softness, and such things didn't belong in a world like Galiza.

Olson and I stared at one another, exchanging understanding looks.

Log gazed at each one of us in turn as the scent of fresh grilled stakona and shǔma filled my nostrils.

Served together, they make a meal called argetti, and resembled something you might consider surf and turf. I raised my eyebrows and smiled.

"Ah, I think dinner's ready. Who's hungry?" I stood up before anyone answered and headed into the kitchen.

XX
An Undesired Mission

Everything my mother prepared was delicious. The stakona was tender and juicy, the shǔma was crisp and sweet; complemented with mashed, creamy fotties. The family chatter leading up to the meal promptly died down once everyone had a chance to dig in. My mother surveyed the table proudly.

After some time, conversation revitalized, mostly concerning me. My aunt and mother shared stories about the last times they saw me. How Olson and I used to be inseparable growing up. At times, we teased Lara and were raising mayhem, deliberately getting lost on family outings in the wilderness and finding our way back. Often times we found our parents were the ones who would go missing. I scarcely remembered much of it, especially the parts about getting lost with Olson.

"So, tell me, Amat," my uncle said as the conversation started to die down between my mother and aunt. "How was alpha training?"

My father paused his chewing and gave my uncle a sidelong look that he didn't notice.

"Oh, um . . ." Suddenly all eyes were on me. What could be said? 'A waste of time' would sum it up. However, that wouldn't answer the question, nor would it be true. "I'd say, I enjoyed my time at Gallethol and learned a lot."

My father raised his eyebrows momentarily.

"I heard you were close with someone over there," my mother said, giving me a knowing look.

"*Mm*, no, I mostly just kept to myself," I replied.

"Yes, I heard that too, but she didn't."

I choked mid-gulp from my glass. Log, who was sitting beside me, patted me on the back.

"You alright?" he asked.

I raised my hand and nodded my head, catching my breath.

"Who's 'she?'" Lara asked.

"Yeah, you didn't mention anything to me or Log about a girl," Olson chimed in, a intrigued smile stretched across his face.

"I don't think everyone wants to know," Lia said.

"Judi!" my aunt blurted.

"What?" my mom replied.

"Are you seriously prying into your son's . . . love life? That's disgusting," my aunt remarked.

"Thank you, Aunt Sally," Lia said.

"Not where I was aiming to take this conversation," my uncle mumbled.

"No, I'm just sharing what Bod told me while Amat was away. I just wanted to see if it was true," my mom stated.

My father cleared his throat.

"Mm, it seems Dad was filtering me a lot more consistently than he's cared to admit."

My dad took a drink and avoided eye contact with me.

"But, to answer your question, Mom, yes, there was a girl at the base who I was . . . on good terms with."

"What's her name?" Mom gently interrogated.

My mind drifted to her. I was taken back to a rare moment in time when Mae and I were enjoying each other's company outside of training. Her smile, the memory of it tingled my heart. Looking back at that day, she was trying for weeks to get me alone with her. We exchanged a good deal of banter up to that point; although, it wasn't until that day when our chemistry ignited. It didn't take much for it to spark. Even then, I couldn't see that for what it was, what it could have been.

"Mae. Her name is Mae," I answered. Saying her name out loud momentarily brought up feelings I didn't know I had. "Back in training, she was always optimistic and it didn't matter what the routine was for the day, we were always neck and neck, ahead of everyone else. In some situations, she was better than me. She never rubbed it in though. I never went out of my way to talk to her or anyone else in my squadron over there. But in the time we did chat, which she made more of an effort than I, she was a joy to be around."

It was then that I noticed most everyone besides my father and Lia were listening intently to what I was saying.

"Well, she sounds like a very lovely girl, Amat. Though you might have avoided her, it sounds like you were still respectful towards her," my mother said, with a proud smile.

"He was," my father said and gave me an approving nod. Felt like the most approving gesture he gave me in a while.

"The reason I asked about your alpha training, Amat," my uncle interjected, "is because I also went through it at the same age as you."

I raised an eyebrow. "Is that so?"

"It is," my father broke in. "You were gone for two years."

"Two? But it's a five-year program."

"Things were different back then," my uncle said.

"Well, what happened?" I inquired.

"I couldn't keep up with the other alphas in training. Granted, I was good at the start. Halfway into my second year, I started having pain throughout my limbs that didn't go away. It was later that I found out, after having twisted my left knee out of place, that my joints had excessive amounts of wear and tear. At that point, it was no longer sensible for me to continue in the alpha program."

"But when you sign on with the alphas, you're required to take on five years of training and at least two years of service. Well, that was the agreement when I signed on," I said.

"Two years of service was also required of me. So, given that I obviously couldn't fight, I was transferred to work with IID: the Intelligence Interests Division."

"Do you still work there?"

My uncle sighed. "No, unfortunately I wasn't happy working there. I learned some things I wish I didn't and did some things I wasn't proud of. By then, my contract was up; so, I left. Went on to help in the reconstruction program." My uncle gave me a smile.

My uncle's answer piqued my interest. "What exactly scared you off from IID.?"

My uncle hesitated to answer. He glanced at my father, who sighed and motioned approval by nodding his head. However, at that moment, the phone rang.

As my father stood to answer the phone, he quickly changed the subject. "Judi," he said, placing a hand on her back. "Why don't you show Amat what you and the girls have been up to over the last five years."

My mom's face lit up. "I think that's a great idea," she said. My mom motioned everyone to follow her into another section of the house, one filled with various pieces of art.

(Bod)

"Hello?" I said, picking up the phone.

"Hello, jinn-hid," a voice replied.

I paused a moment. The voice of the caller sounded all too familiar. "You have no business calling me. Not at this hour; not at my home . . . Diramal," I said in a furious growl.

"You have no business denying the commands of your superior," the Diramal replied.

"Your orders, as I mentioned to your messenger, are a death sentence. A mere squadron is nowhere near enough to take on the occupants of that ship. By Anua's shadow, I dare say the whole world might not even be enough."

"And would you dare to see what happens if we do nothing?" he queried.

I did not answer with words but a sour grunt.

"Well," the Diramal said after a long moment of silence. "Given your lack of reply, I'm going to assume you would not. I trust then you recall what they are capable—"

"*I want a platoon,*" I growled.

"Oh, still so *hasty,* jinn-hid?"

"Speak for yourself. It's because of *you* that these beings have made enemies of us. You were the one who gave the order to—"

"All such events are behind us now, jinn-hid. I only did what was in the best interest of our crew."

"They were merely on approach while scanning our ship."

"As were we. As you know, our scans showed that they were activating something with a highly concentrated energy field coming from the head of their ship. The scans registered the growing green orb was a weapon capable of detrimental damage."

"Even so, in all those years we spent out there, in the deep reaches of space, never once did we attempted to reason with the species that resided within any of those crafts."

"Their ships were moving faster than any man among us could perceive. Why would I allow our crew to risk investigating one of their damaged ships? Was I not wise to insist that we reserve our curiosities?"

"No, you were a coward. From the moment you gave the order to strike first."

Our conversation paused again.

"Well, you stand where you stand, jinn-hid, but I wonder if you have forgotten my authority. If you refuse to fall into line, then I suppose I have to take measures to ensure it myself. Which would include sending Xaizar and additional cho'zai to . . . crash your little family gathering . . . take them *all* away from you . . . and do as I please with them until you adhere to my command. Despite how unfortunate that would be to sever a potential partnership with your son, it would be necessary nonetheless."

"You're *sick*, Diramal," I growled. "Lest you've forgotten I have already stated I will investigate the ship with a *platoon* under my command—"

"You will have it: twenty troops, no more, no less," the Diramal interrupted.

The bare minimum, not surprising. Does he want this mission to fail?! At the very least, I suppose that's six more troops guaranteed from what I would have with just the squadron.

"We don't want to raise too much cause for concern among the public by seeming . . . overprepared for a 'first contact,'" the Diramal continued. "I arranged for you, the members of your squadron from base Lazithia, *and some* to meet at Vīvothar Base, by six a.m. You will take command of an investigative mission to contact our unannounced visitors. It's as simple as that! Whether it is done through peaceful means *or combative* is no concern of mine. However, I want the ship searched, and whatever life forms that may be on it, I want reasoned with. If that cannot be done, find out what they want; if necessary, annihilate them. Do you think you can manage that, old friend?"

I grunted, irritated with the entire predicament. "Taking command of the mission, I can do. But I will not take *all* of my squadron on this mission. My son will remain *here* on Galiza. I will not willingly endanger him."

"You have no authority to tell *me* what to do, jinn-hid. On the subject of your son, I decided to reinstate his rank of alpha. It is strictly for the purposes of the mission, as I'm sure you understand. Should something unfortunate befall you, the commanding officer on this mission, there will need to be a chain of command to take your place. Your son is the most qualified." The Diramal chuckled subtly. "Especially after what he did less than a year ago on that reconnaissance mission he undertook. You may need the boy more than he'll need you on this mission, jinn-hid. Now, is there anything else you'd like to discuss before we meet tomorrow?"

I wanted to rip the Diramal a new one. By the shadow of Anua, I wanted to go down there, to the Diramal's office, and take his life myself. But I knew all too well such actions would lead nowhere, so I smashed the phone down and hung up.

(Amat)

My father joined us in the art room filled with all sorts of crafts, paintings, and so forth that were made by my mother and sisters. My mother did that kind of thing for a living. Her work wasn't highly reputable, but she was a bit of a local celebrity. With dad having one of the highest paying jobs in the world, she didn't need to make much income anyway.

Despite having my back to him, the scent of my father's anxiety gave him away. I turned to face him; he gave me a smile that was filled with hopelessness, and a gaze of encroaching fear. The thought that 'something could be wrong,' was putting it lightly. I never saw these emotions demonstrated so fiercely by him. Though, I felt it wise not to pry.

My father didn't say much else for the remainder of the evening, not even in silent gestures. When my cousins and aunt and uncle left, my father called me to him in private. I walked over and he placed a hand on my shoulder.

"Amat. Son . . ." he started in a queer tone. He seemed to be struggling to find the words that needed to be said. "Earlier, the Diramal called."

"He did?" I asked in uncertainty.

"Yes."

"Well, what did he say?"

"He gave me . . . well, *us*, a mission to investigate the ship that rests on the body of Anua. It seems you'll get a taste of your dream to become an astrometon after all. Even if you lost the drive for it."

I parted my lips to speak, but before I could, my father continued talking.

"Your rank of alpha was also reinstated and you will be operating as second in command . . . Effective immediately."

"Y-You're serious?"

My father nodded.

"Wow, this is . . . amazing! When do we leave?"

"We're expected to arrive tomorrow, at Vīvothar base, at 06:00. The launch commences at 08:00. So, you should get a good night's rest tonight."

"Yes, sir!" I said with a smile. I rushed to the bathroom to get ready for bed.

(Bod)

Judi slowly walked up to me. She didn't initially take note to the gloom on my face.

"What's Amat so excited about?" she asked. I looked over to her and with one glance she could fully register despair. "What's wrong?"

I faced her and held her hands. "The Diramal gave us no other choice." I paused. "My squadron and I are to report for duty at 06:00 tomorrow to investigate the craft that landed on Anua, which includes Amat."

Judi pulled her hands away while I looked down in shame. She had a furious look on her face. She slapped me, and then again. She attempted to strike me a third time, but I caught her arm and grabbed the other. Judi squirmed and struggled but she did not scream or yell.

"Judi, stop. Don't turn this into a scene for the kids to see!" I growled, as she moved their confrontation out of the house.

"Stop!" Judi shouted as she tore away from my grasp and paced in silent fury. "How could you let the Diramal enlist *our* son on such a futile mission? Especially considering it'll be his first!"

"Judi, I didn't just let the man tell me that's how it was going to be. I told him he had no right, *no* authority, to order our son into harm's way. But if I persisted, he was going to take all of you away. Which included not only you and Amat, but the girls, my brother, his wife, and their children. Where would that leave us then?!"

Judi covered her jowls and crouched down helplessly.

I crouched down beside her. "I don't want this any more than you do, but we don't have any other choice." Judi started crying as I held her hands tightly.

"Isn't there *anything* you can do?" Judi asked, looking up at me, pleading.

"No."

Judi continued sobbing.

"But I can make us this promise." Judi paused her weeping. "If anyone will be *returning* from this mission, it *will* be our son. I will see to that much at least."

"I know you will, and that's why I'm so afraid. Because I know that I'm going to lose at least one of you. I remember what little you told me about—"

"Shh, shh, shh, don't think about that." I soothed my wife as she continued to cry profusely. "I know what to anticipate up there, Anua forbid my expectations should be fulfilled. But if they are . . . Amat will come home and steps have been taken to ensure he knows the truth. And Gordon will know how best to help him."

Judi and I wrapped our arms around another like it was our final embrace. For hours we stood in the yard; neither one of us had the desire to let go of the other . . . ever.

XXI
Pep Talk

The next morning, we all woke up at 03:30. Both my sisters, especially Lia, didn't understand why. My mother got them up to speed over breakfast.

"You're going to see the crown?" Lia asked enthusiastically once Mom finished explaining.

"Yes, Lia, your brother and I are going to see the crown on Anua," my father replied.

"Can I come too?"

"*No*," my father said so sternly it made Lia jump.

Lia's smile turned into a frown and she played with her fingers awkwardly.

My father sighed and shut his eyes to gather his thoughts. "I am sorry, Lia. You cannot come with me and Amat because there wouldn't be any room in the ship."

Lia pouted, pushed her plate away, and crossed her arms.

Lara stayed silent, but no doubt she was also taken aback by the news.

"Lara?" my father asked. "Is there anything you have to say about this? Any questions?"

Lara kept a straight face, but I could see the worry in her eyes as she shook her head.

My father nodded and continued eating his breakfast.

The ambient discomfort of my family finally started to settle in for me. Up until that moment, I was so excited for the mission. Then, I remembered how distraught my father became the previous day, and how my mother was now showing similar signs. I finally realized: *I have no idea what to expect . . .* It was at that moment the neuro-chip flooded my thoughts with glory and how honored I should have felt. That no matter what happened, it would only bring praise to Utopion. Even with our lives at stake, we would be renowned for centuries to come.

"Hey," my father said, patting me on the shoulder. "Come on, eat your food." I blinked and continued eating. "I know all of you feel some way about this, and plainly not in any positive light. I just want you all to know that no matter what happens . . . it's all going to be okay."

His words sounded like desperate gasps of air as they escaped his lips. I'm not sure if anyone, besides Lia, believed them.

***

The drive to the SEF base was quiet. At Vīvothar, the time had come for my father and I to bid our farewells. I started with Lia.

"Okay, little Lia, it's that time," I said as I crouched down at her level.

"But you just came back home!" she protested.

"I know, but we won't be gone for too long," I nearly stumbled on my own words as my uncertainty briefly surfaced. It suddenly dawned on me, the unforeseen nature of the mission. Not just in what it would take to get there, but what we would be encountering and how they would receive us. *There's no guarantee they'll be especially hospitable, when we enter their craft.*

She glanced at me, with her head hanging low, before ramming into me for a hug.

"I don't want you to go, or Daddy," she said, breaking into tears.

I gave a long sigh before replying. "It's gonna be okay. Dad and I will be right back. I promise." I rubbed Lia's back as she sobbed.

My father took a long look at Lia before slowly crouching down to her level, as if he was trying to take in every detail of her face. He gave a light, reassuring smile as he wiped away one of her tears. She fell into him and buried her face into his neck as my father rose, pressing her into his chest.

"You can't leave if I stay stuck to you," Lia sobbed.

My father closed his eyes and took in a deep breath of her fur before he moved to gently unlock her arms around his neck. I moved in to gently remove her from my father, and he whispered something to my little sister

121

before letting her go. Brushing her fur behind her ear, my father gently kissed her on the forehead.

When I approached Lara to hug her, she stopped me.

"What's wrong?" I asked.

"I'm scared," she said.

I took a deep breath and nodded.

"I am too," spoke only low enough for her to hear. "Stepping into the unknown is . . . terrifying, to say the least. However, I have every confidence that we'll make it back."

"How can you be so sure? Haven't you noticed how anxious mom and dad are behaving?"

I took a moment to process the question.

"The ship, whatever it is, hasn't shown any notable hostility. Nothing is ever certain, Lara, but we can always hope for the best. Will you hope with me?" I asked, taking my sister's hand.

As her eyes started to well up, she nodded. I motioned to hug her once again, to which she held up her hand at me.

"I'm sorry, Amat, I-I can't. It feels like I'm saying goodbye forever. And the only way it wouldn't, is if you left with something to return for. A debt of a warm embrace, owed to me by my big brother."

I smiled, reassuringly, as I stepped back. "And you shall have it," I promised.

When my father came up to Lara, he raised his hands to hug her and the look in his eyes asked permission to embrace her. She tentatively placed her hands on his forearms and he rested his hands on her shoulders, brushing them.

"You are strong, Lara. Your mother and I, we've noticed you've been . . . distant lately. I was hoping we'd have time to work on it together, as a family, and I still have every intention to do so. But if—"

"Don't say 'but,' Dad. Don't—"

"But if worse comes to worst, look after the others. Don't let anything from your past hold you back. There's nothing you could do to make either of us love you less than we have and still do. If you ever need help, ask for it."

Lara nodded her head as a tear rolled down her cheek.

My father wiped the tear away with his finger. "Look after your sister."

Lara gestured her understanding as she sniffed.

Finally, when I got to my mother, I hugged her and whispered, "It's going to be okay. I'll watch out for the old man."

"The goddess will watch over you both," my mother remarked.

"Of course. It'll be impossible for her not to."

My mother smiled tenderly. "Don't be overly confident, Amat, please. No one knows what to expect up there."

I smiled and dipped my head.

She combed her fingers through my fur. "My brave boy, I love you."

"I love you too, Mom." I could tell her heart sank as my hand slipped out of her own.

My father came up to her and immediately they took one another's hands in a tight grip.

"Bod—"

"I made a promise, Judi," my father interrupted. "He'll make it home. You have my word."

"I know."

My mother brushed her hand across his face. "But you see to it, with Anua as your witness, that you come back as well." He closed his eyes, held her hand, and kissed it.

"Goodbye," he said, bringing her hands together, slipping out of her grasp.

***

When my father and I entered Vīvothar, we found our way to the rest of the platoon, clustered outside a conference room. I looked around and noticed all but one arrived—Blick.

When I couldn't find Blick, I looked around for Dilek. He was situated in a corner, talking it up with some of the other platoon members. The moment I laid eyes on him, my hands clenched into fists at the thought of what he did to my sister. I walked up to him and blurted, "Dilek!"

The smiles on the faces of the troops surrounding Dilek quickly faded as they noted my expression. Dilek, however, maintained his smile.

"Amat, there you are. Where've you been?"

"Catching up with family. I'd like a word in private, please."

Dilek chuckled. "Of course," he replied and hopped out of his seat. "Sorry, guys, I'll tell you the rest of the story about Lůkig later." Dilek grabbed and put on his uniform coat.

I led him well away from everyone else, into a flight simulation room. I didn't count on anyone walking in on us in the short time I had Dilek to myself.

"So secluded, this must be something really important," Dilek stated with that same stupid grin on his face. "So, what did you want to talk about?"

I walked up to him until he could feel my breath blowing past his face. "Dilek, considering all the time we've known each other, I'm gonna give you *one* chance to admit any secrets you might be hiding from me," I said.

It was barely noticeable, but at my mention of the word "secrets," Dilek's eyes jolted to the side, then back at me. *I've caught him off guard, he's under pressure.*

"Secrets? Amat, what are you talking about? I tell you everything. Not always to the last detail, with my missions and all. But I never withheld much from you."

Much. You never withheld 'much' from me, doesn't mean you haven't withheld anything that might concern me.

"You're not hiding anything?" I questioned.

"No." Dilek chuckled again, as his eyes flashed around briefly.

Your eyes say different . . .

I sighed and gave Dilek a reassuring smile as I patted him on the shoulder. "That's great, man, that's all I needed to hear."

"Alright, should we go back to the platoon?" he asked.

"Yeah, actually," I glanced back behind us and looked at the craft model there. "Are you familiar with one of them?" I gestured to the model with my thumb.

"No, never seen one. Did they ever put you in the cockpit of one of those at Gallethol?"

"They did, as a matter of fact. Why don't we go in real quick; I'll show you around."

"Alright." Dilek chuckled awkwardly again. "Lead the way."

"Ah, it gets pretty cramped as you approach the cockpit inside. You should go first. It'll be easier for you to see."

Dilek hesitated a moment but wasn't outright suspicious. "Alright," he said.

I stayed well behind Dilek as we walked up the ramp to the inside of the ship.

"Yeah, I remember from way back when, you used to say you wanted to be a pilot," I said.

As soon as Dilek was at the top of the ramp . . .

"When did I—"

. . . I pressed my hand on the back of Dilek's scalp and shoved it twice against the frame of the entryway. I pulled Dilek back and let him fall to the ground.

"Ah! Anua's light, Amat! What are you doing?" Dilek shouted, clutching his forehead.

"You don't know?" I said, stepping over him. I grabbed him by the collar and he momentarily uncovered his face. I punched him right in the nose. He cried out, still in too much shock to retaliate.

"I found bruises on my sister's arm yesterday. Judging by the way she covered it up, I suspect there were more she didn't want to show me. Am I right about that?"

Dilek fell silent and breathed heavily as his eyes turned from fright to sardonic. His jaw hung loose as he sighed.

"And do you have any idea why that might be, Amat?" asked Dilek.

I cocked my head slightly, but my eyes stayed locked on Dilek.

"Since our reacquaintance, old friend, you have had nothing but the thought of war on your mind. Submitting yourself to serve among the darkest horrors of the world. Do you know what that can do to a man—"

With his collar sill in my grasp, I rammed him against a wall.

"I could not care less what trauma burdens you, you filth. Whatever ails you, destroyed the friend I once knew, and has left behind a fabrication of whoever you are now. You should have thought twice, before—"

Dilek let out a deep growl as his expression grew dark, illuminating his yellow eyes, and hit me in the face, twice, then shoved me off. He stumbled as we both fell on the ground.

"Maybe you're right, Amat. Maybe I was letting all my steam off on someone who can't understand what I've been through!" He stood over me as I got up on one knee. "Maybe you'll have a better appreciation for it."

I shot up and punched Dilek in the chin, nearly launching him off the ground. He caught me in a head lock, drove his knee into my gut. I maneuvered out of the headlock and pushed him back. He whipped his foot into my waist and punched me. I growled and stomped on his quad. As his leg swung out behind him, I grabbed him by the collar, and slammed him against the plating of the model ship. We bared our fangs at one another.

"There is *nothing* you can say that'll justify assaulting my sister. And while she never said so, I wouldn't be surprised if you forced yourself on her," I growled.

He slowly grinned and chuckled sinisterly.

I quickly clasped my hands around his neck, digging my claws into him, almost to the point of drawing blood. He grabbed hold of my arms as his face grew red. "Under any other circumstance, Dilek, I would kill you here and now, without a second thought."

I pressed so hard I could hear his neck start to crack. As I felt his grip weaken, I let go of him. He coughed for breath as I spun him around, pressed him back into the plating, and pulled on his right arm.

He squirmed and reached back with his other arm, trying to stop me. I pulled his arm more harshly, to the brink of breaking, so that he'd stop resisting. I leaned in close, once he settled.

"Stay away from my sister, or I will turn every last bone in your body to powder and I'll save your skull for last. Do you understand me?"

"Yeah," Dilek grunted.

I threw him to the ground and marched away.

I came out and rejoined the platoon in the waiting room. My father and I locked eyes; he was growing a concerned look on his face. his sight shifted past me and suddenly his expression turned sour.

I looked back and saw Dilek's bruised face. He was hugging his arm as he came out. When I looked back, I lost sight of my father momentarily, until he stopped by my side, took me by the arm, and lead us somewhere more isolated. His grip was tight and rough. I growled and rolled my eyes as we moved forward.

Once we were alone, my father made me face him and asked, *"What happened?"*

I turned away from my dad and frowned.

"Hey, tell me. Or you'll be doing double the drills for a month."

I sighed. "Yesterday, you said you wanted me to see what was wrong with Lara." I looked into my father's eyes. "I found out. And I just took care of it."

My father was puzzled. "Is it something *I* should be concerned about?"

"Not anymore, I suspect."

"You're gonna have to give me more than that, Amat, for me to just look the other way after—"

"Dilek assaulted Lara," I finally said.

My father's lips tightened and his fingers curled. He paced around and raised his fists above his head trying to contain his fury. "When?" he finally asked.

"I'm not sure exactly. My guess is that they got together when Dilek flew back in from Zeta. She couldn't find it in her to talk about it too much. But I asked and her answer suggested it occurred more than once."

My father took a deep breath. "Amat, I can't say I approve of the way you handled this information."

Regardless of his disapproval, in that moment, I felt no shame.

"However, I can't say that if I knew about this myself, and if the opportunity presented itself, that I wouldn't take extreme measures to see Dilek pay a price for . . ." My father finally turned around to face me. "No one else is to know of this and from here on out, you will avoid all contact with Dilek. Understood?"

I nodded. "Yes, sir."

"Nothing will be reported about the events of today between you two. From this moment forward, you will allow me to deal with Dilek."

"Yes, sir," I said.

My father placed a hand on my shoulder and looked into my eyes; his own were sad. He shook his head and walked away.

The doors to the conference room opened shortly after we regrouped with the platoon. From them, emerged the Diramal. "Gentlemen, ladies, if you will all please enter the find your places inside, we can begin the briefing."

We all gathered around a wide, reflective table in the shape of an oval. The Diramal had an odd smile on his face, and if my neuro-chip didn't suggested otherwise, I would have even said the expression was devious. Now that I think back on it, perhaps he was hiding something, and fear would be as good a guess as any.

There was something else about the Diramal's expression that felt . . . stimulating. At the subtle curvature of his lips, suddenly my mind fluttered with thoughts of praise, holding the Diramal in a greater prestige than I would normally care to. There was something about his aura that made me feel abnormally trusting. Though all these things were random, it didn't occur to me in that immediate moment. Something suppressed my dubiousness, deep inside of me and nothing compelled me to question it.

"Gather around, I want to make sure everyone can see what I have to present," the Diramal commanded with ease.

The lights in the room dimmed and a hologram appeared above the reflective table, presenting Galiza and the alien ship upon Anua. Purple waves moved quickly from Anua to Galiza and back. All but my father gasped at the sight of it; he merely widened his eyes and tightened his jaw.

"What you are all seeing here is a gravitational field being produced by the alien craft," the Diramal continued. "From what our best aerospace engineers tell me, the amplified field is five times stronger than the natural gravitational field between the moon and Galiza. If the ship was not producing this, since the body of the craft is so large, our gravitational field would fail and natural disasters would ensue the planet. So, if these beings have any desire to harm us, the presence of their own craft would be enough to wipe out humanity and potentially Galiza itself. Which should hopefully ease some of the thoughts that may be rattling your minds."

I shifted as I stood, intrigued by the Diramal's words.

"The mission you are all about to undertake is considered highly classified. For the sake of time, you will be given access to the CX-17."

The Diramal swiped at the hologram and in place of Anua and Galiza, the CX-17 was displayed. A ship with a similar design to the CX-16. It has a large horizontal cockpit at its center, with two cylindrical wings on either side, and at the front of both wings are two cone-shaped rail guns.

"A far more advanced craft, fit with an MHD accelerator. With this, you should reach the moon in no time." The hologram vanished and the lights became radiant once more. "As far as the public is concerned, this meeting never happened and a second team of scientists will be launching in a CX-16. As I'm sure some of you are already aware, they will orbit the moon until you return with intel on the alien craft, to determine if it is safe for the science team to explore it. As far as your families are concerned, your platoon was shipped overseas on a tour into Zeta. Should you not return from this mission, your families will be informed that you were killed in action and a body could not be recovered. Does everyone understand what's at stake?"

Everyone nodded and replied, "Yes, sir."

"Very good," he said. "You are dismissed. Good luck to you all!"

The rest of the platoon and I started to exit the room.

"Jinn-hid, stay a minute," the Diramal ordered.

As I exited the conference room, I found it odd that the Diramal would want to speak with my father alone. *What could be so confidential that he wouldn't want the rest of the platoon to hear? There's only one way to find out.*

My thought process was suddenly interrupted when someone shoved me out of their way. I tripped onto my knee and, if not for my hand stopping me, I would have hit my head against the wall. I scowled at Dilek as he walked away, looking over his shoulder. I would have done something in response, but now was not the time and I had bigger problems to concern myself with.

If I could get myself to alter time, maybe I could sneak into the room, hide, and listen in on their conversation. I walked up to the office doors.

I did my best to recall how I altered time before. It occurred to me, that on most occasions, it acted as a reflex or a defense mechanism, triggered by stress or dangerous circumstances. However, there were instances when I sparred with Blick, where breathing deeply and having a clear mind focused the ability, made it less overwhelming.

I closed my eyes, freed myself of distraction, and focused on my breathing. When I opened my eyes, my exhale echoed to my ears. My mind felt free of thought, and a paroxysm of disorientation befell me. I raised my hands and looked down at them, which took what felt like minutes. Their movements were obscured in trails, like long strokes of paint on a canvas. I shut my eyes and placed my hand onto the doorknob, took a deep breath, opened my eyes, and turned the knob. I rushed through the opening, closed the door behind me, and hid under the reflective table completely out of sight.

Now the question was: how to pull myself out of it? As I thought about a way to bring me back to a normal flow of time, it gradually happened. The more time I spent distracting myself, removing myself from my deep focus, my breath started getting quicker, my thoughts became louder, and the voice of the Diramal sounded stretched, but progressively got louder and louder. It was almost nauseating, as my inner thoughts and the rising sounds of the outside world intertwined with one another. It was all just noise, noise that rang and pulsed in my eardrums.

"You—" the Diramal was cut short as the sound of the door slamming echoed throughout the room. "*Hmm*, that was odd." The Diramal hardly sounded concerned. "Anyway, as I was saying, jinn-hid, my friend, I—"

"I'm not your friend, Diramal. We were never anything of the sort," my father interrupted.

"Very well then, my acquaintance. You see, I care for you like a brother, and though you might not feel the same way about me, I still feel the need to speak my mind. Regardless of where my hopes lie in praying for your safe return, I assume your priorities will focus on the safety of your son."

My father gave a furious sigh.

"You love your son, don't you, jinn-hid?"

"Yes," my father said with an underlying warning clear in his tone.

"And if anyone tried to harm him, would you stop at nothing to ensure his safety? Even if it meant at the expense of your own life?"

My father hesitated but then simply said, "Yes."

I couldn't see his face, but something in his tone suggested he was uneasy.

The Diramal took heavy steps toward my father. "Well, we both know despite what we'd have everyone else believe, the likelihood of this mission's outcome and it's *not* kind."

Even from where I hid, I could hear my father's breath getting heavier and shaky.

"Neither of us knows what'll happen up there." The Diramal started to circle the table. "Neither of us knows if even one member on this mission will make it back alive, which includes Amat."

I saw the Diramal walk past where I hid, but I couldn't hear his steps. Only the sound of his voice seemed to fill the room when expressed and commanded utter silence when his speech paused.

"So, what does this mean for the boy, jinn-hid? He can't back out of it any more than you or the others can." The Diramal's voice deepened and morphed into another tone that sounded like another language entirely. "What if these beings tracked our species across whatever multitudes of space, from which they originated, to wipe us all out? What if this is all a ploy and they're waiting for us to come to them and strike first, to see what we're capable of? What if we're doing *exactly* what they want us to?"

The Diramal's voice became entrancing. The possibilities of his words felt imminent. My heart grew sick and twisted from the abnormal impact the Diramal's speech had upon me. My head ached as genuine thoughts of fear and distrust of the Diramal were conflicted with praises and images of the Diramal held in high esteem, enforced by the neuro-chip. Yet there was no conflict in my sincere dislike of the Diramal at heart. I couldn't tell exactly if my father felt as disturbed as I did, but when I snuck a peek at him from under the table, I saw that my father was sweating and breathing heavily. The irises of his eyes rapidly trailed from side to side, as if he was visually interpreting everything the Diramal was suggesting right before his very eyes.

"It's highly unlikely they're here to make peace, especially since this is not our first encounter with this species," the Diramal continued. "What little we know about these brutes is the real reason why we shut down SEF. Hoping to avoid the never-ending encounters with them, potentially avoiding a day like this. But I suppose . . . this was fate."

The Diramal slowly turned around and I ducked back under the table. "I guess what I'm trying to say is, be careful; look after your child, just as I would in your position." The Diramal's voice sounded as it did, once again, unaltered. He patted my father on the back.

My father inhaled deeply and slowly as he stood, trembling. "May I leave, sir?" His tone sounded weak and quivery.

"You are dismissed."

He started to exit the room.

"Oh and, jinn-hid . . ."

My father stopped. Standing with his back to the Diramal for a long moment. He then slowly faced him one last time, which seemed like such a struggle.

"Remember, be prepared for anything. Even your own death."

I altered time, ran up to the exit, and opened the door. When I got outside, I was sure to close the door ever so gently, so as not to draw suspicion again.

I ran away, deliberately breathing heavily and filling my head with noise to pull myself out of the altered time state. When I finally snapped out of it, I had to lean against the wall. I felt so out of breath and shocked. *The Diramal just attempted to manipulate my father and sabotage the mission! It seems to have taken a toll on my father's psyche, as it did my own for an instance. Maybe if I didn't go on this mission with him, it would spare my father his anxiety. And be counted as a deserter? No. We have no choice. I must go and look after him.*

XXII
A Dire Manoeuvre

I spent a short period of time wandering around the facility, gathering my thoughts. It was so hard piecing together how I truly felt about the scenario; the Diramal being so manipulative of my father. Every moment of seeing him in a bad light was countered with programming from the neuro-chip. It was constantly justifying his actions and authority. After tirelessly going over it again and again in my head, I gave up trying to make sense of it.

I found my father, all alone, inspecting the CX-17. The craft resembled its predecessor, the CX-16, the craft I piloted for my final test in aerospace training. The energy system of the diamane CX-16 was an efficient and volatile iodisceroid compound. A deep-purple substance found in natural reservoirs beneath Galiza's crust. When subjected to extreme cryogenic temperatures, even trace amounts of iodisceroid underwent a rapid exothermic reaction, producing a sonic detonation that propelled the craft forward. Though once in space, it relied on thrust for movement.

The CX-16, by itself, was a craft with minimal risks—provided pilots maintained precise control over iodisceroid cooling levels. Undercooling of the iodisceroid fuel resulted in insufficient thrust and would cause the craft to lose momentum. Overcooling induced excessive fuel detonation leading to an implosion. Once in space, overcolling remained the primary risk. During this trial of my aerospace training, the mission itself was designed to fail, the test was to see how long I could keep her flying before the deliberate faults in her design proved futile.

It was the final test of my aerospace training, the plating was deliberately dented, worn, and everything mechanical about the ship was handicapped. There was also a failsafe in the ship's programing that would safely return me to the surface, if the ship took on too much damage.

Although, there was never any promise of where the failsafe would land me. Aside from the obvious rough texture at the plating, I couldn't predict what problems would await me about the ship's engineering. But I knew, before strapping myself in, I was being tested on how long I could keep her flying. From the moment I began my aerospace training, I studied tirelessly to understand the CX-16 inside and out. I had no intention of failing that test.

In addition to piloting the CX-16 with all its defects, I was expected to perform a reconnaissance run. After putting myself into orbit, I was required to take photographs of a military base in Zeta, where the xǔté won a major victory against the Zetian and Utopian militaries.

There were two chambers in the CX-16. The main chamber held all the iodisceroid separate from the next one over, which was empty, but maintained a temperature of negative fifty-five degrees Celsius. Every time there was an ignition, some of the chilled air in the second chamber escaped, mildly raising its teperature. Anything below negative fifty and you got a weak ignition. Anything above negative forty-five and you got no reaction whatsoever. Thus, I had three panels in front of me, all with arched meters on them. The right panel measured the temperature of the second chamber, and as needed, if temperatures rose in that chamber, I could simply pull back on the marker, and release cryogenic gas to stabilize the temperatures. The left panel measured the liters of iodisceroid on the craft. The middle panel told me how many meters I climbed per second. Which I wanted to keep around three hundred and fifty meters.

I remember counting down before the takeoff, readying the first pressure ignition, releasing four liters of iodisceroid into the cold chamber. The g-force promptly pulled me back in my seat.

I reached the curved ramp, redirecting my trajectory upward. When the curvature straightened, I leaked another quarter liter, to compensate for the lost speed in the curve. By then the temperature in chamber two rose to negative forty-eight degrees Celsius, so I brought the temperature back down slightly.

Still climbing, the diamane had slowed to about three hundred and forty-five meters per second, so I put another liter into the cold chamber. With a loud *boom* and a great thrust followed, the diamane picked back up to three hundred and sixty meters per second. The craft rocked and the plating moaned. One, two, three, four monitors let out sparks behind me. But the ship's course remained steady. Just over five minutes passed when I finally cleared the atmosphere and slowed down.

The air inside the ship was smoky from the short circuits, fortunately they hadn't started any fires. As I began maneuvering the course of my orbit, I noted the left side thrusters were inactive. Making it almost impossible to maneuver the craft in any direction to the right. I reported my observation to ground control. No response. But that was to be expected, as it was one of the rules of the test. Still, I felt it wise to let them know my status.

I attempted to transfer my reserve thrust to the left wing, but the systems were non-responsive. After a closer examination of the left wing, I observed a sizeable fracture in the plating where the wing was soldered. It wasn't enough to be catastrophic, but I knew, any fancy maneuvers would tear the wing right off. If that were to happen, the failsafe would become useless. As a matter of fact, it was safe to assume the failsafe was already of no help.

I reported this to ground control. This time, there was a response. The signal was poor and white noise blasted over my contact. The fact that I got a response from them was concerning, as they were only allowed to respond to the pilot in the event of an emergency, but I kept my composure. They were constantly monitoring the ship's condition and my activity from within, through camera feeds.

With very little control of my maneuverability, I slowly set the diamane on a course that would pass over the mission area. The landscape quickly swept past the capture frame and provided a challenge in capturing the artillery, sentinels, damage and vulnerabilities in the xǔté's defenses. Now, the easy part was over. The worst had yet to come . . . Landing.

As my orbit brought me back, toward Utopion, the left wing moaned and severed a little more, gradually, making it more difficult to pilot. With sweat dripping from my scalp, I did my best to maintain my focus. Given that the thrust on the left wing was still inactive, the only way I was getting back into the atmosphere would be if I made a vertical entry: flipping the diamane upside down. That meant I couldn't land on a runway, so I needed water. Not the ocean, of course, but perhaps a lake.

I brought up the coordinates for ground control. A hologram of a map appeared before me, and I searched for sources of water near the base. A wide lake was located, about ten miles east of the base, and it ran west. Seeing this as the best option, I quickly put the coordinates into the ship's mainframe, setting up a kind of autopilot. The ship wobbled upon initiation, as it failed to utilize the the left wing thrusters. The ship fell silent, recalibrated, and the right wing flipped the ship over into the atmosphere. Red lights flashed, a siren sounded, and warning signs flashed on the interfaces.

Slowly, the blue hue of Galiza's atmosphere melted away all the darkness of space and dimmed the light of the stars. The ship started to rattle intensely, sounding like it was about to tear apart. The autopilot activated the diamane's flaps and thrust the craft forward slightly; allowing it to glide at an angle and not plummet straight down.

I looked overhead out of the cockpit and observed all the passing details of the ground's surface pass me by. Before long, I could see the water coming up. I braced myself for impact, tightening the straps of my seat. I closed my eyes and prayed to the goddess, not out of fear nor gain of pity, but to call upon her embrace should the landing go poorly. Time seemed to expand and sirens echoed in my ears, but their pace did not changed and their sound didn't grow dim. My body felt airy and relaxed. I couldn't explain it quite precisely, but I felt as if an additional layer, a sort of shield you could say, was hugging every inch of my body.

I don't remember the crash. I hardly remember breathing for that matter. I'm not sure if I even opened my eyes in the time that I spent at the bottom of that lake. But I can, however, recall the sound of water that seemed to envelop me and the occasional bubbles that trickled past. Protected by my suit, I was saved from the water seeping into my lungs, but I only had so much oxygen. When the rescue team came to lift me out, they were all stunned by my survival. They anticipated that I was or would be on the edge of suffocating. My father later informed me the skidding impact of the water flipped the ship right side up and aside from the cockpit, the diamane was barely intact. It took the rescue team four hours to get the supplies and the manpower to pull me out of that lake, and in spite of all this danger I seemed to put myself in. I vividly remember asking Pac Yondugŭl if I could do it again.

Back to the time leading up the launch to Anua, I walked up to my father and gently placed my hand on his shoulder. He jumped at my touch and blurted gibberish as he turned swiftly toward me.

"Oh, it's you," he said.

"Yeah, it's just me," I replied.

My father was sweating intensely and gulped nervously.

"Are you alright?" I asked.

"I'm . . . I'm fine."

He couldn't keep a calm composure; he didn't look the way he claimed.

"The ship is fully equipped and ready. Everyone else is aboard. Are you ready?" he questioned.

"Yes, sir."

"Good, I want to get this over with as soon as possible. I don't have an entirely good feeling about this mission, Amat." He leaned down to my level and placed his hand on my shoulder. "When we get up to that ship, I will need you to be absolutely compliant and cautious. Should things turn out in ways we don't expect, there'll be no time for confrontation. Do you understand why I ask this of you?" My father jerked my shoulders slightly.

I felt afraid and hardly recognized the man before me. For the first time in a long while, I lacked the knowledge to solve a problem set before me. In this case, the problem was my father. He wasn't himself, and should the wrong pieces fall into place, he could get everyone on this mission hurt, or worse . . . over me. The only thing that came to mind was to nod and reassure my father of my understanding.

"Good, let's go then."

My father and I shared control of the ship. There were two pilot seats: he sat in the primary seat where the controls were readily available, while I sat in the co-pilot's seat, where the controls could be switched over at any point.

"Peroma CX-17, this is Vīvothar with ground control, the skies are clear, you are approved for takeoff," a woman's voice said over comms.

"Roger that, Vīvothar. All systems active, Alpha Criptous?" my father asked.

I turned my head and glanced at him; I forgot what it felt like to be referred to as 'alpha.'

"Up and running, sir," I replied.

"Are the trantalium amplifiers stable?" he asked.

"Yes, sir."

"Ready to initiate launch, Vīvothar."

"Roger that, Peroma CX-17, opening bay doors now."

Before us, two grand doors opened wide while my father engaged the Peroma's magnetic field. The ship wobbled and hummed as we slowly hovered outside.

My father was sweating so intensely he looked sick.

"Stand by for initiation. On my mark." My father slowly placed his hand over the throttle. "Ten, nine, eight, seven, six, five, four, three, two, one, mark." He gradually pushed the throttle forward and pulled back on the joystick, ascending through the atmosphere bit by bit.

Overall, we weren't moving that fast, but once we hit the upper atmosphere, suddenly our speed picked up several times faster. The ship started to vibrate so vigorously that even my father's grasp on the controls was frail.

"Vīvothar, this is Peroma. We're experiencing some kind of amplification on our speed. Reaching speeds of three thousand miles per hour and climbing. Over."

I could hear someone replying over comms, but the reception was too distorted.

"Vīvothar, can you repeat that?"

The Peroma's plating started to moan like some terrible beast. I looked at our speed—we were starting to reach nine thousand miles and climbing. The numbers were rising at a surreal rate, eventually each passing second marked a new thousand. Before it was plain to me, the stars and dim contents of the cosmos had stretched and blurred in luminous streaks. My heart thumped like thunder in my ears. I didn't notice it until I turned my head to look over at my father. The weight of the movement felt leaden, as if some incredible force bared down against the mass of every muscle and bone in my body.

Struggling to so much as lift my arm, I strained to reach over and switched the main controls over to my seat. I looked ahead and saw that we were coming up on the moon *fast* and if we didn't move out of the way, we'd probably crash head-on. My eyes tracked the controls *steadily* moving toward me.

All concept of time escaped me as my eyelids became heavy, my arms relaxed, and my mind felt drowsy. Slowly, I felt myself drifting off to sleep. Just before sealing my eyes shut, I shouted at myself in my head. *Don't fall asleep! Wake up! You're going to die, soldier!*

My eyelids forced themselves open, as adrenaline flooded the back of my mind. The G-force, while it was still great, proved a minor challenge as it was no match for the resiliency of my physical strength. My hands clasped around the controls with the body of Anua closing in fast. As one arm veered the ship to the right, the other pulled back on the throttle as hard as it could, easing the speed of the ship.

The ship tilted and started to change course. In my throat, I could feel myself grunt and growl, but I could only hear the faint moans of the Peroma's plating. By the time I steered clear of the moon, we were so close that I could just see small details of rock clusters and large craters and faults across the surface.

Finally, we passed the moon altogether, traveling out of the solar system. A black abyss, with only a few stars in sight, swallowed our plunging trajectory. *I've got to slow her down.* It took all of my strength to continue pulling back on the throttle as I monitored our speed. Through pure grit, the speed of the vessel finally waned enough that we came about, back to the moon. Fortunately, we had not drifted so far that I could not identify our own star. That was my initial reference, for our course, until the moon came into view and Galiza appeared no bigger than an iris. With a steady grip on the throttle, my command of the ship grew more deftly wrought. Sounds became more defined as they once were and the compressive force on my muscles melted away.

Coming back around to Anua, we were still moving too fast for a landing. So, I put the Peroma into orbit around her and circled around twice, in a matter of minutes, before it was finally safe to bring her down. Descending to a plane not far from the alien craft, whereupon I deactivated the Peroma's trantalium amplifiers. The ship's hum was replaced with an obnoxious buzzing, which most likely meant she would need repairs before we took her home.

Everyone else was still asleep. Every tension about my body that had fought the misdirecting forces of the craft, laxed as my arms and spine dropped. I tried to pushing against the armrests, in an effort to lift myself up, but the artificial gravity of the Peroma's interior weighed me down, as if I'd been sedated with some muscle laxative. As my spine arched over my stomach, it churned. Something filled the back of my throat and before I knew it, I hurled all over the floor. The taste in my jowls was bitter and my throat felt prickly. The adrenaline provided me with just enough strength to erect my back against my seat before a profound fatigue became me. I wasn't comfortable, yet I felt too weak and sick to reposition myself. My eyelids collided with one another as the soothing feeling of my calm breathing put me to rest.

XXIII
Patching up Peroma

My father shook me harshly. I woke up to him shouting at me with a look of horror on his face.

"Hey," I groaned, wiping my lips. "How are you?"

"I'm doing much better now that I know you're alright," he said. I smiled at him reassuringly.

"Any idea how long we've all been out for?" he asked.

"No, as soon as I landed the Peroma I passed out."

"I suspected as much. No wonder you were the best in your squadron back in Gallethol, being able to handle all those Gs and pilot the ship."

"It's easier said than done. I almost blacked out myself."

My father frowned and glanced at the alien craft across the way. "Are you well enough to continue with the mission?"

"I've got a bit of a headache, as I'm sure most of us do. But I'll be fine."

"See that you are before we head into that ship, Amat. I won't have you go unless you're feeling sharp as a knife."

I sighed at the superstition clutching at my father's every word. He was anything but himself.

"Yes, sir."

I gestured over to the comms on the control module. "Any luck contacting Vīvothar?" I asked.

"I don't know. I haven't tried reaching them yet." He reached over to the comms and placed his finger over the transmission button. "Vīvothar, this is Peroma CX-17. We made a rough landing, but we're here, on Anua. Do you read me? Over."

There was no answer.

"Vīvothar, do you read? This is Peroma. Over." Again, there was no reply.

"Our comms must be down," I said.

"That or someone's interfering with our signal," he replied, grimacing at the alien craft. "We don't know what to expect when we go in there," his words turned to ash in his mouth as he uttered them. He cleared his throat and continued: "I say we should make sure there's nothing wrong with the Peroma before we enter the alien craft."

"I second that, sir."

"Good."

My father sounded out of breath and gave me a long, hard look. It was as if he felt this would be one of the last times he would be able to look at his son in a moment of peace.

"What is it?" I asked.

"Mm, n-nothing. Let's rally up the team." He slapped me on the shoulder as he walked by.

Many of the squadron were still knocked out; one by one, we woke them all.

My father shouted orders for everyone to get into formation. Those that did so in a rush, hurled all over the plated floor and onto others. Everyone looked sickly and exhausted. Even when we were all in formation, hardly anyone could stand up straight. Dilek and I were among the few that could. Though, it seemed like a greater effort for my former friend, and he merely matched my composure to spite me.

My father took a long moment in silence as he looked over the team, noting their meekness. He sighed and once again glanced back at the alien craft, as it continued to intimidate him.

"Thanks to Alpha Criptous, we have landed safely on the surface of our beloved mother. If not for him, we wouldn't all be standing here now. Likely wouldn't be breathing at all either." The man and the woman standing at either side of me glanced in my direction.

"But, as you all likely noted, the launch from Vīvothar did not go so well. Alpha Criptous and I suspect that the Peroma likely took at least some, if not a detrimental amount of damage during the flight. Despite how effortless the Diramal delineated this mission, we have no idea what to expect once we enter that craft," my father said, pointing back at it. "It is my duty as your commanding officer to see that all precautions are taken before we face the unknown. So, I want you all to look around the ship. I know many of you aren't feeling your best at this moment, so you may go in pairs if you would like. If anything seems the least bit out of place, inform me immediately and measures will be taken to patch up the Peroma. Understood?"

"Yes, sir," all the squadron members groaned in unison.

Some even hurled some more, mid-sentence.

"Those of you feeling too sick to do much of anything, there's a small med bay down the hall." He pointed to his left. "Inside there is a machine called a regenerator. Activate it and you should feel rejuvenated. Dismissed."

Everyone saluted my father and as soon as he turned his back, many wandered down towards the med bay, to find the device he spoke of.

The stench of everyone's vomit quickly filled the Peroma's atmosphere. I wasn't that bothered by it and even if I were, there wasn't anything to clean it up with. As I walked around the craft, I kept a watchful eye on everyone, making sure they weren't getting themselves involved with anything dangerous.

During my rounds, I saw Dilek emerge from the med bay. All the bruises on his face and around his neck were gone. Despite how well Dilek looked, upon seeing one another, he still paused in his stride to give me a menacing glare, which I returned in kind. When Dilek didn't move, I approached him. Dilek stiffened his back and curled his fingers, readying his claws for a swipe at me.

"Jinn-hid and Alpha Criptous!" a woman's voice called from up the ship. I paused my stride, but I didn't look away from Dilek.

"We have a problem!" she continued. Everyone stopped what they were doing and started heading that way.

I looked down at Dilek's fists, back into his eyes, and shook my head in disapproval, then headed in the opposite direction.

A crowd obstructed the opening to the left wing's entrance. Squeezing my way through, I came up to the doors and met with the soldier who called for me.

"Alpha Criptous." She saluted me. "Krollgrum Utůla Quarin, sir."

I saluted back. "Krollgrum Quarin, be at grace. What seems to be the issue?"

"It's this door, sir. It won't open and this area of the ship holds our armory."

"Are systems operating on this side of the ship?"

"No, sir."

"*Hmm*, that means it's not jammed, the left side trantalium orbs must be damaged." It was then that my father came forward and joined the conversation.

"We can't access our armory?"

"No, sir," I answered.

He sighed and folded his arms.

"Any idea how we can fix this?" I asked.

"There is only one way. Someone has to go out and manually replace the trantalium orbs on this side of the ship."

"Do we have a spare pair lying around?"

"There is a compartment within each engine that holds a spare pair of orbs," he replied.

"Alright, I'll suit up."

"No, not you, Amat."

"I'll go!" Dilek broke in. Everyone looked in his direction.

My father nodded his head "Very well, Krollgrum Tregin," he said. "Suit up and await my instru—"

"Are you familiar with any kind of aerospace engineering, Krollgrum Tregin?" I interrupted.

"Amat!" my father said sternly.

I was unfazed and looked Dilek directly into his eyes. Dilek returned an earnest expression, but I could see underlying vexation.

"Answer the question, krollgrum. As one of your superiors on this mission, it is my duty to make sure you are equipped with the knowledge to handle such a complex task," I said.

Dilek, holding that same expression on his face, glanced around the room before answering. "No, I am not," he replied.

"Thought as much." I took a few steps forward into the crowd. "I know of only one person on this vessel capable of carrying out such an errand. And any one of you may correct me if I'm wrong, but so far as I know, that person is me."

No one answered. I turned to my father.

"Alpha Criptous, let us talk in private," my father said, walking past me. I followed my father back to the cockpit.

"Are you trying to put yourself in harm's way here, boy? Do you remember what I told you earlier?" my father blurted out.

I never saw my father so mad. I'd seen him disappointed and sometimes that came with aggression, like when he stripped me of my rank. But this felt like anger, sprouted from insecurity.

"Is there a single member on this platoon, sir, who bears the rank of alpha, aside from me?" I asked plainly but respectfully.

He was thrown off with my reply.

"I don't see what that has to do with our present situation," he replied.

"Aerospace engineering is a set of skills strictly given to alphas in the military. There is no other branch in the military that grants those skills. Not even members of the Air Guard. Unless any one of those men or women is also an alpha, every single one of them is a liability to this task, except me."

My father shifted his stance, looked into my eyes and lifted his finger. "You see one thing out of place out there, you come straight back. No questions asked."

"Yes, sir."

"Go on and get suited up."

I put on a spacesuit made from a liquid glass material known as laquar. Despite being a single-layer construct, the suit effectively regulated thermal insulation and generated a self-sustaining atmosphere. The material was dynamically conforming to fit the wearer. If you tore it, the material would grow back within a matter of kiloseconds, sometimes slightly longer, depending on how great the damage was. While the suit ensured survivability, exposure to vacuum through an open wound posed a common risk: cryodermal necrosis, colloquially termed *frost scab*. As the name suggested, it manifested as a frozen, desiccated layer of tissue—a consequence of rapid heat loss and sublimation in space.

They sealed me off in the right wing.

"Amat, wait," my father spoke before I'd made any attempt to exit the Peroma. "The systems are noncompliant. I can't depressurize the right wing compartment of air. So, hold onto something tight, you'll be met with a vacuum once you open that hatch."

"Understood. Standby."

I located a safety tether, wrapped it tightly around my waist and two handlebars. I made sure the clips were firmly secured.

"Okay," I spoke over comms. "I'm ready. Initiating in three . . . two . . . one . . . Breach!"

The hatch popped just slightly. Air hissed out. Half a second later, the hatch popped open and a violent whoosh of air whirled out out of the compartment, along with some equipment. My grip strained and cramped to keep my fingers bound to the bars. My lower body lifted off the floor, as my feet were hoisted toward the breach.

Two very short seconds later, all the air escaped and I dropped flat on my back against the cold, hard plating. A pained grunt escaped my throat as I tried to steady my breath, shaken by the sheer force that pulled at me.

"Amat!" I heard my father call over comms. "Amat! Are you alright?!"

"Oh! Yeah." I pulled myself off the ground, unlaced myself from the bars, reached up, and started to pry myself through the hatch.

Strangely, right when I was just above the hatch's opening, I felt lighter than air. Everything below my waist felt heavy at first, but once I was fully outside the ship, I was in a complete zero-G environment.

My father and many of the other members of the squadron could see me from the cockpit, staring at me in awe.

"There appears to be no center gravity," I said.

"How is that possible?" someone in the crowd spoke.

"Perhaps it has something to do with the hologram the Diramal showed, during the briefing. That strange amplified exchange in gravity between Anua and Galiza could be the cause for it," I suggested.

"Regardless of the cause, Alpha Criptous, you best strap yourself down onto some aspect of the ship before proceeding," my father commanded.

"Yes, sir." I re-entered the craft and grabbed the safety tether, clipping it to another pair of bars on the outside of the wing.

I pulled on the bars of the right wing to make sure they were secure and launched myself toward the left wing. I glanced at the alien craft. Its mystifying appearance gave me a cold chill down my spine. Exhilaration and trepidation conflicted my intrigue to uncover the enigma of the ship's purpose.

As I approached the left-side wing of Peroma. I grabbed hold of one of the bars about its construct with my extensive tether still secured to the other wing.

"Alright, sir, I'm here. There's a terminal situated on the plating. Do you know the code?" I asked.

"Roger that, Amat. The code is three, one, seven, two, zero, one, two," my father replied.

"Copy that, sir."

There was a deep thud that sounded like several locks unbolting. The plating slowly rose toward me. Heat waves emanated the metal constructs, that were slowly being revealed to me. I moved to set aside the retractable plating.

Spark!

Tiny shards of shrapnel sprung toward me from some, caused by some sporadic short circuit.

My heart leapt, adrenaline coursed through my veins. All sound dimmed and deepened, my sight was transfixed on the still nature of the metal shards, closing in on me… ever so slowly. Time had slowed once again. I hadn't caught on to it as quickly as I would have liked. The sudden hyper-focus that had been brought on me, came with a daze as I idly observed the rigid metal etch closer. It was only until my body reached the tunneled vision of my tracking gaze that I realized the imminent threat moving to pierce my chest.

The shrapnel moved centimeters away from my body. *move out of the way!* I finally thought to myself. My body strained to move with any haste and only managed to move as leisurely as my death sentence. The more I struggled against the invisible forces at work, the more tiresome I grew and just as I started to lax my muscles from fatigue, I fell away with more momentum than the trajectory of the shrapnel. Just enough… to avoid a fatal wound. It started as a breath of the coldest air that escaped my mouth, just as quickly as I could take it in. The rigid metal grazing my shoulder started as tingles that turned to needles and finally a sharp, cold sting that erected my spine. The blood that was shed, barely had any time to ooze from my fresh wound, as the ice-cold temperatures of Anua left a scarring freeze-burn over the laceration.

Time *jolted* back to its normal flow. The pain of ice crystals forming over my wound was so great that I briefly forgot how to breath. My father shouted something at me, but I was so preoccupied with the pain that I couldn't make out the words.

I howled like never before, cursing, shouting, weeping, until I exhausted myself. My thrashing and torment managed to push me off the wing and allowed my body to hover away, with the rope still secured. Facing that starless abyss, as I drifted out toward it; I couldn't say whether my sight darkened, or my stare remained gape.

A sudden tug at my waist and the sound of my father's voice brought me to attention.

"Amat! Amat, can you hear me?"

My voice was so hoarse; I couldn't find the strength to speak. Reaching behind me, I grabbed the tether and twisted myself back to face the Peroma. I didn't notice it immediately, but with every pull of the tether, the cord felt less secure, loosened somehow. I paused and focused my sight down the line of the tether and observed a sizeable tear that looked rather precarious.

I'm still a long way from the ship and it doesn't look like it would take much tension to sever my lifeline here.

I proceeded to carefully wrapped the slack around my arm and *yanked* it as hard as I could.

Rip!

The propulsion was enough to grant me a graceful decent back to the ship. Though, there was still the problem of finding a good grip hold on the ship, with the lifeline being completely severed.

My father pressed his head to the glass, gazing up at me. He'd witnessed the cord snap, his gasp audible over the comms. His eyes never left me, as he observed my descent back toward Peroma.

From my perspective, my descent was on a slightly diagonal trajectory. I wasn't too worried about this, relative to where I started, from up above, I hovered maybe a few meters to the left of the craft and not directly above it. Though, with no motor control, if I drifted too far passed the right side of Peroma, I would have to scramble for a well-grounded rock on Anua's powdered surface.

In the final moments, I came right beside Peroma's right wing. And as I extended my reach as far as it would go… the tips of my left fingers couldn't even graze the plating. I lightly rebounded off the surface.

My survival instincts kicked in, adrenaline threw all logic out the window as I kicked against the soft ground, spurred my rebound off the surface, into a twirl. A curse escaped my lips, in a weak growl. The barking cries of my father were distant echoes as I honed my focus on quickly finding some kind of solid ground to dig my claws into. As my steady spin, directed my view beyond the horizon of Anua, away from Peroma, I observed a nearing dune, supported by a mound of rocks, rooted to the ground. I just hoped I wouldn't ascend too far above it before I could use it to my advantage. After drifting, perhaps ten feet, my window arrived. I'd risen just above the dune peak, one of my feet lightly pushed past the powdery dust, but as I came around, I threw and stretched and reached my arm down as far as it would go and found my salvation.

The rock was hidden beneath the powder but held firm well enough for me to reposition myself. I pressed my feet against the dune and launched myself back to Peroma. My heart and breath finally felt at ease as I drifted back.

"Amat?!" My father's voice was filled with concern and despair but seemed hopeful at the sound of my ragged breath laxing. To reassure him, I grunted and rasped what little words I could in that moment. "I . . . okah . . . reah . . . hip . . ."

Pause.

"You're saying, you reached Peroma?" My father asked.

My hands grasped the bars about Peroma's right wing and for a moment, I thought I'd never felt safer.

"Cock . . . pit . . ." I rasped as I made my way over there.

I saw my father marching back to the cockpit of Peroma as the clustered platoon gazed in awe of me. I waved down my father and signed that my voice had been lost.

"Oh, Anua, you've lost your voice, Alpha?" My father's voice struggled to sound strong as his words trembled. "And your shoulder is wounded!"

I nodded, signed that I was well enough to continue with the repair and made my way back to the panel. I could see, in the last glance I saw of my father, his body tensed to protest, but even he could admit the ship had to be repaired, and promptly.

I resecured the tether in a tightly woven knot around a safety bar before returning to the engine. Two magnetic orbs that appeared burned and rigid to the touch sat in a small compartment.

The orbs are overheated and damaged, I signed to my father who was barely in sight of me.

"Very well, you're going to have to manually cool down the amplifiers, Alpha Criptous. There should be a switch directly above the trantalium orbs, remove the old ones before doing what I tell you next. Don't squeeze either of the orbs too tightly, they'll be very sharp and fragile. Flip the switch and reapply the plating as quickly as possible. The engine is going to momentarily fill with liquid nitrogen and reboot. But don't worry, the liquid nitrogen will drain once the engine is cooled. There will be a blue meter on the terminal that you used to open the plating, which indicates the engine is still filled with liquid nitrogen. Once the meter goes down and turns white, that indicates that all the liquid nitrogen is drained and thawed. Then, you will be safe to reopen the plating and replace the orbs."

I raised a thumb and went to find the plating, which didn't drift far from the ship.

The pain in my arm was numbing, but would spike if I shifted or moved it in certain ways and directions. My conscience was drifting and the longer I went without medical attention the more drowsy I became. Before long, I started to suspect that the ice might have frozen over an artery and was slowing down my blood flow. This made the time I spent waiting for the engine to cool down feel longer than it really was.

The meter turn white, the code on the terminal was entered and I assessed the appearance of the engine.

"Is the engine fully cooled?" my father asked. I nodded my head and raised a thumb. "Alright, look down along the interior of the engine. There should be another terminal there. The code for which is: eight, nine, two, seven, five."

I nodded. The numbers on this second terminal were hard to push, probably stiffened from the liquid nitrogen residue. A small compartment opened, but only halfway, revealing one fresh trantalium orb. I had to force the compartment the rest of the way open with my wounded arm to reach the second. The wound at my shoulder surged in pain when the small door abruptly gave way.

"Amat?" my father said.

Clasping my arm, I took a deep breath and shook my head. I raised a thumb and signed that the fresh trantalium orbs had been located.

"Alright, now, put the new orbs in place."

I nodded and wheezed.

"Now, just flip the switch back up that you used to cool down the engine. A purple light should illuminate the interior and the rocks should start orbiting each other."

With that done, I sealed the plating back over the engine. Little strength remained in me, as I jumped back to the right wing. The hatch sealed over my head as I entered, my legs trembled at my abrupt reunion with gravity inside Peroma. Pressure clouds, in thick white plumes of air enveloped me.

My legs had given out under me. I remained still, too fatigued to move. Harsh bangs rang against the metal door sealing off the wing with muffled yells of worry resounding from my father. As the mist of atmosphere cleared, the door slid open and my father rushed to me with some of the platoon members.

He took me up in his arms and the last thing I heard him shout was, "READY THE REGENERATOR!"

My head ached so harshly I couldn't resist the temptation to close my eyes and drift off after a final, conscious gasp of breath.

XXIV
A Cover up of History

I woke up on the bed of the Peroma's regenerator, with my father sitting beside me. He looked to be praying, his eyes swelling. He raised his attention to me when he saw me awaken. I sat up, free of any pain, but still he urged me to take it slow.

"I'm fine," I said reassuringly, an awkward smile on my face.

"From the analysis there were traces of shrapnel that passed through your arm and it pierced—"

"Some arteries?" I cut in.

My father's expression turned sour. "You knew?"

"I suspected as much."

"And you didn't come in sooner to get receive medical attention? Dammit, boy, what were you thinking?"

"I was thinking about the safety of everyone on this ship, including your own. When you said we couldn't depressurize the right wing of air, that indicated systems were failing on a rapid scale. Who knows what would have happened if I came in before patching up the Peroma. We might have lost our life support."

He gave me a stern look and sighed.

"Hey, at least it'll be a story to tell Mom and—"

"*No,* it will not," he blurted. Even though he was serious, I laughed lightly at his response.

I rubbed my chin quizzicially as I pondered whether this was an opportune time to ask a question that had been stirring my mind since the time of the alien vessel's arrival. "Dad, I know this isn't the first time you've come across something like that craft out there," I said solemnly.

My father took his time responding. "What gives you that impression?"

"Your reaction to the craft when you first saw it. The overbearing protectiveness you've demonstrated toward me. You've grown anxious, which isn't like you."

He looked down at his hands and started playing with his fingers.

"I won't ask you to tell me everything, just this." My father looked up at me. "Where have you seen that ship before?"

His eyes filled with a deep dread I had never seen him wear before as his gaze shifted subtly away from me. He sat back in his seat, rubbing his legs. "You know, sometimes you prove to be too smart for your own good, Amat." I smiled curtly. "Given that I have sworn to always respect your feelings *and* your concerns, I will answer your question. But be warned, you may find it difficult to accept the truth of my response."

I already find it difficult to accept the fact the Diramal attempted to manipulate you. Doesn't change the fact it still happened, I thought.

"It's fine," I said. "I just wanna know what's really going on."

"Alright. As you may already know, Amat, I was recruited at a considerably young age to run a mission for SEF. I was not informed in great detail what would be expected of me, but I was briefed on its purpose: to seek out extraterrestrial life. I was offered the rank of pac and shared a dual command of the mission with the Diramal, who was the jinn-hid at the time. I'm trying to think back on what his name was . . ." He hesitated.

"What?"

"Dah! I can't bring myself to remember it. It's been so long since I heard his real name with everyone calling him Diramal."

I placed a hand on his shoulder. He looked over to me with a plain expression on his face but his eyes were terrified.

"It's alright, tell me more."

He sighed. "At the same time, I was getting to know your mother rather closely. So, I wasn't entirely set on the idea of venturing into the great unknown. Nevertheless, I ended up taking on the mission. I felt the cause was just and your mother trusted me to come home safely. Back then, Galiza was in a fiercer state of global war, more than it is today. Many of our current allies were our enemies. I thought meeting with another intelligence beyond our own could change humanity's perspective of itself. Such that we would realize our problems were minuscule compared to everything the universe had to offer. That we could discover new ways of living among one another. But knowledge is power, Amat, and those who are the first to gain it, don't have to share with anyone who they deem lesser than themselves.

"On the day of the launch, I finally met the Diramal for the first time. He seemed like a well-respected man among the other high commanding officers, including the former Diramal, who was active at the time."

"Kronel Dorpem?" I butted in.

"Yes, and there was something about the current Diramal that suggested he was- is . . . different. The first few months we spent out in deep space; we found no trace of extraterrestrial life. Of course, the methods by which we traversed the cosmos were highly efficient and classified. More innovatory than anything even the Peroma is capable of. On occasion, we would see alien planets and star systems, but we always found them in ruin. No forms of life at all.

"On the twelfth of Beuref 2530, we encountered an alien craft identical to the one that rests across the way from us. It almost seemed to appear out of nowhere. The present Diramal immediately ordered everyone to their battle stations, and I followed this as a precaution. We observed the ship for a time but we never made contact with its inhabitants."

"Why not?" I asked. My father was reluctant to answer. Shame riddled his expression at the memory of what he was about to explain next.

"We never gave them the chance. From what I can assume, the ship and its inhabitants must have detected our presence shortly after we activated our weapons, because it started to approach us at . . . such a high velocity. Our scans detected a large energy source emanating from the head of the craft, which the Diramal perceived as a threat. I suggested we reach out and offer both sides of this rising conflict a chance at diplomacy, as was our mandate. Yet no matter the case I made, no matter how much I pleaded, the Diramal gave the order to assault the alien craft with no other justification beyond blatant ignorance and superstition. There was no hesitation in his decision, as if that was our mandate all along. *Which it wasn't!* The priorities shifted from curiosity to slaughter. *Just like that!*"

He snapped his fingers. "Therefore, the encounter and all the events that followed, were deemed classified in light of the damage that it could have done to the Utopian military's image."

I was heartbroken.

For the briefest moment, the great war hero and patriotic image I held of the Diramal was completely eradicated. But then the chip in my mind restored his prowess. Still, something inside me trusted the word of my father more than the chip's portrayal of the Diramal. Tears trailed down my face, but I could hardly remember the emotion that aroused them. *We could have potentially started anew through what these beings had to offer. How different things would be now if the Diramal hadn't annihilated all possibility of that future?!* A spike of pain surged through my neural network at the accusation. I clasped my head and winced.

"Amat, are you alright?" my father asked.

"I'm fine," I said, wiping tears from my face. "Father, you mentioned that this encounter and the events that *followed* were made classified. What followed after this?"

"An interstellar war lasting nearly three years. After we destroyed the first of many alien crafts, we reported back to SEF on Galiza. I considered handing in my resignation but . . . I still had faith in Anua that a truce could be established between our species and the extraterrestrials. But this never came to be."

My father contemplated something in silence before continuing. "You know, I could never really tell . . ." he said leaning towards me. "among these triangular ships were other abstractly formed crafts who opposed us. It was never confirmed whether the inhabitants of either craft designs were the same or completely different. It was strange; we didn't see much of the triangular crafts during those three years. But when we did, they were no less troublesome. I seem to recall encountering these . . . scrappy looking forms of crafts more often than the triangular ones. They resembled bugs: very dark in color with a gold-beige coloration emanating from within them."

"What ended the conflicts after the three-year period?" I queried.

"They disappeared. Gradually, they started avoiding the areas of space we were exploring, and we never saw any of them again. Maybe we depleted their too much of their interstellar fleets to go on fighting."

A thought occurred to me. "But, if they've found us and they've come to exact retribution upon us, don't you think they might have come in greater numbers, expressing a more bellicose message?" That made my father smile.

"That's a very interesting observation, Amat. We can only pray to the goddess that it's true."

I gulped nervously. "Is it too late in the day to resume the mission?"

"No," my father said.

"Is the crew ready?" I asked.

"They are."

"Then what are we waiting for?"

"Well, you, of course. You've been sitting in this bed for hours on end. The question is: do *you* feel well enough to resume the mission right this very moment?"

"Yes, sir, I do!"

"Alright then, get out of bed and suit up. I'll inform the others."

"Yes, sir!" I slowly got up and out of the regenerator. I dressed in another laquar suit equipped with an electric shock-put 101.

XXV
Wonders and Tragedy

At the time of the platoon's deployment out onto the lunar surface, the gravity had stabilized. Still the gravity was low, and the most effective means of roaming the landscape was to skip, all the way toward the colossal alien craft. I gazed above us and saw the ship of the research team casually drifting across the foreground of the black void of the cosmos.

I marched beside my father at the front of our formation. My heart pounding with excitement. Though, with all I'd recently learned from my father, my mind dabbled in uncertainty and pondered whether it was wise to be thrilled, in any sense, for what we were about to encounter. The march was long and awkwardly quiet.

About halfway through, I asked my father, "Sir?" He didn't respond. I could see through his suit that he was drenched with sweat, heaving as he walked in a daze.

"Sir? Dad!" I placed my hand on his shoulder and finally he turned his head toward me.

"W-w-what?" He briefly closed his eyes and licked his lips nervously. "What is it, Amat?"

"I was just thinking. Shouldn't something be said before we go in there?" I asked.

"Such as?"

"I don't know, some sort of speech to keep the platoon's spirits up." And by the platoon, I meant him.

"I'm afraid, n-nothing comes to mind, Amat. But if you feel it will help, step up and say what must be said."

"Alright, can we stop a minute?"

"S-s-sure." He raised his arm, halting the platoon.

The two of us walked up the slope of a crater and turned toward them.

"Krollgums, Alpha Criptous would like to say some words before we enter the alien craft." He glanced at me, then momentarily down at his feet. "If any of you are worried about what we may face in there, I would urge you to hear him out. My son has grown into a young man capable of swaying the hearts of others for the better." He smiled at me proudly and stood down from the slope.

It felt strange being at the center of attention in this sort of circumstance. All those desperate, fearful faces looking up at me to give them courage. My father and some others said over the years that I had the potential to be a leader, but I never saw myself as such. Yet, there I stood, in the position of a leader, a small beacon of hope.

My mind drew a blank, unsure of where to start. All I knew was what I felt: afraid. Just as afraid as everyone else standing before me. *Why do I feel so afraid? I shouldn't be. My heart knows I've wished for something like this to happen for a long time.*

Suddenly, a realization dawned on me and I smiled in the delight of it.

"It's funny, I stand here, looking at each of you and seeing all the same emotions. Fear, anxiety, caution, anger, uncertainty . . . But what is there to fear other than the assumptions conjured within our own minds?" I looked directly at my father and moved my gaze on. "This is not a day to be feared. It is a day of opportunity. This is not only a day of history, but of discovery and potential understanding. Our great mother, Anua, may be gifted the chance to see us forge a union! Do not fear the things you do not understand, but rather seek out the answers to the enigmas that have eluded our comprehension."

There were no rousing cheers, but rather a quiet acceptance in their expressions of hope.

There was no immediate response from the craft when we reached it. A thought occurred to my father as we waited in silence. He looked over everyone in line, studying the low ridges not far from where we stood.

"Gitz, Drealla, Jarla, and Rork."

"Yes, sir?" they all responded.

"You're all armed with moonsights. Even though there doesn't appear to be any openings within the plating of the ship, I want you all to individually take positions at . . ."

My father designated positions for the men and women to take at the top of these small ridges, not far from our location.

". . . about this craft. See if you can pick up anything using your infrared scopes, but don't go testing the strength of the ship's armor. The last thing we need is to rile up the inhabitants of the vessel. Still, it's best to have you out here as a precaution."

"Yes, sir!" they all responded once more.

Just as those four krollgums started heading off to their positions, a large opening made way at the base of the alien ship, right in front of us. The interior was not lit, though there did appear to be some very small blue and yellow lights that flashed here and there. Within it rested a tall, wide room that appeared spacious enough to fit the rest of us inside. The walls were a very dark-gray and appeared smooth to the touch, which hardly seemed welcoming.

My father turned toward Gitz, Rork, Jarla, and Drealla and saw that they paused at the ship's activity. "Go on now, all of you. To your positions."

The four krollgrums turned their backs and continued to skip across the lunar surface, to their assigned positions, while the rest of us entered the craft.

As the opening slowly closed behind us, the room fell into shadow. Quarrelsome emotions continued to stir within me, at the thought of meeting whoever occupied the craft. The ground jolted and a dizzying shift in gravity thwarted our hips, as if we'd been turned sideways, but somehow still managed to stand upright.

"Be on your guard," my father said.

The doors opened to what seemed to be the engineering room. My father signaled for us all to form up behind him and scout the area.

"Stay close to each other, especially you, Alpha Criptous. You are not to leave my side," he commanded.

"Yes, sir," was the answer.

One of the first things we saw, appeared to be the machine that was generating the enhanced gravity field between Anua and Galiza. The entire room had a dark-blue hue, with small, red lights curving up in parallel formation. There were many plugs, vents, and loose-hanging wires everywhere on either side of our path. I paused a moment to admire the disarrayed engineering and architecture. A subtle yet harsh enough bump from an unforeseen shoulder knocked me off balance. Catching my balance, I looked ahead, meeting with Dilek's mocking gaze. I bore my fangs at him with a low growl as he turned away and wandered forward.

A little further up the way we saw the core engine, probably the most wondrous thing I saw in that ship. A grand beam of white light with little hints of red, yellow, and green. Despite how fascinating it was to observe, my father almost immediately ordered us to move on past the beam.

I leaned over the railing to view it more closely. Though I was in a suit, I could still hear soft gushes of wind blowing past. A thin spray of haze trailed up with the light. Stretching my hand out as far as it could go without me tumbling over the railing gave me just enough reach to interact with the sprinkled haze. As the haze moved past my fingers, glitters of many more colors manifested. I smiled and chuckled before I felt a hand vigorously shoved against my back.

I quickly caught my balance and pulled the passing soldier back towards me. Sure enough, I was met with Dilek. My right hand moved fluidly to unholster my pistol.

"Do something like that one more time, Dilek . . ."—I bent him over the rail and pressed the barrel of my pistol against the back of his head—". . . and you're gonna have an accident." Dilek grunted.

"Hold on, who are we missing? Amat? Dilek?" I overheard my father call out.

I restrained myself from taking my actions any further and caught up with the group.

"We're coming, jinn-hid," I replied, not waiting for Dilek.

We found our way to the ship's armory. The setting seemed to make my father more uneasy than ever. He opened a channel over comms and tried to reach Drealla.

"Drealla, this is Jinn-hid Criptous. We're still inside the ship. We've located what appears to be an armory. Despite appearances, I suspect we're not the only occupants inside the ship. Have you or any of the others picked up any odd heat signatures on your scopes? Over." He waited in silence for a moment, then tried to contact Drealla again.

"Drealla! Do you copy? Over." When the silence persisted, he closed the channel and said, "The comms are down . . . hopefully. There's only one other reason why they wouldn't be responding."

"Let's not jump to conclusions, sir, or make any assumptions that would compel us to do something rash."

He sighed. "Amat!" His tone immediately sounded rough and desperate. "You don't—"

Something caught his attention that made his skin crawl. His eyes were wide with a gaze of horror. His body tensed up and his eyelid twitched.

He immediately whipped his pistol from its holster and aimed it at something nearby, but did not fire. Suddenly, the room felt colder.

"Whoa! Dad! What's wrong?"

"We're leaving," he said in a quiet, trembling voice. He walked toward me.

"Well, what did you just see?" I blurted.

"NOW! ALL OF YOU!" he barked. He pulled me by the arm and led us all back the way we came. "Fall in behind me!"

As we walked, my father turned his head this way and that, constantly searching for any signs of an intelligence beyond our own. Even with the exit in sight, he searched frantically for any nearby threat. He started to hyperventilate so fast and loud it seemed to echo throughout the ship. Every gasp of breath sounded strained. I was relieved to see that we were almost back at the entrance, that we would shortly be out of that ship . . . for my father's sake. Once more, something roused his attention, and unnerved him so greatly that he raised his gun and fired. He began shouting and screaming as he saw this . . . being that was somehow pinning itself to the wall.

I never saw what it looked like exactly, but I could see a large limp body fall from the wall and down below the rails. Shocked, I tried to catch a better glimpse of it out of guilt and concern. My intuition told me that the being meant us no harm. A brief glimpse of the being was all I was allowed before my father pulled me back to him, growling furiously.

"Amat!" my father blurted. He paused and everyone looked around the ship as the interior filled with horrid screeches. "Come on! Get in the elevator!"

He sounded like a madman.

Despite how swiftly he and I moved toward the elevator, it was sealed shut before we could enter.

"Oh no!" I gasped, my voice just above a whisper. My mind drew a blank as the courage drained from my body. A queasy tremble shot through my muscles, as if they shriveled.

My father blurted a curse. He looked around wildly and focused on two krollgrums. "Strev! Arlen! Get over here and use your torches to split this door open, ASAP! The rest of you, form up around them and shoot at anything that moves! Amat, stand by me! Let's go! Move it! Move it! Move it!"

There was hardly any space to properly handle my weapon, provided the tight formation of the platoon. I could hardly see ahead of myself. The screeches were getting louder . . . closer . . . more intimidating. Clicking purrs and a crunchy stampede surrounded us in every direction: ahead, above, below, and to each side of us. *Silence . . .* We held our positions. I could smell the anxious stench around me, coupled with heavy breathing. The men and women standing next to me shifted in place, panning the lights of their weapons over their surroundings. Not a single sentient sign in sight.

Dilek glanced back at me, grimacing. He shook his head as he returned his gaze ahead of himself. "Coward," he whispered, though not very quietly.

I gave Dilek a snide as he turned his back to me, but said nothing. *Whoosh!*

"AAAAAAaaaah—*Ugch!*"

A blur *snatched* Dilek. One of the beings hoisted him into the shadows of the ship. Deep gulps and throaty clicks came after the sound of Dilek's entrails flooding from his gullet.

It was so fast that he hardly had time to scream. The troops tensed, shifting in place, barking anxiously.

"Steady!" my father blurted.

Whoosh! The scream of a krollgrum rang throughout the ship. All turned in the direction of the fading cries and fired their weapons. The rounds hit various aspects within our immediate area of the ship. It created sparks from the loose plugs and tubes about the interior, fogging the atmosphere in a hot steam. *ZAP!* Someone's rounds ricocheted and created a great spark that lit up the interior of the ship as it rumbled; the metal moaned. A deep power surge rang in the craft like a bell, as if something was shut down. Whatever was hit, was obviously important.

The screeches started again. One of them here, another there. One by one my squad members were being taken out by something we could not see. One, by one, by one, by one, by one . . . I didn't hear many howling cries, but saw the mutilation of their bodies being torn apart and drained of blood. With only a handful of us remaining, the rest, aside from myself, turned rabid. Howling and pleading for the doors to open, firing aimlessly. My father tried to get them to settle, but they were also taken just as quickly by this unperceivable threat.

Eventually it came down to just me, Strev, Arlen, and my father.

"Hurry up on that door!" my father shouted.

I was trembling with fear; I couldn't keep my aim steady. We stood our ground a few feet away from the elevator. Seconds later, Strev and Arlen burned an opening in the door.

"It's open!" Strev said as he kicked around the outline and pushed the metal through. Strev and Arlen rushed toward the opening and I followed right behind them.

My father must have seen something. "Amat, wait!" He grabbed my shoulders and together we fell back to the ground. Strev and Arlen were swept off their feet, following the rest in death.

As Strev and Arlen howled in terror, my father grabbed my arms, lifted me off the ground, and forced me to my feet. He pushed me forward as we sprinted for the exit.

"Come on, go, go!"

As we approached the exit, the screams fell silent. My father continued yelling as he pushed me into the elevator. The moment I stepped through the opening, I heard something sharp tear through flesh, followed by a weak whimper. I almost couldn't look back, but I did it anyway, because I knew what I would see.

Facing my father, I saw four sharp claws protruding through his chest, with a dark figure standing behind him. Fright became me. He looked at me with so much joy and peace, despite the pain he must have felt. Tears rolled down his cheeks as he smiled at me one last time.

"I . . . I love you . . . son," my father said.

He looked to his side and forcefully reached for a button on the wall that brought me hurtling back down towards the surface.

"NNNNOOOOOOOOOOOOOOO!" I screamed at the top of my voice as the elevator dropped down.

My strength dissolved and my body went limp. I cried and cried as if I would never stop. Loud metal wails resounded from the elevator as it seemed to descend at a rapid rate. When the shift in gravity returned it was so great I was tossed against a wall, slamming my shoulder. The wound aided in shifting my grief from sadness to unbridled rage. I curled my fingers into fists, so tightly that my fingernails dug into my flesh and bloodied my palms. I knew all along that this mission was not going as it should have, and it got my father killed. I would not allow my father's suffering and sacrifice to be for nothing. I now had reason to hate and to fight. There'd be no stopping me from entering *this* war.

XXVI
Battling the Waves

I was sitting up against the elevator wall, dwelling over the loss of my father, when I was returned to the surface of Anua. The doorway slowly rose open and the bright powdered surface of the moon was revealed to me. I raised my hand to shield my face from the bright, reflective powder. My eyes glanced up at the doors, they halted and were starting to close back up. I dashed for the opening and just managed to squeeze myself through the narrowing gap.

The gravity of the moon felt a lot heavier than before and I hit the ground tumbling. The weight of my own body was almost unbearable as I pushed myself off the ground.

"Hey, someone's returned from the ship!" Drealla shouted over comms.

"There's only one though!" Jarla said fearfully.

"Can anyone identify him?" Drealla asked.

"Negative," Rork said. "But he looks like he could be injured."

"Copy that. Gitz, can you identify the individual?" Jarla asked.

"Affirmative, that's the jinn-hid's son," Gitz replied.

"Roger that. Alpha Criptous, do you read me? This is Jarla, at sixty-five degrees about the alien craft's entrance. Over."

I slowly turned toward the direction Jarla gave me; my knees bent and quivered every time I stomped my foot against the soft ground.

"Sir?" Jarla asked.

"This is Alpha Criptous, I read you," I said, holding my hand up.

"Alpha Criptous, where's the rest of the crew?" Jarla asked.

"Dead, the beings . . . killed them . . . all of them," I said, short of breath.

I stumbled my way towards the Peroma.

"What?! How?!" Drealla blurted.

"Calm yourself, Drealla," Jarla said. "Alpha Criptous, sir, do you require assistance getting back to Peroma?"

"*No*. I'll get there myself. Rendezvous inside of her, we're going home," I replied, picking up my pace as much as I could, towards the Peroma with a stagger in each step.

"Roger that, sir. We'll have your back till you're safely behind our lines," Jarla said.

I chuckled at that—if one of those things were to come out and attack me, I highly doubted Drealla or any of the others could catch it in time to protect me.

I made it into the ship, strapped into the pilot's seat, and took off once the others were strapped down as well. The Peroma rose gracefully off the surface as I turned her back toward Galiza, minding the sensitivity of the throttle. Gaining distance from Anua, I felt it safe to slowly test the speed of the Peroma, only to be met with rising turbulence. The faster I pushed her, the harder it was to keep her on course. The plating moaned and the interior shook. Yet we weren't moving all that swiftly.

The amplified gravity shifting between Galiza and Anua must be the cause of this... I thought.

Slowly, the turbulence eased and eventually ended; I adjusted our course toward Galiza. The plating began roaring loudly and the ship started to shake more violently than before.

"Hold on!" I barked. The front of the ship was lifted and directed back toward the moon. We were thrown way off course, retaliating force was short lived. Once again, I adjusted course. I was sweating as my mind gaged how safe it was to push the limits of Peroma's speed in this scenario and close the hundred-fifty-thousand mile gap.

The plating continued howling and shaking as the speedometer picked up from the propulsion of the amplified gravitational field. The joystick briefly became stiff and harder to control.

"Brace yourselves!" I exclaimed. This time the front of the ship was forced forward and on a course to Galiza's southern hemisphere. I gave a throaty *growl* as I pulled back on the joystick with both hands to correct our course.

"What is going on?" I heard Gitz ask.

"The enhanced gravity field is shifting back and forth from the alien ship to Galiza, it's fluxing the anti-gravity of the ship!" I barked.

As we approached the atmosphere of Galiza, we were once again forced back toward the moon, thwarting us from the runway towards the SEF base. This time, it was harder to recover because Galiza was now hurling us straight down toward her. The Peroma was falling flat and dropping so fast that I struggled to force it in any other direction. At first, I considered throttling the Peroma forward, but then I thought that would be a chancy move. It could tear the ship apart. However, another idea occurred to me. *What if I aim the face of the ship down, open the flaps on the wings, and pull up? That could work!*

The flaps were made primarily for braking in an emergency landing, which could come in handy if you had an atmosphere. Given their design, they could be repositioned to catch the air flow underneath them. And, in turn, would make it easier on me to pull up the Peroma's nose.

I pulled back on the throttle and forced the joystick forward. The front of the ship gradually aimed itself toward the surface. There wasn't much time to make that final adjustment. When the front of the ship was aimed about forty-five degrees toward the surface, I positioned the flaps and waited a few moments to make sure they got some air current underneath them. I then eased the throttle forward and pulled up. Hovering just above a tree line, I finally managed to bring the ship on a horizontal projection. As something scraped the bottom of the ship, I eased off the throttle, and pulled back even more harshly as we regained some altitude.

I slowed the ship to a cruising speed and set a course for the autopilot to take us back to the SEF base.

"We're okay!" I shouted to the others. I lied back in my chair, closed my weary eyes, and to the sound of Gitz, Jarla, Drealla, and Rork cheering in celebration, I drifted into a deep slumber.

XXVII
Two Guilty Parties

My stinging eyes cracked open to the sound of a monitor steadily beeping beside me. Everything was a blurry haze until my eyes adjusted to the sight of Vīvothar's infirmary. Across the way from me, painted on the wall, I could see the SEF insignia.

My gaze panned all around me until I saw the Diramal sitting in a chair, staring at me with those deep-red irises of his—so patient and calm. There was no break in his expression, even after we made eye contact. I pulled myself up in my bed and calmly said, "Diramal."

"Alpha Criptous," he replied.

"How long have I been asleep?"

"Almost four days since your return from the moon. The time is eight p.m.," the Diramal answered as he glanced at a clock on the wall.

"Is my family alright, sir? Has there been any activity from the craft?"

"Calm yourself, alpha. Your family is fine. Since you and your platoon left for the moon, there's been no further activity from the alien craft specifically. Although, for reasons we can't quite explain, there's been an upheaval in seismic and tidal activity across the globe. Not enough to be entirely catastrophic but it is concerning how wide this activity has spread. Our scans also showed your ascent to the moon. Once the Peroma exceeded the mesosphere, you were caught in one of the gravity shifts that acted as a sling shot, propelling you towards the moon at an amplified velocity. Many of us are surprised to see you back. I do trust that *you* are the reason you're sitting where you are now. I read the reports of your test with the CX-16. Quite impressive. You have astonishing credentials as an aerospace pilot!"

I realized the Diramal failed to mention something. "Sir, you said that you were surprised to see *me* back, but what of the others?"

"Others?" The Diramal had a puzzled look on his face.

"I believe there were four other members of my platoon who made it back with me. Gitz, Jarla, Drealla, and Rork."

"I know of no such names or platoon members who came out of the Peroma with you. You, Amat, were the only member of this mission who returned."

I looked down at my legs, contemplating what I knew to be true in my mind: those men and women *were* all in the Peroma with me when I flew back to Galiza.

"This can't be."

"I assure you, Amat. It is the truth."

Suddenly I was reminded of something. "The truth, is it?" I asked, squinting, my tone shifting deeper. As I began to question his authority, my mind ached with conflicting thoughts of trust and uncertainty. He hardly seemed concerned at the sight of my discomfort.

"Well yes, of course, Amat. What reason would I have to lie to you?"

"Well, sir, I don't know. What reason *would* you have to lie to me? After all, I've known you to deceive people before."

"Before? Alpha Criptous, what are you—"

"Befo—*Ah!*" The pain in my mind intensified. A sensation in my head roared the command, *Stop!* But I wouldn't, I would speak the truth, I would confront the Diramal.

"Before the briefing . . ." I started heaving. ". . . we had in the conference room . . . regarding the mission . . . my father seemed so sure of himself, as a jinn-hid should be. But after you spoke with him . . . in private . . . *Ahhh!*" I clenched my fingers into fists and dug them into the scabs on my palms.

He seemed slightly amused, even though he bore no smile or grin on his face. In fact, he held a very empathetic expression, but his eyes were overjoyed at the sight of my struggle.

"I could tell . . . at first glance . . . that my father was no longer himself. His strength . . . and surety . . . left him. I saw it in his face during every moment of the mission. I know what you said to him, to manipulate him. You couldn't have known . . . it would end in tragedy . . . yet you enforced that idea so deeply it drove him . . . to do something terrible.

Something . . . that killed him." I grunted harshly and bent forward as spasms coursed through me.

Do not question him further! the neuro-chip commanded.

"So, before you tell me . . . that his death was an accident, enlighten me on how you knew the extraterrestrials would be preemptively hostile toward us, when it was my father who shot first!"

The Diramal sighed as he looked down at my fist, bloodied once again. "Amat, you should know that I treated your father like a brother, and that it pains me to know he is dead. I assure you that—"

"Spare me your sureties, Diramal!" Pain shot across the top of my scalp.

Do not speak out of turn! the neuro-chip commanded.

I growled. "You're the reason . . . my father's dead. Though, you're not the one who gutted him, you might as well have. And your end . . ." My mind felt like it was splitting. ". . . will come soon enough," I managed to muster out. I suddenly started to shiver. I felt cold and sick, much like on that flight when I transferred to Lazithia. Only this time it was so overwhelming I thought I might black out.

The Diramal's face darkened. "Are you threatening me, boy?" he asked.

"Without a doubt . . . *I am!*"

"You are foolish, Alpha Criptous. *You have no idea what force you threaten to oppose.*" His voice changed in tone and seemingly in dialect. I understood the words, yet somehow, they felt foreign to me and they seemed to possess an eerie will that crept over me.

"I have some idea. In spite of that, I hardly trust you have any idea what I'm capable of."

The Diramal laughed mockingly, leaning his face inches from mine. "Hardly enough to bring me any trouble, I'm sure."

Our stare persisted in silence, neither one of us betraying the slightest flicker of a blink.

"As your superior officer, Amat, I would advise you to tread more cautiously from here on out."

"And as your b-b-*bane*, Diramal, I would advise you to do the same."

The Diramal calmly stepped away. Before exiting, he paused and said, "Did your father choke on his own words as well?" I growled in reply. The Diramal chuckled. "Don't shame yourself, Amat, they always do, those who confront me. When I decide it, they grow weak, like your father did . . . like you are now."

I wanted to jump out of my bed and have at the Diramal then and there; however, a physical and psychological barrier forbade me. It wasn't the neuro-chip, its code wasn't capable of restraining me like that. No, this was something else. My stare was somehow transfixed, as if it'd been possessed, holding firm on the Diramal's sly, unblinking, red eyes.

"I didn't kill your father, Amat, he did. If he hadn't shot first, as you said he did, maybe he would have been at your side in my stead, here, now."

I managed a twitch that shook my bed, but I still couldn't move. Suddenly my diaphragm locked and my chest pulled forward—I couldn't breathe.

"I can see you're agitated. I'll let you rest now; it appears you need it."

No matter how hard I tried, I couldn't manage an inhale until the Diramal left the room and he did, ever so slowly.

By the time I was able to breathe again, it felt like I'd forgotten how. Air caught in my throat as I coughed it out. Pulling myself together, I stepped out of my bed and stumbled to the door and yanked it open, expecting to see the Diramal walking away, but he was nowhere in sight. *What . . . what did he do to me?* Surely it must have been the Diramal's doing—people don't just forget how to breathe.

***

That night was restless, my mind was a riotous quarrel, scheming ways to take down the Diramal and having each of those thoughts thwarted of their machinations by my neuro-chip. The early morning finally came, as the sun started to warm the horizon. *The cafeteria should be opening soon . . . I might as well get up now.*

The halls of the base were vastly empty. It struck me, how the unstirring solitude of my room, in the infirmary, had been disrupted by intrusive thoughts, relative to this quiet walk. The only sound was the entrancing clicking of my boots, echoing through the halls, soothing the chatter in my mind. That's why I found it strange when other sets of footsteps came clicking behind me. Growing louder, nearer by the second, as if I was being stalked.

At first, I thought they were just standard officers of the base, perhaps dukas in training who were heading my way to pick up some breakfast or to a department within the base. Though, they weren't speaking . . . not even in whispers. *Seems like they might be on a less casual stroll or patrol through the base . . .*

Even if I was being superstitious, it didn't feel wise to act on it. My suspicion was so roused. My eyes darted to a public bathroom, just a few steps ahead of me, and I leisurely entered. *If they follow me in, I'll take them for trouble.*

I immediately went to the sink and started to wash my hands, that way, if they followed me, I would appear unsuspicious of them. I started breathing deeper from my diaphragm, in an attempt to channel a time alteration.

The bathroom door opened and my heart skipped a beat as I heard two sets of footsteps enter. *How could this be happening, truly? Being hunted by my own countrymen . . .* I kept my eyes down, but quick glances up in the mirror allowed me to see up to their waists. The two men kept their distance, yet they still stood too close for comfort on either side of me.

Catching on to what was about to unfold, I said nothing to either of them. I was merely waiting for the right time to act. My eyes raised to the mirror and caught a glimpse of the left man's shoulder. His jacket bore the insignia of krollgrum: two parallel curved blades, with three points at the lower ends. In between them rested a six-pointed star; the bottom point was the widest, stretching down, and at either side of the star were two great curved wings.

The krollgrum's movements had already been slowed to my eyes, before he started reaching behind his back. My heart continued to beat steadily but also strongly. Every pump palpitated my chest. He slowly approached me as his arm revealed a knife from behind his back, graciously raising it over his head. I spun around to face him, baring my jagged teeth, raising and extending my knee as my foot impacted his chest. The blow sent the krollgrum through one of the stall doors across the room.

The second krollgrum moved quicker, almost matching my speed. He was already in front of me before I had time to notice him, knife in hand. I dodged back at every swipe and swing of his arm, until my grip locked around his wrist, crushing it harshly. He hardly seemed thwarted by the pain of his bones and joints being crushed. I broke our menacing grimaces with a swift fist to his face. The blow left him with a feeble grip on his blade that it dropped from his grasp. The blade's descent was hardly noticeable, almost as if it were suspended. I leaned down and swiped the weapon into my grasp. In a smooth spin, I stabbed the man in the leg and kicked him to the ground. The first krollgum returned, grabbing and spinning me from behind. He launched his fist and it connected with my chin, knocking me back. He traced back, found his knife, and stood over me. In a quick movement, he swung the blade down towards my head, but I grabbed his wrist and broke it too. The opening for a critical blow presented itself as I launched the palm of my hand up into his snout.

As I slowly found my way to my feet, the second krollgrum found his way behind me and wrapped his arms around my neck, squeezing tight. I struggled to pull away, but the longer my lungs went without air, the harder it was to maintain my altered state. A pressure built up in my chest and I couldn't hold on to the flow any longer. My strangler pulled both my arms back as I coughed and caught my breath.

The krollgrum, whose nose I broke, got up with his knife in hand. Before approaching me, he adjusted his wrist back into place, again hardly phased by the pain. He threw a mighty punch in my chest that left me heaving. I gasped and coughed loudly. The krollgum before me pressed the edge of the knife between my legs, right at my groin. A shiver crawled up my spine that made me as stiff as a statue.

"Look at me!" said the krollgrum in front of me.

I narrowed my gaze as I bore my fangs at him. My mind noted one of his irises were red, like the Diramal's, and the white of that red eye was bleeding. It was very subtle, but the blood that covered his face seemed darker than it should have been. His opposite eye was light blue, but that must have been some kind of faulty contact he was wearing. These weren't krollgrums, they were Anua's cho'zai. That explained their resiliency.

"You're cho'zai."

"How do you know that?" the one in front of me growled.

"If I didn't before, I do now from the way you phrased your question. One of your contacts got knocked loose in our rumble," I replied.

He looked into the mirror and saw the true color of his one eye was revealed.

The cho'zai turned back toward me, hit me in the face, and pressed the edge of his knife against my perinium once again.

"You're very observant, Alpha Criptous," he stated as he put his hand on my throat and started to choke me. "You should have learned by now where observations get you." He let go of my neck and punched me in the stomach.

"Perhaps we can take advantage of the situation, now that he knows who we are. He assaulted two of Anua's cho'zai. Such an offense can't go unpunished," the one behind me said.

"No, it can't and it's a high price to pay, I should think," the cho'zai in front of me said, lifting the knife more firmly up against my perinium.

The pain spiked, and my heart was beating out of my chest. I tried to calm myself down and focus on my breathing again. Remaining in the normal flow of time wouldn't get me anywhere in this situation.

The cho'zai continued talking, but his voice became deeper and slower. Moments later, the sound of my breath filled my ears. All motion slowed down to a crawl. From there, I used both my legs to shift my weight back onto the cho'zai restraining my arms. Once my legs were high enough, I kicked the cho'zai in front of me in the chest, launching him across the bathroom and into the wall. As I landed, I leaned forward and used my momentum to break the second cho'zai's knee. He let go of me instantly and howled out in pain. I turned around, choked the second cho'zai while he was down, and did so until he was knocked out. The sheer strain and force I inflicted through my arms and onto the cho'zai's neck, steadily balanced out the flow of time.

Stumbling to my feet, I turned around to find the first cho'zai moaning and trying to stand up. Picking up his knife off the floor, I quickly threw it at his hand, nailing it to the wall. The man yelled in agony, but I didn't want that attracting any attention, so I ran up to him and covered his muzzle.

"Who hired you to kill me?" I growled.

The cho'zai looked at me defiantly with his blood-red eye, jerked my hand away with a twitch of his head, and spat in my face.

I wiped his saliva away and vigorously gripped my hand around the cho'zai's neck. My other hand placed itself on the knife hilt. He glanced at the blade then back at me.

"What are you doing?" he asked, half choking.

"This," I said, forcefully twisting the blade inside the man's hand. He growled.

"Any names come to mind now?" I quizzed.

He grasped my jacket tightly with his free hand, digging his claws into my shoulder, so I twisted the knife even more. He was gripping my clothes so tightly that they started to tear. I glanced over at my torn jacket and stopped. "I can stand here all day till I drill a hole through *both* of your palms. I'm not all that fond of torture, too messy for my liking; however, if you won't give me what I want . . ." I turned the blade more and I could hear bones snapping. He growled a little more loudly. ". . . I have no problem with it. So, do us both a favor, tell me what I want to know and I let you walk."

The cho'zai nodded his head reluctantly. As I uncovered his muzzle, he sighed and said, "It was Blick."

What? I thought baffled.

"Blick who? Vykin? How would he even have the authority to send two cho'zai after me?" I growled, twisting the blade further.

"Aaah! He . . . he's got more than you may realize."

I was unfazed by the cho'zai's answer; I didn't believe him.

"There's more to him than his brutish appearance and combat skill."

I leaned in close and whispered to him, "We both know who really sent you. I don't need to hear his name to be satisfied. But if you or your friend approach me again, I don't care whose orders you're under, I will finish what you started here."

I carelessly let him go and plucked the knife from his hand. He squeezed it and held pressure over his oozing wound.

"I suggest you visit the infirmary, get that checked out. Wouldn't want you to bleed out. Your friend is still alive, by the way, just knocked out."

"You didn't kill him?" The cho'zai sounded surprised.

I glanced back at him. "I could never bring myself to kill a sentinel of Anua's cho'zai." With that said, I left them behind and marched to the Diramal's office to confront him about his hit on me.

XXVIII
Trusting a Stranger

I found the Diramal in a conference room. I burst through the doors in altered time, revealing the company who surrounded him. My stride broke, the flow of time abruptly regulated, and a sudden observation froze me in place. The Diramal was surrounded by a council of men and women, all bearing decorated coats and the insignia of the jinn. Each of them had one thing in common: the red eyes of the cho'zai. I didn't know what that meant then and there, but at that moment, I felt dangerously outnumbered. All of their gazes fixated on me with varying expressions. Some seemed threatened or offended while others appeared to be in awe or frightened and a select few had devious grins.

The guards who I barged passed stood erect to the Diramal. "We apologize, sir, Alpha Criptous managed to . . . rush past us before we could stop him," one of the guards said.

The Diramal, bearing a subtle smirk, nodded to the guard.

"Not a problem, Cho'zai Nophrea," said the Diramal. "My good jinns, we shall conclude our discussion of how best to resolve the alien vessel upon the moon, at a later date. I sense, Alpha Criptous has a rather pressing matter to discuss with me . . ."

The jinns leisurely and silently moved passed me as they made their way out of the room, their eyes still passing over me. The doors finally shut, the hologram of the alien vessel on the moon cut and left the room in a shroud.

There was something unnerving in the Diramal's unwavering persistence in keeping the room dark. The only thing I could make out was the mellow glow of his eyes.

"Well, Criptous, what brings you to me?" asked the Diramal.

The question caught me off guard as my defensive instincts started to kick in.

"You…" I said, gathering my thoughts.

"Me?" asked the Diramal, his boots started to click around the table, coming nearer.

"You are the only person with the authority in the entire country to give commands to the cho'zai," I finally said.

"That I am." The Diramal's voice shifted, melding between two different dialects simultaneously.

The neuro-chip in my mind was somehow triggered. Suddenly, my thoughts and speech felt constrained.

"So, why then, would one of your cho'zai tell me that a fellow soldier gave two of them commands to assault me?" I asked.

Thump, *thump!* The Diramal's boots rested before me and his gaze lowered to my eye line.

"You were assaulted?" The Diramal's voice was still meshed. His words compelled me to answer him bluntly.

"I was this morning, not too long ago. But I know it was—" I replied.

"That is quite concerning, Amat . . ." The Diramal interjected. Despite desperately wanting to, I couldn't retaliate. ". . . why don't you have a seat and tell me more." The Diramal guided me to a chair and sat me down.

"There . . . there was a name they gave me," I said.

"Who's?" he asked.

A shuddering breath was all I could manage in hesitation, before some invisible force compelled me to utter: "Vykin. Blick Vykin."

"Vykin?" he said, standing up. "I understand you two have a history with one another. Quite a brutal one."

I cleared my throat. "Yes, sir," no other words came to mind.

"It just so happens that I had a meeting with Blick Vykin not an hour ago. He came in for a debriefing on his mission at Entropolis in Zeta. Doesn't quite explain how he managed to send two cho'zai after you, but he is here and he does have a certain level of authority most are unfamiliar with."

The Diramal seemed oddly empathetic, but there was still demand in his tone, some sort of . . . influence in his speech that choked me from speaking my mind.

"Rest here for now, Criptous, while I recall Vykin and get this sorted."

I remained frozen in place while the Diramal returned to the table at the center of the room. He activated the base intercom and beckoned Blick to the conference room.

"Don't worry, Amat, we'll get this resolved," he said while I sat, struggling with my own impulses.

It was such a mental barrier to even conceptualize anything outside sitting in that chair. I couldn't compel myself to do anything else, no matter how hard I tried. Any effort to combat the Diramal's suggestions nearly left me faint.

Not much time passed before Blick arrived, escorted into the room by two cho'zai who stood guard outside the conference room.

"Sir," Blick said. "Was there something else you wished to discuss with me?" I couldn't see Blick with my back turned to him, still frozen in place. The room remained unlit and Blick's tone gave away his unease at the ambience of it.

Steady footsteps filled the room. "Mr. Vykin," the Diramal said," "As a matter of fact, there was. Not long after your dismissal, I was made aware of a rather disturbing report."

"What report, sir?" He sounded bemused.

The lights finally flickered on, briefly blinding me as my eyes adjusted.

"I believe you're familiar with Alpha Criptous," said the Diramal.

"Eh—I do. What does this have to do with the information you received, sir?" he asked.

It wasn't him! I thought to myself.

I couldn't divert my attention away from the wall, no matter how much I wanted to. The only thing I could control was the harshness of my grip on the armrests and my breathing.

"The son of the recently deceased jinn-hid, shared how he was attacked by two cho'zai. One of whom, reportedly mentioned your name." The Diramal held a silence as two hands slapped on Blick's shoulders, holding him down, presumably by a cho'zai. Blick *growled* in reply. "Why did you hire those cho'zai to attack Amat, Blick?"

"What two cho'zai? When did this happen?" Blick asked, confused.

The Diramal held another silence and whispered something inaudible.

"I didn't do anything! I didn't hire anyone to go after you, Amat!"

I know you didn't! Curse the Diramal and his tricks, how can I not move?! I thought.

I didn't see which one, but I could hear the loud *smack* of the punch that hit Blick in the jaw. Promptly, I heard someone choking, oddly the strangled gasps didn't sound like Blick. I would have looked back to see who it was but I remained immobile. *Great Mother, forgive me. I can't will myself to stop this. I am so sorry, Blick,* I prayed.

"Amat!" the Diramal called. "Will you look here, boy?"

I turned my head slowly and defiantly towards the Diramal and the men holding Blick down, realizing I could only just now move at the command of the Diramal.

"Look into Blick's eyes for me, Amat, and tell me . . ."

Our gazes locked, mine and Blick's. I tried to communicate, through mere expression, that I knew he was innocent. Even if he did terrible things to me in the past, this was not one of them.

"*Is he innocent?*" The Diramal's voice sounded morphed.

Yes! I wanted to blurt so desperately, as I struggled to part my muzzle. A single tear trailed down my face.

"It's fine, Amat," the Diramal said, ever so reassuringly. "You don't need to answer. *Turn back around son, it's best you don't see this.*"

Subconsciously, my body started to turn away from Blick and faced the wall once again. The pace of my heart picked up as my neuro-chip reenforced the commands of the Diramal, striving to fight against them.

The Diramal sighed. "It pains me to say this, Blick, but it appears, Amat feels you are too great a threat to him. As the son of the jinn-hid, he is all too great an asset to this militia to be trifled."

A gun cocked back. Adrenaline surged through my veins as I attempted to stand and face the Diramal, but I couldn't outmatch this restraint holding me back.

"I'll give you one chance to defend yourself. Let's assume for a minute, Blick, that you didn't hire the cho'zai to assault Amat. Do you have anyone in mind who would want to frame you for this attack?"

"I wouldn't know of any specific names, *sir.* I made a lot of enemies in my time. I did some . . . horrible things to fellow soldiers who I deemed lesser than myself. However, *never once* have I had the intent of killing *anyone*. That is the truth. Forgive me if my explanation is not satisfactory to your questioning."

The Diramal ordered him to be hit again. It sounded like the was hit so hard his head was knocked loose.

"How else would one of them know your name if you weren't in on it?" the Diramal asked, deviously.

"You know how," he growled, frustratedly.

Another loud *smack*.

"You would be wise to restrain that train of thought," said the Diramal. He sighed.

What did he mean by that? I thought.

"Since you cannot put produce any evidence that we should otherwise dismiss your apparent corroboration in this dilemma, you must be met with a consequence. Any conspiracy to assassinate or mortally wound a fellow soldier is punishable . . ." He dislodged the safety on his weapon. ". . . only by death."

Wait! No, stop! I wanted to blurt out, yet my voice remained constrained.

No matter how hard I tried to volition myself to move or speak, the neuro-chip completely overwrote everything. The more I fought against my physical constraint, the more my body tensed.

Just when all hope seemed lost, I felt a chilling sensation on my shoulder, followed by a faint whisper of my name. It alleviated me from my agitation. Gradually, my muscles relaxed and the voice sounded again. The walls blocking off my neurological pathways broke down and the voice beckoned, *"Close your eyes . . . breathe."*

My hands were trembling as they slowly lifted from the armrests. All sound echoed away into a soft wind.

My eyes broke open and suddenly my lungs expanded with new found depth. Beathing with my diaphragm, the pace of time finally started to ease around me. I was able to ground one foot after the other beneath me and stand tall. I faced the Diramal, who aimed his gun down at Blick. I could see his finger steadily squeezing the trigger.

"*Now, run!*" the voice said in a hush.

I sprinted for the Diramal, keeping my eye on the trigger. Reaching him, I extended my arm forth and pushed his arm over his head, toward the ceiling, as he shot the gun. Almost immediately after I touched him, time burst back to normal.

"NO!" I shouted as I tore the weapon from the Diramal's grasp, after he fired his third shot.

"Amat! Ho—What are you doing?" The Diramal was in awe of me.

"Stop playing dumb, Diramal! I tolerated enough of your harassment for one day! You never heard my position on Blick's charges and I state it now. There is no way Blick has the authority to command two cho'zai, let alone *one* to carry out any sort of errand for him—ill-willed or good—considering it is you who has absolute authority and control over their rank."

He smirked with a sinister look in his eyes and said, "An astute observation, Amat. Your father was the same way and you would be wise not to forget where that got him."

"No, an idea killed my father, a simple phrase you uttered to him and I quote, 'Be prepared for anything, even your own death.' And he was. I spent my final hours with a man who merely wore the mask of my father. You destroyed him before we went on that mission, knowing where that would lead him."

"Did *I* destroy him, or did *you?* Was it your simple existence and the idea of losing you that killed him?"

I wanted to kill him right there. After all, the gun was still in my hand. My index finger lightly tapped the side of the gun. He looked down and noted my unease.

"What thoughts occupy your mind, boy?" He gave a cunning grin, knowing full well what was on my mind. "There should still be seven rounds in that magazine. There would be no better opportunity than the one you have now. Of course, there would be consequences, but you'd be doing the world a favor, wouldn't you? Best of all, in your eyes, you will be doing right by your father. *Avenging him,*"

My hold on the gun was no longer firm and my arm quivered so vigorously that I couldn't aim.

The Diramal looked behind me and ordered his men to stand down. Before I was aware of it, I aimed the gun at the Diramal's head.

"That's it . . . good man. Now, execute the shot . . . just kill him . . . he killed your father. It's what your family would want," a sadistic voice in my egged me on. It was an inner monologue, an archetype of sort I never heard before.

It almost felt like another entity living within me, encouraging my vengeful temptations. However, the calm, chilling . . . presence returned as well and argued against killing the Diramal. When I first encountered the soothing voice, it felt like a stranger, but now it felt familiar. As if maybe it could have been my father himself. Embracing the council of this kinder presence allowed me to lower my guard; my rage ceased.

"You changed your mind, have you?" the Diramal said.

"My mind was never fixed on killing you. You tempted me, but I didn't give in." I dropped the gun on the floor. The Diramal glanced down and then slowly picked up the pistol.

"You know, Amat, I don't see what all this fuss was *really* about. After all, what harm can . . ." the Diramal whipped his arm up and aimed the pistol at my chest, point blank range. I stepped back and tripped, falling onto the floor. He fired the pistol. ". . . blanks do?" He laughed sinisterly.

Lying on the ground, I could finally see that even though there were shots aimed at the ceiling, there were no holes. Heaving, I stood up and got a handle on myself. "You can leave now, the both of you. I'll be speaking with you later, Alpha Criptous," he stated.

Together, Blick and I exited the room.

"Where are we going?" Blick asked, massaging his bruised jaw.

"The cafeteria. I haven't had a thing to eat all day and we could both use a drink," I said.

"Sounds good to me."

On our way to the cafeteria, we ran into Olson and Log. The three of us raced toward one another, meeting in embrace. Taking in all that happened the past couple of days made it feel like I hadn't seen them in weeks. Weeps of rejoice were shared in our reunion.

"We heard only one made it back, but we didn't find out it was you until today. We would have come to visit you sooner otherwise," Log said.

"I wasn't the only one to make it back. I was the only one to escape the interior of the ship, but four others remained outside the alien craft. They came back with me. I know they did, but the Diramal insists I was the only one to return. That, and several other recent events have me questioning the Diramal in a variety of ways, but that is a discussion for a later time. A lot has happened and my stomach longs for its first meal of the day. Blick and I were just making our way to the cafeteria." I turned to acknowledge Blick. "If you're comfortable with him, you both could join us."

My cousins noted his bruised face as they took in his appearance.

"That's fine with me," Olson said. "It seems like you two might have been through some recent hardships."

"Hardships is putting it lightly," Blick spoke up.

Olson turned toward his younger brother. "Log, are you alright with sharing Blick's company? I know you two had some . . . confrontations."

Log examined Blick. "You still lookin' to cause anymore havoc?" he asked.

"No. I'm sorry for what I put you through almost every other time we've met. Not only to you, Log, but also to you, Amat. I've been through some hefty times myself, as I'm sure you noticed at this point. But I recognize the error of my ways and how I've isolated myself. And . . . someone important to me wouldn't want me to continue living that way and I won't. Will you forgive me?"

"I will," I said.

Log nodded his head. "As will I, assuming your word is true and you do want to change."

"I do."

"Shake on it." Log offered his hand and the two kindly shook their grasps.

With that, we all started anew, as equals.

XXIX
Harnessing Time

Olson, Log, and Blick leaned in close as I discussed what happened on the mission. Although, Olson and Log seemed more in awe of the details than Blick, who held an unreadable expression. My cousins had questions for everything I didn't have answers to.

"You mentioned Uncle Bod wasn't himself; how did that happen?" Log asked, his eyes heavy with tears.

"He was . . . overly concerned with my safety," I said, also shedding a tear. "I wasn't concerned enough with his."

"That is not true, Amat," Olson said with sad eyes. "He was your father. He had a responsibility to keep you safe, which did not extend to you, onto him."

"You didn't see how he was, Olson," I said, sniffling. "It wasn't fair the way he went; he was so paranoid. So much would have been different if the Diramal didn't weigh my possible death in his mind. That's what put him on edge."

"So . . . if the Diramal compromised the mission by manipulating its senior officer, what would be the benefit in doing that?" Log asked.

"I'm not sure. But it means Utopian has an iniquitous man at her head."

"You sound ready to do something about that." Olson sounded concerned.

"I may very well be, especially if he does anything else to harm me or our family," I said, taking a drink.

"I hope you're not planning on doing anything rash. He may be corrupt but to do anything about that would require planning and *patience*," Olson said.

"What I plan to do, Olson, is keep you and everyone else in our family *safe*. And I will take whatever measures are necessary to do just that."

"As you should," Olson stated. "But consider where you stand, Amat. You are an alpha, a high value military asset with limited authority on what you can enforce outside the autocratic agenda. Attempting any kind of impeachment, or worse, would require time and likely a full-on insurrection with the constructs of our society."

"Amat Criptous. Amat Luciph Criptous, please report to the main entrance. You have a visitor," a voice announced on the intercom.

"A visitor . . ." *Mom,* I thought. "I think I know who. I should go, I'll see you guys later."

"Amat," Olson called, sternly. "Don't do anything your father wouldn't. This conversation's not over."

I nodded my head respectfully, and shook Olson's hand. "I won't."

Olson nodded in reply. "If Aunt Judi's here to see you, tell her we said, 'Hi,' and . . . pass on our condolences," he said.

"I will." I turned to Log to say goodbye and shake his hand. Then I turned to Blick.

"Thanks for earlier . . ." he said and extended his hand to me ". . . friend."

I shook his hand. "Friend," I replied with a smile.

I left the table and headed to the main entrance. During my stroll, I reflected on the voices in my head that spoke to me in the Diramal's office. Never did I encounter anything like that before. But then, in all my life up to that point, I never questioned the authority of my country. In that sense, I suppose it was to be expected, struggling so hard to speak freely. However, there was still the mystery of the voice that guided me to withstand the Diramal's commands and their strange restraint over me. Why did it feel like my father? How could that be?

I caught sight of my mother the moment the base's entrance came into view. Her expression was filled with relief. She rushed toward me with open arms and I to her.

"Oh, my boy!" she cried with joy. "I've been waiting here for hours on end trying to find some way to see you. I didn't know much, they told me this morning, you were the only one in your platoon to make it back. Anua blesses me to see you well." My mother broke into tears and held me tight.

"I'm really happy to see you too, Mom!"

My mother eased herself away from me to look into my eyes. A deep dread filled her own, as she struggled to voice her next words.

"Did your . . . did your father go peacefully?" my mother asked.

My heart sank at the recollection of that final moment, seeing those claws protruding through my father's chest, seeing the life fade from his eyes and that final, tranquil moment.

"He did," I replied, struggling to admit it.

Best to keep the extra details from her, it wouldn't serve well to tell her. I thought.

My mother broke down, taking me back into her embrace.

"I'm so sorry you had to witness that, Amat. I'm so glad we still have you." My mother whimpered.

"I'm sorry I couldn't bring him back with me."

"No. No, sweetheart, that wasn't your responsibility. Don't . . . don't bear the weight of that. Your father promised, if no one else, *you* would make it home safely and that's what he did," my mother replied.

Why? The question dawned on me so abruptly. *My father was everything to this family and to so many others on Galiza. People I'll likely never know. I left all of them behind as soon as I could without a second thought and with no intention of seeing them again . . . Why should I have been allowed to come back?*

Just as quickly, the answer I received didn't come through in words, so much as it did as a feeling. My senses told me it was 'protection,' to protect . . . everyone. It was hard to pinpoint who 'everyone' was, as it didn't feel specific to just my family. Nevertheless, it was a call to action, to serve a purpose greater than the one I made up for myself.

"It might not have been my fault, but a responsibility fell onto me; I *will* ensure our safety," I told my mom.

She stroked my fur around my head and finally started to calm down.

"Then let's start by brining you home," my mother said.

I nodded.

"First, I want to see if there's anything in my room at the infirmary worth recovering. I'll meet you back here in fifteen minutes, alright?" I asked.

"Okay," my mother said with a smile, kissing me on the forehead. With that I ran back to my room.

I couldn't recall if there was anything worth recovering from my room. I just wanted some time to myself to scheme how I would keep my family safe from the Diramal, knowing he wouldn't let me just walk away. Even if I resigned, that would only make me more powerless to his authority over us all. A permanent solution was necessary. To my surprise there was a decade-old photo of my father and I. *I never noticed this sitting here,* I thought, picking it up. He seemed so happy, so at peace, holding me over his shoulders.

I picked up the portrait and rushed back to my mother. Returning to the front entrance of the base, I saw her conversing with the Diramal in an argument. From where I stood their conversation was inaudible. Moving closer to hear their voices, I saw the Diramal raise a fist. My heart skipped a beat as my fingers tightened into fists. My teeth clenched against one another as my lips flexed into a gnarling growl. Rage filled my heart and my mind flooded with all the things I wanted to do the Diramal at that moment. Time quickly halted to a near complete stop and brought me to my knees. It was as if my own weight toppled over me, holding me down.

"*Amat . . .*" the soft voice whispered into my ears. The first time I ignored it. Too fixated and struggling just to lift my head and gaze up at the unfolding assault the Diramal was carrying out onto my mother.

"*Amat!*" it called again, this time a little more urgently. I took one deep anxious breath as I gradually started to focus more closely on the voice. My heart strained with every beat pulsating throughout my body, and my chest was tight and cramped.

"*Stand up!*" the voice blurted. I felt the chill on my shoulder again.

"I can't," I replied.

"*Yes . . . you can.*"

"I'm too weak, I don't know how to control this . . . manipulation of time."

"*You can control it . . . but you can't force it.*"

"How?"

"*You know how . . . focus your breath. You've done it before . . . do it again.*"

I closed my eyes.

"*Breathe . . .*"

I closed my eyes and took a deep breath through my diaphragm, which seemed to relieve a lot of the tension in my heart.

"*Now . . . stand! Your mother . . .*"

I gasped and whipped my head up. I saw that the Diramal's fist was growing nearer and nearer to my mother's face by the second, little by little.

I pushed myself off the ground and pulled out a knife from my side. My eyes tracked his fist, inches away from connecting with my mother's face. I moved toward him with long quick strides. When I was just out of arms reach of the Diramal, I tackled into him so hard we flew across the room, through a glass wall, and went tumbling across the lawn as the altered time wore off.

Once we stopped rolling, I sat over the Diramal and put the edge of my knife tightly to his throat.

"YOU! YOU TOOK ONE OF MY FAMILY MEMBERS AWAY FROM ME, AND YOU WILL *NOT* TAKE ANOTHER!" I yelled. "YOU WANT TO HURT SOMEONE, YOU HURT ME. UNDERSTAND?!" I said, spitting in the Diramal's face.

The Diramal squinted and laughed hysterically. "You feel relieved now, don't you, with all that rage at your disposal. I bet you'd feel a whole lot better about yourself if you moved that knife across my throat. Why don't you try it and see what happens?"

A small group of cho'zai came rushing out of the broken glass opening, but he ordered them to halt with a slight raise of his hand.

This is it, Amat! The moment you've been waiting for! the sinister voice in my head said. *The Diramal has called off his men. This is your chance! Take it! Your father would have done the same for you!*

I started to shake again. I didn't hear or feel the chilling presence, but I did what I thought it would have wanted me to do. I took a deep breath and said, "No, it's not. My father would have wanted justice, not vengeance. I won't destroy the path he set me on."

"And what path was that?" the Diramal said with a mocking smile. I retracted the blade from the Diramal's throat and stared at him down. *Whack!* The throw of my arm was so loose, I barely noticed that I threw the punch. The Diramal clasped his face with his hands as he growled. "To not let people like you get into my head and make up my mind for me," I said.

I walked back over to my mom, catching the eye of a very prominent cho'zai, Zothra, who was said to be the Diramal's best. He looked me up and down with a slight mocking curl to his lips. He gave a slight scoff and tended to the Diramal. My gaze returned to the direction of my mother and my heart nearly stopped at the sight of several doctors surrounding her body.

"Get out of the way!" I shouted, pulling aside one of the doctors. He tried to hold me back, but his words were inaudible to me. "Move!" I barked, throwing the man off his feet and out of my way.

I went to my mother's side and inspected her. She was still breathing, but in short, rapid breaths; she was unconscious. Although, there was no sign of injury.

Unless she's concussed. I thought.

"Is she going to be alright?" I asked desperately. I observed in anticipation as another doctor examined my mother.

The third doctor went to inspect the other doctor I just tossed aside. His well-being didn't much concern me at that given moment, but I paid him a quick glance back and saw he was uninjured and on his feet before long.

"She'll be fine. She just passed out. It'll only be a matter of time before she wakes."

"How long do you think that will be?"

"Can't say, but we'll get her in a bed and scan her neural feed to ensure there's no internal hemorrhaging." The doctor glanced up at me and finally noted the level of concern on my face. "Don't worry, sir, we'll look after your mother."

"Thank you."

"Of course, sir. I'm Doctor Mixil. If you have any further problems or concerns, call for me."

I nodded my head as Mixil signaled for the other two doctors to get my mom on a gurney and rushed her to the infirmary. I turned and marched back to the Diramal as Cho'zai Zothra helped him to find his feet. Before I could get within five feet of the other two cho'zai, who had their backs to me, Zothra called their attention to me and they promptly widened their stances.

"Criptous! You would be wise to stay right where you are. You've already assaulted the Diramal, let's not make it worse by going in for round two," said the cho'zai standing to my left.

"I could say the same to the man you defend at your back, cho'zai. He almost assaulted my mother."

"Can you testify to what prompted the Diramal's reaction?" the cho'zai on the right asked.

I tilted my head at her.

"Not what was said, but—"

"Then I'm sure the Diramal had his reasons," she returned.

I slowly stepped forward.

"And as the son of the late jinn-hid, what exactly would stop me from behaving any differently onto those who protect this predator?" I asked.

Thump. I was abruptly stopped in my tracks when I sensed the presence of yet another cho'zai coming within inches of me. My eyes shifted to his, taking in the features of his masked pleasantness.

"Even if you were the son of the active jinn-hid, Criptous . . ." said Zothra, maintaining a piercing gaze with a confident smile. ". . . it would not excuse you from publicly assaulting three members of Anua's cho'zai, in addition to the Diramal. It would be in your interest to walk away. Now."

The Diramal's nostrils had rivers of blood flowing from them. I didn't notice it in the moment, but the color of his blood seemed peculiarly dark, like the cho'zai who attacked me in the bathroom. I raised my finger to the tyrant and spoke, "If you ever come near my family again, Diramal, I will ensure you raise your fists to no man or woman ever again."

The Diramal curled his lips, maintaining his grim stare. I looked back to Cho'zai Zothra, stepping back, only turning away when I deemed it safe.

"I'll relish the day you hold yourself to that promise, Criptous," he blurted with a choked cough.

I stopped in my tracks and momentarily clenched my fists as I turned my head back just enough to see the cho'zai's hands on their holsters. With a growl I pressed on and went to look after my mother.

You won't have any of your maniacal guards around you when I do.

XXX
A Fixed Deal

My mother was still asleep, but Dr. Mixil assured me she was stable and would awake in due time. I pulled up a chair and held my mother's hand, resting my head on the bed beside her, and slept until she woke. She stroked her fingers through my fur. I lifted my head almost immediately, crying with relief to see her well.

"Thank goodness, you're not hurt! I thought I lost you too," I said as we hugged each other tightly. I pulled away from our embrace to inspect her. "You don't feel pain anywhere, do you?"

She shook her head.

"Not really. Somehow, the Diramal didn't strike me. I was blown back though, by something and I fell faint," she replied.

I was hesitant in my reply, as I didn't want to unveil my newfound ability to her. *I don't know enough about it yet to give her a proper explanation . . .*

"What were you and the Diramal arguing about?" I asked, trying to change the subject.

"You. Apparently, he was filtering your neuro-chip and discovered that you were leaving with me. He said he wouldn't allow me to take you away. When I confronted him, he threatened to never let me see you again and that's when . . . things got out of hand."

I looked down at my mother's hand and held it tight. *By Anua, what would have happened if I didn't come sooner?*

"I'll find a way to stop this, I promise," I said.

My mother gave a faint smile, as she put her hand over our grasp.

"As long as it doesn't come at the cost of losing you," she said. "Under any other circumstance, I would say 'no,' but our options are scarce. We *all* have to tread carefully as we move through this world."

Just as we reached the car, I heard a voice calling out to me.

"Amat, Amat!"

I turned around and saw a familiar face.

"Blick? Is everything alright?"

"I wanted to tell you something," he said.

"You have my attention."

"I have something to confess. I've . . . been a ward to the Diramal for many years now. What you've witnessed today is not entirely out of the norm for me. In light of recent events, things have changed, and I never felt at greater risk."

I wasn't sure where Blick was taking this conversation, but I was intrigued nonetheless.

"Go on."

"I . . . I need to leave,"

"You mean desert?"

"Yes."

I took a deep breath and shut my eyes as I processed this. The chip in my head yelled commands, tempting me to report Blick. It passed and I opened my eyes once again.

"I can see where this conversation's going, and I understand why. But, Blick, I have a family and I need to keep them safe, now more than ever."

"I understand that, truly, I do. All I would ask of you is one night. One night and by morning I'll be gone, having my next step figured out."

I shook my head. "I'm gonna need a *really* good reason for it, Blick. Regardless of the fact that we're on better terms with one another." I turned my back, crossing my arms.

"My parents knew your father," his speech did not falter.

I tilted my head.

"They worked together to conspire against the Diramal," he continued. "I remember, when I was very young, seeing your father visit our home on several occasions." He came up close to me and spoke in a cautious tone. "One night, I vaguely remember hearing my parents talking about some kind of unethical, classified files, detailing human experiments approved by the Diramal. Together my parents and your father were going to use this to strip the Diramal of his rank and authority. My parents were killed two days later, veered off a windy road; bodies were 'unidentifiable.'

For reasons unknown to me, I was promptly taken in as the Diramal's ward. Perhaps he pitied me. As the years went by, I *endured* the Diramal and worked tirelessly to insert myself under the command of your father, the only other man I trusted in this world."

"Did my father know who you were?" I asked.

"I never told him. Though, it was curious how willingly the Diramal let me train under your father. In fact, the only time in all the years I spent training under your father, the Diramal only ever asked me to do one thing."

"To do what?" I asked.

"To keep tabs on you. He didn't say why or how, but days before you showed up, those were my orders,"

"What have you reported to him?"

Blick sighed.

"I can't . . . explain it, but I noted certain peculiarities about you, Amat. At the time, I couldn't care less for what it might mean for you, given how things started out between us. Had I known it would lead to where we are now, I would've thought twice. I admired your father, Amat, and I never desired any ill-will for him,"

I nodded my head in agreement. "One night."

"One night."

I looked around to make sure there weren't any guards or militia to observe what would happen next. "We'll need to move fast. You'll keep your eyes shut on the way to my family's house and you will not open them until I say otherwise. You will not engage with my family, nor will they with you. In the house, you'll be blindfolded. These are my conditions to minimize the risk of anyone locating you through your neuro-chip feed."

"I understand," Blick said.

"Alright, wait here. I'm going to tell my mom the plan."

The ride home was silent, just as I wanted it to be. I didn't want anyone who might be filtering Blick to identify the voices of myself or my mother.

When we got home, my sisters were already asleep. My mother said we would wait until morning to tell them what became of our father. I retrieved a long cloth and tied it around Blick's head, shielding his eyes.

I led him to a large, empty closet with a mattress and some blankets. I left him with some cards and a pen; I wrote something on one of them. It said, *If you need anything, knock and slip a note under the door. I'll be up all night.*

Sitting by the window on the second floor of the house, I watched perceptively for any sign of the Diramal's subjects. The phone rang unexpectedly, at a late hour. I went to answer it.

"Hello?"

"Criptous," the Diramal replied on the other end.

I raised my head and my eyes widened. "The audacity of you, Diramal, calling my home after the events of today."

He chuckled.

"You've grown to share your father's audacity in how you speak to your superiors. How impudent you Criptouses are," he said.

"What do you want, Diramal?" I demanded.

"I want my ward back, and you at SEF tomorrow for the next mission to the alien vessel."

"What makes you think I have your ward?"

"Don't take me for a fool, Amat. Then again, I sensed you would reply in this manner. So, I called with more than just a demand. Have you ever compromised before, Amat? Debating a middle ground with someone to get what you both want?"

"I would rather take my chances trying to reason with our invaders than make a bargain with you."

"Well, before you make an attempt at that suicide mission, let me explain something. There are four of my best cho'zai stationed just across the street from your home. I believe you interacted with one of them today: Cho'zai Zothra. They await my command to storm your house, take Blick, and do whatever they feel is necessary to the other occupants of your home."

I marched to the front window, peered out, and saw the car he spoke of, with three men and one woman.

"I can call them off *if*, and only if, you cooperate with me."

I sighed. "If I do this for you, this will be my last mission for the Utopian Military. I will be resigning upon my return."

"You have no option to resign. You are under contract."

"You're asking me to lead an assault against a far superior alien race. Such a service should pay, in *full*, whatever debt I owe to Utopion."

"There are many at my disposal who are capable of far more than you, Amat. All the same, I am willing to hear out any other conditions you might have that would be of less expense to me."

"If more capable troops are at your disposal then what value do I hold to you?"

"There is much about yourself that you are not aware, Amat. Things that only myself and a select few know, regarding *your abilities*. That makes you an invaluable asset. But as I said, I am willing to make *smaller* accommodations that are to your liking."

An eerie horror crept up my spine at the implications of the Diramal's words. I didn't doubt, the inherent "abilities" he spoke of were in regards to the strange time alteration I was learning to master. The thought had crossed my mind to question him further and seek the answers he presumably possessed. My tongue stayed itself at the recollection of the Diramal's qualities for being an adept manipulator and a likely pathological liar. Whatever the reasons behind my innate peculiarities, I doubted the Diramal would have been transparent about them, in any sense.

With no other choice left to me, I contemplated what else the Diramal could be bartered for. "Very well, I want full command and ownership of the Peroma. For sentimental and personal reasons, I would like the luxury of taking her for a spin any time I choose."

"Done."

"I also want a platoon of alphas assigned to me on this mission."

"Those are both reasonable requests, Amat. I think I'll add a condition of my own, so everyone walks away happy in this exchange."

"And what would that be?"

"That Blick goes with you on the mission. If he survives, he will gain his freedom; I will denounce my ownership over his person."

A snarling grunt escaped my throat. Despite how dangerous it sounded, it seemed a half reasonable offer. "Alright."

"Good. Considering the loss of your father, I'll do you and your family the courtesy of having the morning to yourselves," He spoke condescendingly. "You and Blick will be expected to return to the base no later than noon, tomorrow. Now, before I go, is there anything else you would have of me?"

I slammed the phone down and then watched from the window as the Diramal's cho'zai left my home. I called for Blick and my mom and told them what was going to happen the next day. Blick, though he was notably disappointed, took his involvement with the mission well.

"If I still had my family, I would have done the same," he said.

We all went to bed in silence shortly after.

XXXI
Undeify Anua

At six a.m., my alarm sounded. An emptiness filled the house, not because I was the only one awake, but because something . . . someone was missing from it. However, there was a subtle feeling of comfort in the silence. The calm before the storm.

I went out to the living room, took a seat on the couch, and opened a photo album that sat on the coffee table. Ironically, most of the pictures were of me and my father. In the first few pages, the pictures were of me when I must have been about five. I couldn't help but notice the many smiles and merry expressions on our faces. They were so true and unburdened by tension and conformity. Memories from the various parks, shores, mountain ranges, and events we attended together whirled through my mind. I was able to recall how joyous my father and I were together.

As the pictures went onto more recent years, the photos of my family were less spirited. Even when I caught a smile from my mother or sisters, they seemed less genuine. The pictures were taken in more local areas and the expressions shared between myself and my father became more stern. I began to feel alienated by my own image. I found myself whipping through the album until I couldn't take it anymore. I realized how unrecognizable I became and threw the album across the room.

Noting the rise and fall of my chest, I closed my eyes and started to control my breath. My attention honed in on the crushing pain in my heart. The feeling dissipated with every breath I took. When it was gone, I got up and headed to the kitchen to make a quick breakfast.

Blick came out shortly after and helped himself to some food as well. We didn't say much to each other as I was too deep in thought to start a conversation of any kind.

"Are you ready for today?" he asked.

I looked over at him with a bland expression. "I'm mentally preparing for it," I replied. "Are you?"

He gave a heavy sigh. "I truth, I don't know how I feel about it, any of it. I think there have been enough funerals and K.I.A. pertaining to this mission."

Something in the way he spoke suggested he was referring to more than just the alien craft. However, I was too preoccupied to concern myself with what else he might have meant.

Before long, my mother came out and greeted us.

"Are the girls up yet?" she asked.

"I haven't seen them," I replied.

"What time do you have to be at Vīvothar?"

"We're expected at noon."

My mother looked over to the nearest clock. "Alright, I'll go get Lia and Lara up."

I nodded.

My mother returned with Lia and Lara at her side. They were both surprised to see Blick in the house. As they took their seats at the table, I made quick introductions.

"Where's daddy?" Lia asked innocently, seemingly oblivious to Blick.

That almost made it harder to tell them how it all happened. I had to pause before continuing and Lara's eyes filled with tears as she noted my hesitation. It was then that Blick excused himself from the table.

I closed my eyes, and my mother took my hand. Lara listened very intently as Lia seemed to drown in her sorrow, staring blankly at the table. Lara stiffened at my telling of how Dilek died. When I finally told them of how our father had passed, sacrificing himself to save me, Lara immediately broke down into tears. Lia, at first, grew a frown on her face and walked up to me. I took her up on my lap and she cried into my chest. From there, our mother took the floor and did her best to soothe the girls' weeping. Tears rolled down my cheeks, but I did not sob.

I glanced at the clock in the kitchen and noticed that time was running out before Blick and I had to be at the base. I stood from the table, still holding my sister. "I'm going to get ready."

My mother nodded as she took Lia from me and cradled both my sisters, rocking them back and forth. Before my mother would allow me to leave, however, she reached out toward me and gently pressed my head against her lips.

The ride to the SEF base was much like the one before it, but with a superior gloom shared between us all.

Upon arrival, the Diramal was at the head of the base, awaiting us with a mocking smirk on his face.

"Good morning, Mrs. Criptous. Allow me to express my sympathies. I don't believe I had the opportunity of expressing them when last we spoke," he said. My mother gave him an indignant look and nodded. "And hello, Lara, Lia, Amat, and Blick!" he said with enthusiasm.

We all acknowledged the Diramal in our own way. Then, silence passed over us all until Lia spoke.

"Why did you say those mean things to my daddy?"

He looked down at her with an oddly satisfied expression.

"Amat, Blick, why don't you boys follow the Diramal and we'll return home," Mom said.

"Right," I replied.

"But, Mommy, I want to—"

"Come on, Lia," my mother spoke sternly. "Say goodbye, now."

I hugged my sisters goodbye and said I loved them both. However, when it came time to hug my mother, I said something different.

"I'm still coming back, same as last time. I'll do everything in my power to bring as many as possible back with me."

"You just make sure you stay safe above all else, Amat," she replied. Her eyes said what she dared not; *anyone else is obsolete in this.*

"I will."

Blick and I were escorted to the Peroma by the Diramal, walking on either side of him. No words were spoken between us. Once we reached the ship, the Diramal wished us luck.

"May you have a safe journey, and return home with glory," he said.

Neither Blick nor I replied except for a reluctant salute. The Diramal then left us.

Blick and I walked into the Peroma. I glanced at a nearby clock and saw it was approaching noon. Before prepping for the launch, I inspected the crew to ensure that everyone was on board before we left.

"Amat . . . Amat Criptous," a voice called from behind.

I turned around to see who beckoned me. I was unsure of their identities, but promptly recognized who they represented. They were scientists from MIST—Military Investigative Sciences and Technology.

"Are you sure you're on the right ship, gentlemen?" I asked.

"Yes, we are bioengineers from MIS—"

"I know who you are, I'm wondering why you're here," I said, cutting off the representative.

"Well, we've been assigned under your command to salvage what we can from these . . . beings. To study them. By the way, I'm—"

"Doctor Hanker, yes. I can see that on your nametag. I also see that your associate is Doctor Rogen. I recognize your names and your reputations. You are the developers of the vi-warmigols as well as many other bioweapons used in the Afeiketan war. I read about you when I was twelve."

"That is correct, sir."

I was not impressed. My suspicion of the scientists and their true purpose for being there stirred silent judgments in my mind.

"I assume you are here under order of the Diramal," I said.

"Uh, yessir, correct again," Doctor Hanker said with a dumb smile on his face.

I sighed. "Alright, here's the deal. Regardless of what your orders are, you are under my command now. If I decide on something that doesn't suit your agenda, hold your complaints for the Diramal. Am I understood?"

"Mr. Criptous, please. There's no need for—"

"My rank is alpha and you will address me as such! Lastly, should either of you pose a threat to me, my troops, or this mission, I will not hesitate to execute either of you where you stand. Now, find your seats, all of you!"

Everyone quickly found a seat and strapped themselves in, aside from the bioengineers who so awkwardly secured themselves.

I walked over to the main controls and activated the trantalium orbs. Blick sat beside me as my co-pilot.

"How are the systems looking?" I asked.

"Fully operational, sir," Blick replied.

"What about the engine?"

"Humming soundly."

"Weapons?"

"Locked and loaded, sir."

"Good, let's get this done." I opened a comms channel. "Vīvothar, this is Peroma CX-17, we are prepped and ready for takeoff. Over."

"Roger that, Peroma CX-17," a man's voice said on the other side of the channel. "Opening bay doors now."

I eased the throttle forward, hovering our way outside. I pulled back on the joystick to aim us at the moon and propelled us forward.

This launch was a bit different in the sense that we weren't going toward the moon, as it was not directly overhead. We approached it from the side to avoid getting caught in the wake of the enhanced magnetic field again. Though, the Peroma shook and was thwarted from my control as we neared the lunar body.

I decided it safer to hold our position for a time until the opposition to our course subsided. Staring out at the goddess, Blick and I noticed something very odd about her movement.

"Are you seeing what I'm seeing?" I asked Blick.

"I am. Anua's rotation is extraordinarily fast."

"What do the scans show on the current state of Anua's magnetic field, Blick?"

He ran a scan on the moon. "It's all over the place. I'd be surprised if it's the wish of the aliens to hold their position for much longer, which would amplify this field. This increased rotation of the moon is dragging it closer to Galiza."

I leaned back in my seat and contemplated something for a moment.

"What?" he asked.

"It's something the Diramal mentioned. He said there's been an increase in seismic and tidal activity across the world. Do you know what happens when a moon gets closer to its planet, Blick?"

His eyes went wide. "A surge in natural disasters."

"To start, yes. However, if the moon continues to get closer, and we're lucky, it will impact Galiza," I said. "A worse and more likely scenario: it will shoot itself out of orbit from our planet. Sea life would diminish; tidal activity would drop drastically. Currents would cease to mix arctic waters with tropics and the global climate would steadily rise before plummeting into an ice age."

Blick took a few heavy breaths as he made another observation.

"Not only that, but this also drastically hinders our stratagem flexibility. At the velocity Anua spins, we'll have a minimal window before the ship and the surface surrounding it fall in and out of shadow," he said.

"We can't wait for an opportune time. Every moment the craft stays active it will continue to drag the Anua closer to Galiza. We need to get down there now," I said, pushing the throttle forward.

I almost cursed the aliens in that moment. The idea that they would willingly stay, merely to see our planet destroyed and our people with it. Then, I remembered that spark and power surge within the alien craft. *Did we dismantle something that has compromised their technology and backfired on us all?*

It wouldn't be totally out of the question. If there was any chance of these cosmic visitors having peaceful intentions, after our first encounter, it would make more sense for them to leave. Although, if we somehow disabled their craft . . . Would they have any choice?

I lowered the Peroma onto the lunar surface, out of sight, behind a rocky hill close to the alien craft.

"Alright, alphas, gear up and equip yourselves with heat vision goggles! We may need them," I commanded.

As I stepped up from my seat, the ground beneath our feet rumbled, and a deep, thunderous zapping sounded in the direction of the craft. It only lasted a few seconds, but it was enough to rile my troops all the same, howling and backing amongst themselves at the disturbance. I was riled myself, as conflicting impulses tugged at my reactions. I went from glancing out of the cockpit and back to my troops. The instant some speech came to the tip of my tongue, a strong curiosity allured my attention back to the top half of the craft as some strange dark-blue aura emanated at the middle of the craft.

"Settle yourselves, that's enough!" my voice towered over them. "It's done, carry on with your orders, all of you."

With my heart still thumping, I took a second to catch my breath as Blick came up to me.

"Sir, do you think that came from the ship?" he asked in uncertainty.

I wiped my snout as I shifted in place. "At this rate, we can't know for sure. But we might be able to find out."

My troops observed the alien craft from the ridge of the hill that hid our ship from their view. It was *mountainous,* the alien vessel, with no clear signs of translucency. It seemed as though they had no immediate means of detecting our position.

"The only known way in is through the main entrance . . ." I spoke over comms. ". . . which is a spacious elevator. It leads into this . . . engineering room. Considering how my last encounter ended with these beings, I doubt approaching the front door is a viable strategy. What we're looking for are any openings, moving components, or flaws about the craft that we can use to our advantage."

"Did the ship itself demonstrate any activity, at all, in your first mission to it, sir?" asked Blick.

"No, but while we were inside, someone might have inadvertently hindered the craft. In our time spent forcing an exit strategy, a set of rounds ricocheted and hit something that presumably combusted crucial components of the ship. Depending on the severity of the damage and whether or not it's been repaired, is what we're trying to—whoa!"

The ground beneath us shook and our bodies started to levitate up off the surface; a deep rumble filled our ears.

"Grab hold of the hill!" I yelled direly.

The gravity on the surface fluctuated once again, rapidly declining to zero.

"The goddess casts us from her!" I heard one of my troops howl in terror.

The rumble turned into a roaring horn, in a spurting frequency, as if some drill or other mechanism were causing this great disturbance.

"She grows impatient, this craft has vandalized her image for too long!" another troop cried. "She seeks to repel it from her!"

My fingertips were strained by their grip on the lunar surface. Steadily slipping away, with no firm placement, the frail rocks beneath us gave away. I flexed every muscle in my upper body to remain anchored down. Everyone's legs lifted to the void above. There was a squeal of a bark from one of the women as her grip gave out and she ascended to the stars. The commotion thwarted my focus. Half a second later, I lost my own grasp on the surface. Eyes wide in a gasp, I felt myself getting higher and higher off the ground. I stretched and reached my arm back toward the ground with no avail. *Yank!* Blick grunted while he fought to maintain his grasp on me with one arm, and his grasp on the surface with the other.

Just then, something lured my eyes toward the ship. I could see the lunar dust sparkling and blowing off the surface in a thin cloud. Beyond that, a vibrating, dark-blue aura was faintly visible at the base of the ship. My heart lifted with relief at the sight. *They're trying to leave!* My thoughts raced with the possibilities of what that could mean. However, before I could explore the train of thought too deeply, the quaking force from the ship dissipated and my troops settled back onto the surface. The first thing I did was gaze up to the void above, hoping to see that none still lingered there.

Before my eyes reached her, I knew she drifted too far from the surface, as her screams were heard in the diminishing comm signal. Her body steadily tumbled higher and higher, growing smaller and smaller until the signal was finally lost.

A silence fell over the troops; I was at a loss for words. All our heads were weighed down in respect of her service and the life she gave.

"Does anyone know her name?" asked Blick.

My troops were hesitant to answer.

"Yeina," one of my troops spoke up, sorrow clear in her voice. "Yeina Smotolf."

"May the goddess embrace her spirit," I replied.

The thought crossed my mind to pilot the Peroma and recover the trailing alpha. But I sensed it was too risky, especially if it would require a speedy maneuver, given how unpredictable the gravity shifts were becoming. And time was already running out for us all, as Galiza had gotten notably closer since the previous mission.

My ears perked up at something new: a cavernous cracking in the crust. I saw the slightest plume of dust, and my eyes darted to Peroma. A fracture surged towards her, destabilizing the landing zone

My heart skipped a beat as my focused narrowed. Feeling time alter, I shouted to Blick before I was moving too fast for him to comprehend what I was saying, "Hold here, Vykin!"

I ran as fast as I could, trying to get out of sight. I needed to move quick enough so the others would not notice. Time seemed to be at its slowest flow by the time I turned the corner of the ship's wing and entered the ramp.

With Hanker and Rogen still inside, I would have to regulate time and scramble to the cockpit. It was that or they would see me in my altered time state.

Interfacing with the control module, I activated the Peroma's systems just as her plating started to moan and the floor seemed to shift.

"It's a sink hole; she's falling, sir. Hurry!" Blick barked over comms.

Taking the pilot's seat, my bottom lifted off as quickly as it sat down. The Peroma dipped in a plummet. The trantalium orbs activated and the Peroma trembled against the force of her free-fall. Slowly pulling her up, dust clouds shrouded my sight. I was surprised to see how high the lunar murk had stretched by the time we ascended it. I brought the Peroma about, to inspect the . . . it's not a sink hole?

"What is that?" asked Rogen.

I glanced to the doctor who gazed down at the lunar surface from over my shoulder.

"Not a sink hole," I replied. "Can you see the lights too, Vykin?" I asked.

"Yessir, we can, vaguely. There must be some kind of . . . power source under the crust," he replied.

"Technology within the goddess herself?" Rogen gasped.

How could that be? I pondered.

"What an astonishing discovery this is. The mother of all life is . . . artificial!" Hanker chimed in.

My reality shattered. I was pondering so many questions that I didn't know which to focus on.

"Should we investigate the opening, sir?" asked Blick, refocusing my attention.

"Stand by, Vykin. I have to find a new landing site for Peroma. We'll investigate the opening together, once I rendezvous back to you."

"Yessir," Blick replied.

XXXII

Beneath Anua's Powdered Skin

I landed the Peroma in a crater a few yards out from the hole, still keeping her out of sight from the alien craft.

"We would like to join your excavation under Anua's crust," said Hanker as I marched for the ramp.

Halting in my tracks, I sighed begrudgingly and turned back to the men.

"Does the possibility of everything you thought you knew to be true, turning out erroneous, not frighten you?" I interrogated. "The idea of immediate technological advancement - that may prove something others before you thought impossible – laid bare for your minds to study. It doesn't infuriate you?"

Hanker tilted his head while Rogen let out a light chuckle.

"Of course not," said Rogen. "Is that not the purpose of science? Discovery?"

I held a silence, analyzing their expressions and I looked into their eyes to see their true intentions.

"Alright. Suit up and meet me outside the ship."

I lead the doctors back to Blick and the others, who crowded the rim of the opening, taking in its contents.

"Vykin," I beckoned. He turned and met with me.

"Sir."

"Has there been any activity from within the opening?"

"No, sir, but there is something down there," he answered.

"Show me."

I came to the rim of the opening and saw bright lights reflecting off white floors. It was filled with columns of data banks, completely operational, stretching in every direction.

One by one, we made our way down beneath the crust and took in our surroundings.

"What is all of this?" I asked.

"A much more interesting question, Alpha Criptous," Hanker said, "is who engineered all of it?"

"We may never know."

"Sir?" asked Rogen. "Look closely here."

I went to Rogen's side, studying one of the machines.

"Notice this grid pattern? It's consistent across all the other banks," Rogen continued.

I glanced around at the other chest-high data banks and noted tiny trails of lights flowing in the same direction along each machine.

"Perhaps they lead somewhere, to some kind of core engine or a motherboard," he suggested.

"You may be on to something there, doctor," I said, turning to my troops. "Be on your guard, we're going to follow the grid flow."

We marched in the same direction with no obscurities in our path. Eventually, we came upon a reactor, stretching up to the hollowed lunar crust above. It generated cold, moist clouds that dissipated in the air. Our proximity to the reactor did not make us colder, but thin layers of ice formed over our suits.

"What a marvel!" Rogen gasped as Hanker took a device from the case he was carrying.

"Uh, Alpha Criptous," Hanker said.

I turned around to acknowledge him.

"As convenient as this may sound, my geo-tracker is telling me this reactor should be right underneath the alien craft," he continued.

Blick formulated a hypothesis, "That might make sense if this reactor is linked to the core of the moon. It may serve as a sort of antenna, a medium that helps the alien craft manipulate the gravitational fields between Anua and Galiza."

Hanker finished tapping away at the device. He ran some different simulations and calculations.

"You're not too far off, sir," Hanker said to Blick. "The core of Anua is composed of ice, and this machine is a harvester and thermo-converter. Somehow it is ice, or perhaps the temperature of ice, that seems to be powering the technology here."

"Well, I am assuming this technology has been active for thousands, perhaps millions of years. If it could be so ancient, how is it that the core of Anua hasn't been depleted of its natural source of ice?" I asked.

I examined the reactor and began to silently conjure a plan.

"That I don't know," said Hanker.

"We would have to reverse engineer a lot of what's here and get a close-up view of how it renews its source of ice," Rogen butted in.

"Anua etches closer to Galiza by the minute." I towered my voice over his. "We don't have time to waste on research, doctor." I reverted my attention back to Hanker. "If we ruptured the stability of this reactor and burst the crust from underneath the alien vessel, what would be the adverse effects?"

Doctor Hanker grew a concerned look on his face.

"Well, sir, hypothetically it may be enough to sever the amplified magnetic field between the moon, Galiza, and the craft. However, the added mass of the craft itself, may cause other variables to consider with the negated, amplified magnetic field."

I didn't have to press for further knowledge on what Hanker meant by that. With the gap having already closed between Anua and Galiza, the added mass of the alien ship would nearly double Anua's and would increase tidal activity more than eight times over on our planet.

The only way we could possibly make this work is if—"Whoa!"

A synthesized sound echoed from above. The ground beneath our feet trembled again, and the shift in gravity levitated our boots off the ground.

"Grab hold of something!" I ordered.

While there wasn't any risk of us being repelled from the gravitational pull of the moon, once this gravity flux settled, the crust above us was roughly seventy feet high. Suffice to say, if any one of my troops got anywhere close to that height, they would be dead, or too gravely injured to proceed with the mission. Fortunately, the complex manufactured surroundings were more plentiful in anchor points. Most of my troops were able to latch onto something without getting more than thirty feet off the ground.

This drop in gravity was shorter lived than the last. Unlike the previous instance, where the noise and rumbling remained consistent until an abrupt halt, the sounds and treble dissipated gradually. All my troops gently descended back to the ground with grace.

I couldn't be sure, but something felt different about that last gravitational flux. A sixth sense alerting me that something . . . changed.

"Top side," I said, alluring the eyes of everyone around me. "Back to the surface. Let's move!"

On the surface of the moon, powering back to the top of the ridge, we saw the top-half of the alien vessel had severed itself from the bottom.

What happened to—my eyes trailed up to the stars and there it was, suspended above the surface. In a tumbling rotation, a rippling aura was heading towards the alien ship. The active craft was frozen in place and the head point was transfixed in the direction of the incoming aura. The illumination stretched for what seemed like lightyears, until the back end of it slungshot forth in the blink of an eye.

Goddess! I let out a gasp. I was at a loss for words, but a deep sense of dread fell upon me.

"W-w-what . . . what does that mean?" one of my troops asked.

I looked ahead to the horizon as the sun swiftly dropped behind it. A few moments later, the first quarter of Galiza quickly rose into sight from the east. I looked further beyond, to the stars and nebulas, and even they were still moving all too fast for the moon's rotation to be considered remotely regular. I sighed with my head hung low.

"It doesn't matter what it means. With any luck, it means all the occupants of the ship fled within the upper half of their craft, leaving us with the troublesome base of it.

"We're left with no other options. We have to destroy it, or Anua will leave Galiza's orbit, drastically changing her axis, and the world will fall into an unrecoverable ice age. Vykin, see to it that charges are set directly underneath the alien vessel and as far up as can be reached."

"Yessir," he said.

"The rest of you . . . help where you can." I knew how defeated I sounded, but it didn't matter. Very little did at that moment, in light of what we just witnessed.

I walked back to the Peroma, to which I was followed by doctors Hanker and Rogen.

"Doctor, I know exactly what you're going to say," I finally replied to Hanker as we reached the ramp to the Peroma. "But the safety of our kin is more important than any data and information you and your associate plan to suppress and study in secret."

"Sir, I'm not here to make demands of you, I ju—"

"What don't you understand about the extinction of the human race, doctors?!" I barked. "Not to mention the top half of the craft has fled to goddess knows where; what we do here may not even matter"

"I understand full well, sir, the weight of our circumstances. I'm also considering the benefits of having a clear enough understanding of this lunar technology to use to our advantage," Hanker pleaded.

"You mean when your friends at MIST learn how to enhance and weaponize it?"

"Considering what else might be coming to our planet, if need be, yes!" he replied.

"What are you more afraid of, sir? An underprepared human front against an invading alien presence? Or a closing lunar body that has the potential to destroy our world, but we have the means to stop?" Rogen spoke up.

I slowly turned my head towards the doctor, scowling. "From what I understand, you are both brilliant men, but you are also MIST personnel. Which means you comply rather closely with the Diramal and the other high commanding officers of the Utopian military. I don't know if either of you heard, but as of recently, the Diramal has made a rival of me. Therefore, as liaisons to him, I can't trust you."

Hanker motioned to speak again, the color of his face shifted to a light pink from the rage that boiled within him. Rogen raised his hand to him and proceeded to talk with me.

"I can understand where you're coming from, sir. I don't know all that's happened between you and our nation's leader, but it's no mystery at this point that you've lost your father. That's enough justification for your opposing conduct," Doctor Rogen said in a calmer tone. "If you don't trust us, trust the sense I convey to you now. I have a daughter, her name is Rika, she's around your age. Do you honestly think I want her to endure a frozen demise? Do you think I want her to face a war that we are defenseless to counteract? Or even the tyrannical world we live in today, where no one has the right to think for themselves? Where few benefit at the suffering of the majority? Where resistance to conform leads to death or worse? No. I would rather live a hundred miserable lives, before I tolerate my child living in a world like that. Understand, Alpha Criptous, we may be working under the Diramal, but we are *not* working on his side, just like you."

I thought about it for a moment and considered what Doctor Rogen said. "When was your daughter born, doctor?"

Rogen stood tall and smiled as he recited his child's birthdate without hesitation. "Apik twenty-fifth, twenty-five thirty-seven."

There was no hesitancy in his answer and his voice was confident. I sensed no lie . . . in the fact that he at least had a child. "Very well, learn what you can from the reactor. However much time it takes for my troops to set the charges, you will have an additional thirty minutes to study the reactor. Possibly more depending on whether or not our battlefield will be illumined or shrouded. If there are still beings aboard the base of the craft, we'll need all the daylight we can get to face them."

"Yessir. Thank you, sir," he said and motioned to the other doctor to leave the ship.

Alone in the Peroma, the tension of the conversation and the stress of the mission compelled me to recline in the pilot's seat while my troops went about their business.

A dream of what seemed to be a destined future, came to me. It was a lucid vision. The skies were darkened by countless alien vessels identical to the one that landed on Anua. There was already a frenzy among the people before I set my eyes upon the street I strolled. Theft, fights, and delirious drivers muddied the streets, while others scurried to barricade their homes and surrounding buildings. Some just accepted what was happening, with hopeless looks on their faces, praying to the goddess to ascend them with open arms.

Military formations rushed in behind me, their guns aimed to the sky, as blurring crafts whipped through the airspace and even faster beings annihilated the armed forces. Every human who stood against the invaders died in their wake. A sharp pain *spiked* between my shoulder blades and a cold chill surged through my chest. I looked down, and as my mouth tasted of copper, I observed the same wound that killed my father, inflicted upon me. As my gaze darkened, I looked to the sky, dropped to my knees, and witnessed a grand explosion. Light beamed down onto the world again, but it was not a glorious moment. For ships were emerging from within Galiza, leaving behind countless innocent lives, helpless to save themselves.

I was pulled from my nightmare when Blick woke me.

"Amat! Sir! Wake up!" I slowly opened my eyes. "The charges are set."

My eyes took their time orienting my surroundings as I searched for a view of the outside. A few moments passed, and my eyes just couldn't focus or perceive outlines of anything. Not because it was too dark, it was the exact opposite. Everything was oversaturated with faint outlines in blue and purple hues.

What is happening?!

An aching pain persisted in the back of my eyes and in my frontal lobe.

"Ah, are there lights on?" I asked.

"Uh, yes, of course sir," Blick replied.

"Shut them off," I commanded.

He took a few steps from me and at the flick of a switch, my eyes finally adjusted. However, everything was still . . . illuminated somehow, but not blaringly. I could decipher the outlines of the rocks and everything about the lunar plane. Standing over the control module, I must have looked odd, to say the least, from Blick's perspective.

"I-uh . . . it . . ." It was on the tip of my tongue to ask Blick: *Is it still dark out there?* Regardless of whether or not it was, I'm sure it would have been an estranging question. Provided that he shut off the lights within the Peroma, I assumed the landscape outside was pitch black.

"Have, uh, the MIST doctors been given their thirty minute grace period to investigate the reactor?" I asked.

"So, you did allow them that?" he asked.

"I did."

"Well," he cleared his throat. "In that case, they should have roughly twenty minutes left."

"Have you calculated the intervals between how long it takes the moon to rotate back toward the sun?" I asked.

"Yessir, I did. According to a scan of Anua's rotation, the 'days' if you will, last just under an hour and a half."

"Well, then we're not going out there any time soon. how long ago did our position come into the moon's shadow?" I asked.

"Right around when we started planting the charges, which would have been . . ." he glanced down at his watch. ". . . twenty-four minutes, sir."

"Tell Rogan and Hanker they have till the ten-minute mark of the lunar dawn to get back to Peroma. In case there's any further repercussions to getting that ship closer to the lunar core, we'll need all the daylight we can get."

"Yessir, right away." He turned to march away. "Oh, before I go, I think you'll be wanting this. It's the detonator, sir. I figured no one else here deserved to set off the charges more than you."

When the time finally came to set off the charges, my troops and I took positions back atop the ridge. Blick saw to it that Rogen and Hanker made it back to Peroma safely. Two minutes before the sun rose from the horizon, Blick rendezvoused back to the ridge. I counted down the seconds, looking for that bright shine in the foreground of the trailing stars. Thirty seconds early, we witnessed the rays stretch out beyond the outline of the alien craft. Without giving it a second thought, I triggered the detonator. A loud wave *whooshed* over the land, pluming the lunar dust above the alien vessel as it fell straight down. The ship moaned and went ablaze at its puncture, which was swiftly doused. Its impact quaked the ground. The silence of space crept back into our eardrums. I held our positions, eyes fixed on the motionless craft, much of it still in view.

Nothing happened. In fact, there seemed to be no response from the alien forces whatsoever.
It seems to be a successful assault, but look to the stars. They trail even faster than before. Something tells me the stillness we now hear is but the calm before a storm.

XXXIII
The Lunar Clash

Time was running out. Anua's silhouette was growing nearer by the minute and wouldn't be long before it reached us. The shadow of the moon was roughly a little less than ten miles out and in closing fast.

To ensure the mission was accomplished, I ordered three of my troops to go and investigate the craft at the opening we made in the plating.

"Alpha Criptous, sir, this is Alpha Güdrid. Come in. Over," one of the women called the on comms.

By this time, the blanket of Anua's shadow was seen creeping over the lunar surface, etching closer behind the craft as the sun panned overhead. The stars began coming back into view among the various green, yellow, and pink nebulas.

"This is Alpha Criptous. I read you, Güdrid. Over."

"Sir, the ship has sustained heavy damage. If it wasn't before, it's now marooned. There're electrical arcs, spewing from loose hanging and torn cables; they're likely the cause of the fires in here."

"Stay on your guard in there, it could still be inhabited by our unwelcomed guests," I said.

"Yes, sir. We see multiple enemy casualties. There has been no sighting of any live hostiles."

My gaze turned to Blick, who gave me a reassuring nod.

"Roger that. Keep close together. Over."

"Yes, sir."

In the background of the comm channel there was audible clanking, screeching, and banging. "Alpha Güdrid, your comm is picking up a lot of background noise. Is everything alright in there?"

"*Sir!*" Güdrid's panting filled my ears. "Live hostiles remain in the ship, a lot of them! We found 'em trying to put out the fires and repair their ship! We're getting out of here!"

"Wait! Don't run! You—"

In the middle of my warning, I heard an explosion over the comms. The screams of my team members attracted the beings, and all I could hear after that were their horrifying shrieks. With her dying breath, Güdrid warned us of the assault headed our way. I could faintly hear her skin sizzling and her throat gurgling, as the aliens finished her off.

I stood atop the rim of the crater in silence for a moment, and quietly called to Anua to embrace the souls of my fellow alphas. I prayed they would be well looked after; that their suffering would not go unacknowledged.

"Amat? What do we do?" Blick asked.

I stood and turned to my troops. Their expressions were more confident than those on the first mission. However, they had no idea what they were about to face. *Most, if not all, of these men and women will never return home, and that may very well include me.*

Suddenly, I heard something rumbling across the lunar surface, like some great drill mining just below the crust.

As I stood there, I felt the chilling presence of the dark-blue aura return, faintly highlighting the edges of the alien craft.

"Ready yourselves . . ." I finally said. ". . . and say your prayers."

Across the way, as the invaders rose and dashed toward us, many small, dust clouds plumed across the field between us and them .

"Prepare yourself, Amat . . . breathe . . ."

I breathed deeply into my diaphragm in a calm, steady rhythm. As the masses of alien bodies came into focus, and time began to slowly alter. I raised my hand and yelled to my troops, "Attaaaaaaack!" They rushed down the slope, all of them trailing behind me, firing their weapons.

At the start, some of my troops' shots hit their targets. However, as most of them easily dodged the volley of fire; I knew each of those kills were only blind luck.

I fought right and left, trying to keep as many of my alphas safe from the inescapable onslaught as possible. Although, no matter how many invaders I removed from the battle field, my platoon was swiftly being cut down, one by one.

Despite moving in altered time, I never had a clear visual of the invaders, but I could see they bore no weapons and seemed to rely on their claws for their attacks. For a split second, the distinction of how fast I moved, relative to the invaders, made me wonder if the aliens had some other superficial means of exerting their high-velocity movements. The moment passed and I couldn't spend another microsecond contemplating it. All my focus was to be reserved for that fight and that fight alone.

As the conflict died down, and my forces came to their near-depletion, the shadow of Anua darkened the battlefield; it completely blinded all of the alphas who were not torn apart by these creatures. As the shadow cast itself over my back, my sight went black, my heart skipped a beat, and—*slice!*

Just as quickly as my howl cried over the moon, I choked and keeled over from my own pain. I clutched the fresh wound at my side, frozen over by the icy cold of space. The force of the blow twirled me around to face the other way, as I came to a knee.

Slice!

Another blurring enemy swept past me, cleaving my goggles off my suit; however, it did not rupture the integrity of the laquar material. I was shoved to the ground and onto my back. Growling with my eyes shut, terrified of the possibility that I was blinded. Helpless to myself, let alone anyone else, I remained on the ground, ready to die.

"Amat . . ." The calm voice returned. "*Open your eyes . . .*"

"*What's the point? I won't be able to see anything!*" I protested.

"*Amat, open them . . . you will see.*"

I scoffed at myself.

Look at me, arguing with myself at a time like this . . . pathetic!

The voice was silent for a moment. "*I am not a mere extension of your conscience, Amat . . . do you not recognize my voice?*"

I stopped to consider the question. I noticed it didn't seem like the voice was coming from within my mind, but outside of it. I concentrated harder on the sound of the voice and drew a conclusion on its identity.

Father?

Yes, he responded.

But . . . how—

We don't have time to discuss it, Amat, your troops around you are dying, and you need to open your eyes.

Slowly, my eyelids cracked open and as before, when I awoke from my dream in the Peroma, the lunar plane around me was illuminated in purple and blue hues of light.

Now . . . stand, my son.

I panned my vision around me and witnessed one of my troops standing his ground, firing blatantly, with no sense of aim. My breath caught in my throat as I saw a trailing figure rush past him, let out a brief spew if purple liquid, and my soldier fell limp to the ground.

Go, Amat! Fight!

I unholstered my pistol, charged the closest extraterrestrial, and shot it in the back. My sight was drawn beside me just in time to catch another hostile dashing toward me. With my free hand, I reached for my electric shock-put 101, took aim, and shot the creature between the pincers around its mouth. My sixth sense averted my attention to two more creatures charging me. Holstering my ESP-101, I took out one of my knives. I lunged right back at the aliens. When I was close enough, I slid beside one of them and sliced at its knee. Falling behind them, I pulled out and aimed my pistol back around at the other and fired. The wounded alien turned and limped toward me, but I threw my blade at the center of its chest and tore the knife out of the dead alien as I ran past it.

Two more aliens rushed in from either side of me, both extending their arms at me as they galloped across the ground. Just before one of them reached me, I holstered my pistol and grabbed the alien by the wrists, thwarting it to face its ally. The second alien fell on its side, scraping its claws against the one I restrained.

I put my knife to the first alien's neck, and slashed through its throat. Shoving it aside, the second alien rushed back up to me. I tucked and rolled behind it, slicing its waist as I tumbled by. I extended my leg and tripped the alien back onto the ground; in a smooth transition, I arched my blade in its skull. A third alien leaped over me with its claws extended out. I spun out of the way and our gazes met. We were less than a foot away from each other. The alien back-handed a dust cloud up in my face, flexing its claws toward my head, as I dodged back and found my feet. It sped toward me, hunched forward with its horns ramming at me. At the last moment, I shifted to the side and swiped my blade up into its chest. A fourth creature got the jump on me and rammed its head into my back. It pinned me to the ground; however, before I was rendered useless, I managed to squirm somewhat upright.

The alien quickly recovered, enveloped its four arms around me, and tore its claws across my chest and ribs on either side. Again, my howling cry was cut short by the brief ice-cold of space flooding into my suit for fractions of a second. Though it sent spikes of pain up my body, I contorted back toward the creature and swiped my blade at its face as viciously as I could. The creature fell on its back and clutched at its wound. Raddled, I winced at the tight and sensitive tug of my fresh wounds, heaving. I pinned the alien's arms and forcefully plunged my blade into its abdomen. Its limbs clenched and stiffened after the final shuddering ceased.

My eyes studied the knife in my grasp and the frozen blue blood that coated it.

I looked around, praying that it was over. A weary sigh left my lips at the sight of nine more aliens spread across the battlefield, occupied with the last of my fellow alphas.

I am alone . . . The severity of the situation finally settled in.

Sheathing my knife, I unholstered both my guns, and shot the remaining alien bodies as they closed in on me. In the time it took them to reach me, I was able to take down three other targets before the rest were within range. My fingers let loose the grips of my guns and I replaced them with knives, once again. The aliens surrounded me, but were met with my steel simultaneously.

Coming head on with the first of the remaining hostiles, I slid to the side and punched the edge of my knife through its ribs. The blue blood that spewed from its wound, just as quickly froze before it tumbled to the dusty, lunar ground. The next came beside me. Using the momentum of my drift, I spun off my knee and threw my blades into its gut. The fading momentum of its final steps carried my blades back to me.

A third came from behind, grabbing at my shoulder and reached for my neck. With my blades still deeply rooted in the second alien's body beside me, I pulled it toward me, dodging out of the way of its fall, and let it collide with the enemy at my back. Its grip continued to hold firm and was only briefly distracted as it cast aside its fallen brethren with its lower, right arm. Seizing the moment of its hesitation, I pierced one of my blades into its groin and pulled away from it. Unable to finish off the third, as my eyes were lured to a fourth, which was broader in size and somewhat taller than the others. I launched off the ground, raising the blades above my head. Coming down, the larger alien caught me in my descent and squeeze my ribs. I plunged my knives down into its shoulders, tucked my knees, pressing my boots against its chest, and kicked away from its hold on me, all while I was splitting its shoulders open.

The third alien clutched at its wound, contorting, going into shock from the gripping cold. Gazing ahead, two more remained, one trailing the other, with a gap between the two. I charged at them with all my speed, kicking up moon dust in my wake. I stopped dead in my tracks before meeting with the first, it swiped at me with its two left arms, and I swiped back at one of its hands. Clutching at its wound, I swung both my blades up into its jaw, pulled it down to its knees, and launched off its shoulder at the final foe. Sailing through the air, I crossed my arms as the alien stood its ground with its arms raised. It motioned to strike me, but as I swung out wide, the force of my elbows fractured the creature's feeble arms. As the swing of my blades followed through, the final alien was left decapitated.

With the battle won, I allowed myself to topple over the dusty surface as time slowly returned to its normal flow. While it wasn't my full weight that I fell on, it was enough to send pain through my wounds and sores as I rolled. Adrenaline dulled my pain during the battle, but the agony was rushing back. Finally, as I was lying still, fatigue crept over me. I nearly forgot how to breathe, but I was too stiff to move. My eyes glanced around at the bodies that congested the surface. When I caught my breath, I shouted over comms to see if anyone was still alive. No one answered. Mustering the strength to find my feet, I whined and growled at the pain. Though I lived and was still breathing, it still felt like the battle was lost.

XXXIV
Neuro-Frenzy

The white plane of Anua was riddled with the blue and red blood of the dead. I limped across the surface, hopelessly searching for survivors to no avail. It didn't occur to me, the weight of responsibility that came with losing soldiers under my command. It was always a simulation or a drill. *It's hard to feel accomplished or any sense of pride when they don't come back up . . .*

I only wished to bring at least *one* back with me. *Had things gone differently on the first mission, perhaps none of this would have come to pass.* In my daze, I realized that if the entire team was wiped out, that would have to mean Blick was dead too. For the promise I made to him, if he was dead, I would at least recover his body. Though, I prayed he was still breathing.

"Blick! Blick!" I trudged along the battlefield as quickly as I could. Every corpse I inspected that wasn't Blick's, while it should have left me relieved in some sense, it only stretched my despair. There was no sign of my friend until some movement, within a pile of bodies, piqued my interest.

Closing in, I saw an arm making attempts to push away the alien corpses that swathed it. My pace quickened towards the disturbance, and when I removed one of the bodies myself, I uncovered . . .

"Blick! Are you alright?!" I asked.

"Well . . ." Blick wheezed. ". . . I'm k-kinda c-cold."

"Can you stand?" I pulled him up on his arm.

He growled as I started hoisting him to his feet. "N-n-no! Stop!" He let out an exasperated sigh as he panted.

I let go of him and parted the heep of alien corpses. At his oblique, I saw that one of the aliens firmly planted its claws. The laquar suit made an airtight seal around the mortal wound.

I cursed under my breath and shifted in place while I calculated the best course of action. *I can't risk prying the claws from him. He would go into shock and die if the arteries near the wound were frozen over.*

Blick shook his head, his eyelids weighing down as his voice rasped, "It's . . . it's . . . fine, Amat. Y-y-you can l-leave me . . . here,"

"By Anua's shadow, I will not." I started removing the last few bodies piled on him.

"Y-y-you can't . . . t-t-take it . . . out. And you c-can't c-carry . . . b-b-both—"

"As the commanding officer of this mission, I have final say here. There's a regenerator in Peroma . . ." I grunted, carefully lifting both Blick and the alien corpse over my shoulders. Fortunately, the lighter gravity on the moon made the weight of the pair more tolerable. Blick let out a furious growl, as pain surely surged through his wound. ". . . and I'm gonna get you there in no time."

With his fatigue aggravated, Blick's protests slurred into mumbles.

Don't fall asleep my friend, I thought as I took in deep, calming breaths and shut my eyes. The desolate ambience of the lunar plane deepened in my ears. The weight on my shoulders lessened slightly. I opened my eyes. My vision narrowed, hyper focusing on objects in the foreground of my sight.

"Alright, Blick, just hold on."

Every step carried me further than I expected it to. The relative force of altered time granted me accelerated momentum. Blick let out howling cries that were altered in pitch and length. Making my way back up to the ridge was the most challenging part of this hustle. The beats of my heart were closer together and grew more thunderous. My footing occasionally slipped against the ashen surface, but I stabilized myself against the rocks and continued pushing up the hill. In my final steps to the top of the ridge, the altered time gave out and suddenly the weight over my shoulders arched my back. I gasped at the sensation of losing my balance, but quickly found my stability and caught my breath.

The sound of my heart pulsated in my ears. The flow of blood throughout my body seemed to be rushing, as there was a subtle cold tingle throughout my limbs and gut.

"Haaah! By Om—" Blick stopped himself mid-sentence. I could scarcely think of what he was about to say.

"Blick, you alright?" I asked feeling out of breath again.

"I'm f-f-fine!" he growled. "You . . . you're the last . . ."

My ears perked at that and I turned my head towards him.

"I'm what?"

He harumphed. "You're . . . the l-last one . . ." he exhaled the final word.

No! I thought, sensing his body gave out on him.

I altered time, once again, and hurried down the slope to the Peroma. Just before rushing up the ramp, I regulated time.

Doctors Hanker and Rogen rushed to my side as I burst through the airlock, taking the bodies of Blick and the alien from my shoulders. Both were placed gently on the floor after I warned the doctors about the alien's tether to Blick. Hanker and Rogen took steps back to register the entirety of the alien figure.

"We have to get Blick to the ship's regenerator. We should hold from removing the alien's claws until the mechanism is primed. He's already lost a lot of blood," I said.

I kneeled down beside Blick. Drawing one of my knives over my head, I came down and amputated the alien's hand, lodged into his side.

It only just occurred to me that the alien was dressed in a type of suit. The material was thin, black, and smooth looking. A spherical helmet encompassed its head. Only a small clearing at the front of it allowed me to see its eight eyes, all blue. Mechanic extensions about the helmet allowed for the extension and flexing of the alien's pincers.

The alien had eight limbs all together: four arms and four legs. Two horns sprouted from either side of its scalp; pincers arched over either side of the mouth, with hundreds of tiny teeth. The hands, bearing four claws, were small. Its feet, with two claws at the front and one at the heel, were narrow. The overall physique of the being was slim and appeared almost frail.

The doctors were still in awe at the sight of the being and oblivious to my speech.

"Hanker!" I shouted. He shook his head and immediately attended to Blick. With Hanker being the more muscular of the two, he helped me lug Blick to the regenerator, while Rogen marched ahead to prime the machine. Rogen issued a scan, and as a golden curtain of light slowly made its way up Blick's body, I pried the claw from his side.

"He's stable," Rogen said when Blick's wound mended.

My friend remained unconscious and was likely wearied by the drastic reanimation of his flesh.

"We should get you through this too, sir. You don't look to be in good—"

"I'll be fine, Dr. Rogen," I spoke firmly as the heat of the moment was still passing over me. "My wounds won't take me from this life."

"Please, I insist, Alpha Criptous, allow me to at least administer something that will ensure your blood is flowing regularly." Rogen persisted. "Those do not appear to be any mere lacerations of the skin."

Looking down at myself, I noted the faint trails of blood along my ragged clothing and armor. The wounds of which were cauterized by the frozen temperatures of Anua. I looked back to him with a softer gaze and nodded my approval.

"I'll be right back then. Take a seat, sir," he said.

Finding a chair to rest in, he approached me. "How lucky you must be to survive *two* encounters with these entities. Especially, when all others have faced their demise."

His tone didn't suggest he meant it as an accusation, but I nearly suspected so.

"Anua guards my life well," I replied with a shrug, still not sure how to explain the unique attributes about myself.

"And we should be grateful for it," chimed in Rogen, returning with a serum in his hand. "Neither Hanker nor I could hope to pilot this vessel back home."

A tingling pain followed his injection in my neck, while a quick and clean pry relieved me. An irksome growl escaped me.

"Much appreciated, Doctor Rogen," I said, rubbing my neck.

"My pleasure, sir. It would be my advice to prolong our return to Galiza until Mr. Vykin has stabilized, if we can afford to do so."

"That should be fine," I replied.

I stood to return to the alien corpse at the airlock, as the doctors followed behind me.

"I hope that by severing the hand, I haven't completely degraded its use to the both of you. Is there much at your disposal here that can be used to make some early progress?" I questioned, intrigued to know if the alien's biology might provide me with some answers to my supernatural abilities.

"Not at all, sir. There's still much to work with," said Rogen, taking a sample of the dribbling, cold blood from its fresh wound I inflicted. "Though, we certainly lack the proper equipment to make any thorough analysis of this creature here."

"If it would interest you, I could make a physiological assessment, sir," Hanker broke in, his tone filled with eagerness.

Not exactly a promising analysis for the information that I desire about this creature, as I have eyes to see it for myself.

Regardless, I gave my approval. Hanker moved in and kneeled beside the alien corpse, gently moving and feeling about its body for inspection.

"The arms and legs are all very light and delicate, but the specimen's gut, chest, and skull seem to be the strongest aspects of the body. The spine appears to be just slightly exposed outside of the skin, as the spinal column flexes out. The back is also dense in lean muscle, but I would imagine if you were to hit this being dead center of its spinal cord, it could be easily crippled."

I nodded my head, somewhat disappointed. "Well, should we ever have the misfortune of seeing these beings again, I'll be sure to keep all that in mind."

"Yes, but aren't these beings reported as having extraordinary movements?" asked Hanker. "I recall reading the files on the deep space missions of your father, when he first encountered these beings nearly twenty years ago. Personally, I don't think we would have any distinct advantage over them until we can match their movements. It's a shame we've never had an opportunity to gain a more civil understanding of these cosmic visitors."

A wave of dread came over me and suddenly, for a very brief instance, my hate for the beings was alleviated.

"I think we did this time. I'm not sure if they came in peace or perhaps curiosity, given how they kept to the shadows. I question whether it was truly malicious or not . . ." The moment of remorse passed and I shifted to the doctors once again. "Now, you have a body, make sure you put it to good use. Learn as much as you can from it."

"Yes, sir."

I turned around to see Blick walking from around the corner. "Blick," I rejoiced. "It's good to see you well, my friend."

He didn't answer. His eyes gazed plainly, bearing a soulless expression. His lips flexed slowly, as he let out a deep growl behind his teeth. His posture seemed calm, but his diaphragm expanded and deflated rapidly.

I frowned. "Blick?"

Without warning, he barked and charged at me. His movements were so swift I couldn't fully process them. He forced me to the ground, our arms in an interwoven tussle as he snapped his jowls at my face. Hanker and Rogen rushed to pull him from me, but he threw them back with a swing of his arms. Pounding me back onto the floor, he pressed his hands on my neck. Blood instantly clotted as my face filled with tiny, invisible needles prodding at me. I grasped at his wrists, puffing in whatever air I could.

Time warped in and out of its altered flow. The clotting at my throat seemed to thwart the ability. His movements were hardly noticeable, but I felt the choke at my throat alleviate slightly. I witnessed a swift arm extend over his head. My hand stretched to his wrist, slowing his blade's descent toward me.

No matter how hard I pushed against him, or how long I stayed in an altered time flow, Blick's knife slowly made its way down . . . down . . . down. At first, it was a firm press, then an instant later the spike broke through flesh and bone in my chest. Thankfully, it was not over my heart. I gave a deep growl, still fighting with all my strength to push against his assault. The tip of the knife inched slightly deeper, before Doctor Hanker's figure towered over Blick, and knocked him over the head with a gun from a nearby rack. Blick fell limp to the ground, taking his blade with him. As I rolled away, he turned his head to me and exposed a rabid gaze. In a fluid motion, I closed the gap between us. Time finally started to converse around me with every step leading up to my blow that was so great it should have left his neck in a contortion, were it not for his broad build. As I calmed, everything gradually started moving in its natural sequence again.

"What in the name of Anua just happened?" Hanker barked.

"You tell me! Did you give him anything while he was in the regenerator?" I demanded. I promptly grunted as my shouting spiked the pain in my chest.

"No, sir!"

"Is that the truth from both of you?"

"Yes, sir," Rogen said.

I sighed and shook my head. "Well, I've known the bastard to deceive me before. He really convinced me he wanted to change. Those cho'zai from the other day were probably somehow sent by him all along. Strap yourselves in; secure Blick as well," I ordered.

"Yes, sir," the doctors both said.

I quickly strapped in and impatiently started up the Peroma's engine, piloting a course back to Galiza. The ride was hasty and almost reckless. When we broke through the atmosphere, I allowed the ship to carry us the rest of the way on autopilot and land us back at the SEF base.

As we exited the Peroma, we were greeted by a massive crowd of journalists, military officers, and medics. All cheering for our return and victory over the invading presence on the body of our great mother goddess.

XXXV
The Death of a Mother

Powering though the shroud of journalists and the general public, I found my way to the nearby medical personnel. The convolution of shouts, cameras, the apathy in their eyes exasperated me. If only those pestering members of my kin knew, not just the words they desired from my mouth, but the weight of the drowning ache in my heart; the guilt of my conscience. Maybe then, they would truly understand the avidity for silence and recuperation. Despite the obvious raggedness of my uniform, not so much as one pair of eyes glanced down at it or went wide with concern. Each praising pat on my back and slap on my shoulder raddled my wounds and caught my breath.

Finally, reaching a gurney, the medics there were the first to note the true state of me. Collapsing on the gurney was the only sign they needed before the raving mob was promptly dispersed and I was rushed to the infirmary.

The medics tried to comfort me in the assurance that I would get to a regenerator in no time.

"I won't be healed by a regenerator. Stitch me up. For all the trouble I went through, I may as well get something out of it, even it's merely scars," I said.

They gave me an anti-viral injection to clean up whatever infections the moon's frozen temperatures might have granted me and put me under.

***

My family came to see me after the operation . . . with the Diramal falling in behind them. He entered silently and kept to a dark corner of the room. No one else seemed to notice him until the journalists came flooding in, surrounding my bedside.

The Diramal's gaze never left me, nor mine on him. Much of his form was darkened by the damp lighting of the room; his red eyes were the most outstanding feature of him. I almost paid the journalists no mind as they all barked questions at me, but still my gaze on the Diramal held firm.

"Everyone!" I finally bellowed through the room. The journalists quieted. "I am more than willing to answer as many questions as I have the current energy for. However, I will not disclose anything to you until the man I'm staring at . . . leaves this room."

Everyone turned in the direction of my gaze and seemed equally estranged by his presence. The Diramal leisurely exited the room with a sigh and a faint smirk on his face, mostly hidden by the gloom of the room.

Only after I heard the door shut behind the malicious tyrant my story began. First, telling it in full, then I answered clarifying questions after. When they were finally satisfied, the reporters took their leave of the room and I was at last able to catch up with my family. Though it was a dispassionate exchange. All my cordial qualities had faded in light of the brutal and bloody acts I'd received and carried out on sacred ground. My uncle took note of my bland behavior and asked if I preferred to be left alone.

"Yes, that would be nice. Thank you, Uncle Gordon," I said, but it was not for the sole purpose of resting.

"Of course, Amat." He was just about to leave when he stopped and turned back to me. "Amat, there was something I wanted to mention." He leaned in close to me and whispered, "The other day I received a package from your father, and inside, he left a note saying the contents were meant for you to have." That immediately honed my interest. "When you're ready to receive it, come see me." He placed a comforting hand on my shoulder. I nodded and my family slowly exited the room.

"Log, Olson, stay a moment please," I requested.

I was about to do something. It was something I knew could get me killed or worse. Despite its consequences, there was no other choice for me . . . but there was for my cousins and the rest of my family.

When my cousins were at my side, I grabbed both by their collars. "A perilous decision rests before me. It could strip me from all of you, but I see no other way around it. Should I fail, you may need to protect our family from me, as well as the high commanding officers. The Diramal especially."

"Amat—"

"*Listen!*" I snarled at Olson. I gripped both of their collars tighter and pulled them closer. "I . . . I can't let him get away with it." I started to cry. "What *he* did to *him!*"

"Amat!" Log shouted. "You're hurting me!"

Olson hit me and pulled them away from my grasp, tearing off a few of the buttons from his uniform. Log was alienated and Olson was outraged.

"Promise me you'll look after our family!" I barked out to them as they left. "And be prepared to kill me!" The door was long shut.

It broke my heart to drive my cousins away like that. The idea of that meeting being their last possible memory of me furthered my dispirited mood. However, I had to isolate myself from them, I *had to.*

With enough strength returned to me, I got dressed. In the folds of my uniform I kept a pistol from the Peroma's armory stowed away and concealed it on my person. The base was livelier this day, unsurprisingly. Thus, I had to keep my head down as I marched passed guards, staff and high ranking officials. The flap of my hat shielded most of my face from those whose attention I sought to avoid. My aimless wandering finally got me in earshot of the Diramal's beckoning voice.

A peek inside the room from a small, square window built into the door granted me sight of a meeting. The Diramal was in the company of some of the highest commanding officers of the world. Countries we were at war with had representatives present. At the time, I didn't process enough of what was happening, or being said, to say why they were there; I didn't care. My priority was to kill the Diramal. Though my vision was limited, I noted there were four cho'zai in the room: one for each corner. If I was going to make my move here, it would be best if I waited for them to exit with the other officers.

Just as I moved to take a hidden position, I overheard the Diramal starting to discuss Anua. A decision was made in that instance, with not a second thought, among the people in that room.

The leaders of Galiza agreed to utilize a secret weapon capable of not only destroying the alien ship, but also Anua herself. My ears flattened at the utterance of this congruous decision. This was now bigger than just avenging me and my father. Stopping the Diramal meant keeping our sacred Anua from being harmed.

The officers remained oblivious to me as they exited the room. Those final moments to myself were spent strategizing how I was going to kill my target. Perhaps I should just use the element of stealth to my advantage. I can alter time, if I'm able, and take the Diramal out before anyone could even see me. Maybe I could take care of a few other high commanding officers as well. Except, the Diramal did not come out of the conference room; the halls were empty . . . too empty.

I unholstered my gun and slowly entered the room. Deep, steady breaths muffled my anxiety. I first aimed to the far left of the room, where I thought the Diramal might be; however, the room was, in fact, entirely vacant.

My guard was dropped by my bafflement, until my gaze saw the room extended a little further behind me. I stiffened and my ears twitched, as the fabric of the floor shifted ever so slightly. Hardly a moment's hesitation . . . *Spin!* My feet attempted to jolt me back, as I held my gun close, but the Diramal grasped my arm. I grimaced, bearing my jagged teeth. He smiled and clutched his grasp so tight, the strength in my hand faded. It was unnerving how greatly his strength superseded my own.

A whine escaped my lips as I struggled to re-aim the gun at him with my other hand. The barrel had been torn from my grasp. The grip of the gun *whipped* across my check. Stumbling back, my head rang and conflicting thoughts raged inside my head. My tongue squirmed around my mouth, the taste of copper filling my mouth as I felt around chipped and cracked teeth that I spat at my foe's feet.

He threw the gun aside and addressed me, "I was hoping this could be avoided, but I am no less enthused by where this will lead."

I took a deep breath and stood idle for a time as he approached me. Adrenaline rushed through my veins, but I couldn't feel my father's presence and time hardly seemed to slow. I threw a punch at him; he caught my arm once again. A howling cry raddled my throat my arm violently contorted.

The chip in my head seemed to be impeding my movements. My chest rose and fell in distress. I pulled back to throw another punch with my good arm. He threw his punch quicker and hit me in the face so hard I was lifted off the ground. My back slammed against an oval table. My nose was filled with blood and one of my cheekbones felt fractured. My head buzzed and my ears rang.

"Funny, I expected you to put up more of a fight, despite the neuro-chip's programming to hinder anyone's ill intent toward me," he mocked. Walking over to me, he picked me up off the table. "Come with me," he growled, as he pulled me over his shoulder. He carried me outside to an alley, where no one could see us.

As my strength slowly returned, I hit him in the back of his head. The blow only enraged him further, and he pulled me off his back by my ankles. It was as if the ground had escaped from under me at the rate my back struck against the canister's edge. A defiant glare was all I could manage as I recovered and time finally seemed slow enough to count in this fight.

Shooting up from the ground, my fist whipped up at his chin, but he dodged out of the way. Stumbling forward, I tried to turn and raise my right arm for another hit, but it was too weak for me to even clench my fist. I couldn't even turn properly; the middle of my spine surged in pain and infirmed me from moving fluidly.

The Diramal crouched, extended and whipped his leg out against my ankles. The ground impacting my chest burst the air from my lungs. Slowly, I found my feet, then I felt something. *Snap!* He dislocated my shoulder, pulling my good arm behind my back. A fierce, howling cry trembled in my throat, which lashed time back to normal. He hoisted me off the ground, before I felt it escape my feet, crushing my arms into my sides. Excruciating pain strained and tested the integrity of my ribcage. *Pop! Crack!* I tried to gasp for air.

The Diramal finally threw me against a wall and kicked me relentlessly. He let off for only an instant. The dead weight of my broken shoulder rolled me onto my chest; I coughed up blood and was huffing every breath. I yelled internally at myself to get up and keep fighting. Pressing my forehead against the pavement, I eased my left arm beneath me. On last attempt . . . *Stomp!* My spine fractured, leaving me completely limp and numb as my conscience drifted.

A low but world shaking rumble stirred my attentiveness. It took every ounce of strength I had left to lift my head and gaze to the sky. I raised my eyes, only to witness a grand shockwave warping to the heavens. The moment the peculiar pillar of light faded, Anua cracked and burst apart, along with what was left of the alien craft. An 'X' shape, dual halo of debris, dispersed from the integrity of the moon. My jaw dropped and my eyes filled with tears. My head dropped helplessly back to the pavement. I let out a defeated howl in the mourning of our beloved Mother before the Diramal silenced me.

***

I awoke paralyzed from the neck down. The Diramal likely continued to mutilate my body after I was knocked out. A dark room enshrouded me and a mechanism was holding my body upright.

Growing nearer, footsteps echoed throughout the dark room. The first thing I saw was the Diramal's red eyes, piercing through the dark. A little closer and the rest of his figure was revealed in the muted light.

"Alpha, how do you feel?" he asked.

I gathered up some blood in my mouth and spat it towards his feet. It didn't get very far, but it said a lot. The Diramal glanced down at the bloody saliva, then back at me.

"Don't be surprised at the circumstances of my retribution over you, Amat," he remarked. "You've conspired against me, your leader, and stole my ward. You made underlying threats to me directly, assaulted me even. You had to know there would be repercussions. But I brought you here, in hopes that we might . . . start anew."

I gave him a cold-blooded, rancorous stare. He walked up to me and moved his snout close to mine.

"A new war is underway, Amat. A war that will unite all of our peoples. But, for it to be efficient and successful, I'll need you to obey my commands, and put aside our . . . complications. For the greater good of humanity."

I spat in his face. "I would sooner let the frail state of my body take me to the luminous paradise that awaits me."

He gave a light chuckle as he wiped my gory spit from his face.

"Even with the current state of Anua?" He smirked sinisterly. "You never cease to disappoint me, Amat. You never make anything easy for anyone, including *yourself.*"

I heard another set of footsteps come in from behind me.

"Ah! There you are, doctor." The doctor looked old and frail, with a hunched back. "Amat, this is Doctor Skrilk, one of the very few people on this planet who knows how to operate the very machine you're strapped into."

Machine? I thought. I glanced around as much as possible, to discover what I could about the mechanism to which I was secured. Flexing mechanical arms moved into position, arching over me. It was then I realized: *This is a first model regenerator, developed in the twenty-third century!* It was such an ancient and dangerous technology that it was no longer in use. The automated limbs about me served various functions, so if the patient was not *highly* sedated, they could die of shock, due to the overwhelming pain brought on by the machine.

"Oh, Anua, please tell me I'm—"

"You are not sedated, Amat. Not in the slightest. Oh, but don't worry, I trust you won't need it," the Diramal interrupted, leaning in toward me. "Of course, it won't be any less painful than what you're expecting," he whispered with a smug smile.

The doctor finished surveying the machine and booted it up. The syringes filled with fluids as the arms slowly bent down toward me. A flat, yellow light scanned across my body.

"No! Please! Stoooo—OOOOWWWWWWW!" I howled and screamed as my bones were snapped back into place, one immediately after the other. The adjustments were promptly follow by injections that pierced deep into my tissue and cramped my muscles. However, my chest was the worst. The small, robotic hands pulled back on the bones, to stretch it out, and then set it back into place. A large needle pierced into my heart and injected it with a pink liquid. Certain areas on my legs and arms were cut open, where the robotic limbs reached in to mend broken bones and torn arteries.

At the procedure's conclusion, the Diramal raised his hand to Doctor Skrilk. The machines were stilled. He nodded his head at the doctor and injected a serum that instantly deprived me of sensation.

"The only reason why I numb you now, is because I fear you wouldn't be able to psychologically recover from what is about to happen next," he stated. "And you're no good to me as a vegetable." He looked over to the doctor. "Continue."

A razor moved across my scalp and shaved off all my fur. Left with a bald scalp, a high-pitched *zing* sounded from behind me. My skull began to vibrate harshly. I didn't feel any pain, but I was horrified and nearly gagged at the thought of what was being done to my head. A piece of my skull was removed and put aside. An opening to my brainstem was made to attach a code nine neuro-chip it its center. The code nine neuro-chip took effect moments after it was embedded. I lost all sense of who I was . . . I no longer saw myself as anything other than a product of the Diramal. With my only purpose being to obey his every command, nothing else mattered—not Anua, not my friends, not even my family.

I calmly waited for the procedure to be over and felt no other discomfort as the robotic arms fused my skull back together with a laser. My body naturally relaxed, and my eyes were suddenly dry of tears. The aches in my bones, muscles, tendons and joints, dissipated. My heart was no longer skipping beats or beating rapidly. My breathing remained a constant.

The doctor removed my restraints. I stepped forward from the old regenerator with my balance fully functional. My stance was tranquil and my every action awaited the Diramal's word.

"Oh, look at you now, Amat. What a spectacle you are!" he said with a patronizing appeal.

I said nothing, I didn't even acknowledge the Diramal with a glance, as I was now programmed to do, and awaited further orders.

"Give me your name, rank, and who your superior is," he commanded.

"Amat Luciph Criptous. Alpha. My superior officer is you, the Diramal, sir," I responded instinctually.

"Finally," he said, pleased with the outcome. "Congratulations, Amat, at last, you accept your place at my side." He placed his hands on my shoulders. "Together, with you as my greatest weapon and me as your trusted . . . leader, we are going to accomplish wonders. I can see so much in store for us further down the road, and I would like to reward you ahead of time. As you must know, I am still short a jinn-hid. How would you like to take your father's rank? Lead our armies against any and all current and future battles, in the effort to spread the Utopion autocracy?"

"I consider it a high honor, sir."

"Good." He chuckled.

Suddenly, red lights started to flash and a loud siren sounded off. The Diramal glanced up, his lips curled into a curious, yet knowledgeable grin.

"Come, Amat, let us see what all the fuss is about."

"Yes, sir."

He led the way outside. We saw many more of the dual-triangular ships clouding the skies by the hundreds. The Diramal laughed dastardly.

"They came, Amat! It's working! Ha-ha-ha! Now . . ." he turned to face me. "I want you to ready our armies. Today, humanity will know of a new war! We must be ready to defend against these savages, however futile they might be."

"Yes, sir!"

I moved with urgency to carry out his bidding.

Before long, the surface of Galiza became pitch black. All of the alien crafts converged and connected over the sky, blocking out every bit of sunlight. My ultraviolet vision activated and I could safely see my way back into the SEF base. There, I rallied up what troops I could find in response to the invasion of my world . . . in the name of the Diramal.

Epilogue
(The Diramal)

I entered a large hollow building where all one hundred thirty-seven of my high-ranking operatives, from around the world, awaited me. All of them were assigned leaders from each country on Galiza. All stood at attention to my arrival, welcoming me with a prompt salute.

"At grace, jinns," I said with a confident smile. I stood atop a stage, before a podium, and spoke aloud for all to hear. "Throughout its entirety, we have *dominated* this war. But, in all the countless years that have stretched for megaannums, there has been no day like today. A mai'sahara was within our control before the other Hanu could reach him."

The jinns nodded and shared whispers of approval.

"In light of our current circumstance, we are unable to move him, or any of the other humans under our control, to Serakis. It is being moved to the Quaron system as we speak. Once it is in position, arrangements will be made to see Amat transported to the planet, as well as anyone among his kin who we can convert."

"What are we to do in the meantime, Diramal?" one of the jinns spoke up. "Our infiltration among the humans is compromised. Surely, we've become high priority targets—"

"Has that stopped us before, Jinn Aorokrith? From the dawn of this war, we've been outnumbered, and look at all the *ancient one* helped us to accomplish. The humans, even in their mutilated, physical forms, reduced to rabid canines, remain the strongest members of the Hanu. And their unconscious willingness to adhere our desires will serve as a durable buffer to defend us from the Zelton forces.

"Speaking of whom, in addition to blocking out the sun, the Zeltons formed a newly amplified magnetic field around Galiza to maintain its orbit. The compressed gravitational force will sustain cooler, but still bearable temperatures for the greater portion of humanity to endure. Especially because most of them will be abandoned to the outside world.

The rest of us, and those with military connections, shall take residency within the underground fortifications we built in preparation for this day."

Another member among the jinns stood slowly and hesitantly posed a question to me.

"With all due respect, Diramal, knowing full well your relationship to Blick Vykin, many of us are growing concerned with his efforts to leave your side. And now, with the Zeltons so close, can we trust that he won't give any of us away?" Jinn Prodiclaín asked.

My blood boiled at the sight of him. I slowly moved from the podium and approached him.

"If we couldn't . . . I'm curious as to what you would have me do with him, Jinn Prodiclaín."

The jinn glanced around nervously in my approach.

"Well, for the time being, until he can be moved back to the Boufü system, perhaps we can return him to cryostasis." Jinn Prodiclaín continued.

The jinn stood inches from my chest as he gazed up at me. He was wise to choose his words carefully. Prodiclaín had no idea how close he was to meeting with my wrath. I never killed anyone under my command and never planned to, but the suggestiveness in Prodiclaín's tone had me considering . . . devious consequences.

"Hm." I smiled cunningly. "You make a reasonable request, Prodiclaín. I'm sure many of you feel similarly, having heard two concerns at this point. Vykin assaulted his commanding officer during the last mission to the moon, upon activation of his code three neuro-chip. While this incident was my doing, having triggered his rabid outburst, he will be met with certain repercussions. And, rest assured, if he demonstrates any further *rogue* behavior, your suggestion will be granted, Jinn Prodiclaín."

The officers all nodded in agreement. I continued to speak as I made my way back to the podium.

"Now, moving on to a more pressing matter—how we are going to supply a technology that will allow the humans to fight the Zeltons in their altered time flows. A technology which we already possess. However, to minimize suspicion, we will have Doctors Hanker and Rogen take the lead on studying the Zelton corpse they retrieved from the moon. They will be assisted by a few of our own specialists to expedite the tech's development.

Upon completion, Hanker and Rogen will be met with certain . . . incidents. We discovered, while filtering Amat's feed, these men are conspirators against our domain here."

The officers nodded and mumbled words between themselves.

"On one final note, I am proud to announce that we have finally found a way to fully transmute the humans into members of the Varx."

I gestured to my left, opening my hand to the first four human Varxs. They stood to either side of me, still bearing their human forms, but with notable black, bulging veins around their heads and arms. The same four surviving members who arrived back with Amat from the first launch.

The jinns stood and applauded.

"And in the coming weeks, we can expect to see them joining us on the enshrouded battlefield. As a precaution, to keep their existence a secret, their missions will be isolated from any and all human interaction."

The officers gave approving smiles.

"It fills me with pride to finally say the time of the Hanu is ending . . ." I said as I started to remove my human skin-suit. ". . . And the time of the Vix, has come."

Do not place faith in the corrupt.
To Be Continued . . .

Photo taken by Jingjing Huntley

About the Author

James McGettigan is a young and ambitious writer and filmmaker. He started writing this series in early 2012, when he was just eleven years old. At the age of twenty-three, he managed to put together three complete books, and has dozens of other various fictional genres in the works. He has also gained an immense amount of experience in the domain of filmmaking by working with various artists like the Trestles, Lyndon-Enow, and Goofee Jay. As James learned alongside of them, he was able to produce original content of his own. He is in the midst of putting together a comedy TV series. He is currently studying to get his Bachelor of Arts degree in video editing at the Academy of Art in San Francisco, California. James has intentions of one day converting the Altered Moon series into a film franchise, among other stories he is currently working on.

The author would also like to express his sincerest thanks to the readers for supporting this series. It has been ten-plus years in the making.

He would also like to invite the readers to share their thoughts and leave reviews of his books on the platforms that sell them. This would be greatly appreciated and will further support James in his ability to publish the many stories he has in store for the world. Thank you!

Glossary

Ankavi: A xǔté tank.

Cho'zai: The most blessed soldiers on Anua's scorched Galiza. Born with natural and rare dark-red irises, they are bred for war from the day they were born. They are sworn to the Diramal before their country and its civilians. Their obedience lies solely with the one who bears the Diramal rank. Complicating their own ranking, they are considered less skilled than an alpha, but fiercer brawlers. They do not answer to any rank other rank; however, they cannot govern themselves.

Cryodermal Necrosis: A form of localized tissue death resulting from extreme cold exposure in a vacuum or near-absolute-zero environments. This condition occurs when bodily fluids rapidly freeze, causing ice crystallization, cellular rupture, and subsequent necrosis.

The Diramal: An autocrat who holds executive authority over the people of Utopian and its soil. They decide whether or not to declare war, attend foreign meetings, and maintain foreign relations. There is almost no limit to their power and authority, so long as they don't get caught doing something illegal or morally wrong. They have the final say on what the public is allowed to know or to remain oblivious to, thus they keep close relations with members from IID and MIST.

ESP 101 (Electric Shock-put 101): A human weapon that shoots small, concentrated globes of lightning, fires at high velocities, and is held in three-by-three-inch square quartz crystals. The rounds can and will tear through any material—unless the gun is set to stun. However, the denser the material that the round hits, the more quickly the electric entanglement of the round dissipates.

Humans: The humans of Galiza are not how you might think. While there is a distant connection the humans of Earth share with the humans of Galiza, they are not directly correlated. The features of the Galizian humans are spliced with canine features: snouts, tall ears, their eyes, fur about their bodies, physique, endurance, and many other factors which separate us from them. However, the humans of Galiza know no other form or knowledge of any distant ancestors, to reference how they might have such extreme physiological contrasts.

IID (Information of Interests Department): A Utopian government agency. They are responsible for tracking and filing all military operations, as well as economic and scientific data.

MIST (Military Investigative Sciences and Technology): A military corporation responsible for the investigation and development of advanced technologies and weaponry. Much of these things are classified. They do, however, help the progress of the Utopian society as a whole. They also manage Utopian allies, create cleaner and safer means of transportation, health care, and energy usage.

Jinn-hid: The second most powerful ranked official on Utopian and in its military. Only one person can hold this rank at a time. They report directly to the Diramal. It is not usual for the jinn-hid to command brigades or train soldiers, in addition to their standard duties. Both Amat and Bod Criptous are peculiar in this way. They are the Diramal's spokesman, advisor, and remain in close contact with the jinns. They hold the power to reserve the Utopian armies and to organize brigades overseas. For instance, if the Diramal declares war on another country, the jinn-hid decides the where and when troops will deploy. Also, they say how many soldiers are sent off and how many remain on home soil. In theory, they know everything the Diramal does.

Laquar: A durable, liquid shielding used for a variety of purposes. Formed in part by liquid oxygen, plasma, muon particle, and a high enough volume of melted magnetite that it creates a stable forcefield from liquid and gaseous elements. In addition to that, when in the form of a suit or domed shielding at the bottom of the ocean, the two continuously counteract one another to provide its shelled interior with gaseous oxygen. Metals or sharp edges will break the integrity of the substance. However, the substance is incredibly durable, so in the event it is torn or broken, it will rapidly reform itself in a matter of microseconds. Well, so long as it's not totally obliterated.

Neuro-chips: A rectangular device that ranges in size, depending on the code. It is installed at birth and is designed to grow in part with the brain. A standard, code one neuro-chip is small and takes on a thin, webbed shape, which spans over the top of the brain. Whereas a code nine can take up almost a tenth of the brain's anatomy and compensate for the functions in either hemisphere of which it is placed. Any neuro-chip upgrade is used as a means of repercussions in the Utopian society. Each one would further limit an individual's freedom and control over their own biology, thoughts, and emotions.

Pac: A moderately ranked officer. They hold command over the base armory and oversee inventory, along with rations. Their responsibilities extend to ensuring that fades are loaded with proper equipment and accessories before a launch. They can also serve as training officers among various lower ranked troops.

Wasper: A heavy, mounted gun that shoots 10,000 rounds of ten petawatt concentrated laser beams per minute. Even the slightest contact with one round would at least combust or even vaporize a human being.

The Altered Moon's Making

The Altered Moon is the first story I ever came up with. I was eleven, almost twelve, when I got the idea for it. I was at a point where I was struggling in school and was trying to figure out what I wanted to do with my life. I was under a lot of stress. I was not doing well in certain academic subjects and I was scared of flunking out of school. Around the middle of sixth grade, in 2012, I had a dream one night.

My dream had the same narrative. In particular, it had the same ending as this story, but it wasn't as complicated. Although, the alien ship was in the dream, of course. Amat's sisters, mother, and father were in the dream. Yes, Amat's father did die in the dream, the same way he dies in the book.

The other characters and aspects that I did not mention were not present in the dream: Blick, the Diramal, Amat's cousins, uncle, and aunt, etc. Amat also didn't go to a military base in the dream. He was sort of "hand selected" at random and given training to lead the mission. A process which took what seemed like months, but he wasn't military.

There was also a point in the dream when Amat overshot the moon and had to maneuver back around to it. He actually landed on the back side of the moon when it was very dark. He had to hike past these tall, narrow, cone-shaped structures. Dreaming that aspect of the story was fun and intriguing, but I didn't see how I could incorporate it in the book.

Amat did not get tortured at the end of the dream, that was also added. I have enhanced this story, giving it *a lot* of development over the thirteen years or so that I have been writing it.

I originally hand wrote this a few years ago, as well as the other stories that are connected to it, which are more than two to three hundred pages long. This has been a hard, but interesting process. This book is my world and my future. I have spent a lot of time developing it and can't wait to get the rest of it out there.

Don't worry, this is not the end of Amat's character.

The Editors

The editors for this story are numerous; I've taken *many* people's feedback and advice. All of this brought the story to this final draft. The most committed editors of this story and the ones that had the most impact were my parents, Judy and Tony McGettigan.

My dad was a direct advisor and completely open with his perspective on the story. He voiced what he thought was wrong with the story, just as openly as he did his fondness. In the grand scheme of things, that was just what I needed to make this story what it is today; however, it also made him difficult to work with at times. The way he criticized it made me feel like there was too much wrong with the story for it to be a success. Fortunately, my passion for writing helped me to repair various issues within the narrative. The catch was, every time I made improvements, I felt obligated to go over the *entire* book again and again, which essentially came down to rewriting it over and over again. But if I had to go through it all again, I would.

What I appreciated about my mom's editing is how she wasn't as directly critical. She contributed basic editing and made corrective notes that I would then type onto the current draft. She had a subtler way of critiquing it, which probably isn't as good for development. Although, her editing style kept me committed in giving me more reassurance that I was doing well.

My Grandfather, Alan Patmore, who is my mom's dad, also helped to edit this book. He gave amazing feedback, particularly on the terminology that I used in my story. His remarks helped to create a more unique feel to the world of Galiza. For example, he provided the idea to separate Amat's society from our own. Although he is human, his race of beings are more of an ancient time in the universe.

Steve Sortino, my old tutor and friend, helped to edit this book. He helped to point out a few loose plot points in portions of the story and assisted me in making it a little more complex. He also pointed out a lack of female characters and strength in this portion of the story. To which I did my best to make subtle adaptions. The reason why there is a lack of female strength and characters is that this book is tied solely to Amat's perspective, his journey, and his conflicts. This naturally leads to a lot of masculinity and egocentrism, but that was not the intended mood for the overall story. Rest assured, to any readers who may have taken note or offense to this, more female characters will be introduced in the second book. One in particular, mentioned in an earlier point of this book, Mae Kalbrook will be returning with a more crucial and stronger role to the story, in the next book.

Alex McGilvery gave the most professional and concise feedback on this book. While I didn't work all that closely with him, he still played a critical role in the overall outcome. His advice particularly influenced what is now the first eleven chapters of the book. Which, prior to his feedback, did not exist. He encouraged me to make a more engaging start to the story. The book now starts with a lot more action, whereas before, it started more slowly with a lot of contextual explanation. He also contributed to the adjustment of several character dynamics and developments in the story.

Angie Greth, has been a superb individual to work with as my main editor for this second edition. Her patience and support have been well noted throughout my process of getting this new and improved version of Altered Moon out into the world. I am greatly thankful to be working with her on this and future books to come. Thank you so much Angie!

The characters, at least the key characters in each of my stories, are editors as much as they are the true story tellers. Because, I as the writer, I merely interpret and envision the details my characters' experience.

Sometimes, I can misinterpret things and or envision a scene poorly. Usually when this happens, I'll get a certain indication that I should have written out differently as an action, feeling, expression, etc.

It's been a very creative and collaborative journey and for that, I am grateful. This is only the beginning of a *very* long history . . .